GO ALL OUT

SCARLETT FINN

Also by Scarlett Finn

NOTHING TO...
NOTHING TO HIDE
NOTHING TO LOSE
NOTHING IN BETWEEN: ONE
NOTHING TO DECLARE
NOTHING TO US
NOTHING IN BETWEEN: TWO
NOTHING TO SAY
NOTHING TO GAIN
NOTHING IN BETWEEN: THREE
NOTHING TO YOU
NOTHING TO THIS PREQUEL: ONE WILD NIGHT
NOTHING TO THIS
NOTHING IN BETWEEN: FOUR
NOTHING TO DO
NOTHING TO FEAR
NOTHING IN BETWEEN: FIVE
NOTHING TO DENY

GO NOVELS
GO WITH IT
GO IT ALONE
GO ALL OUT
GO ALL IN
GO FULL CIRCLE

KINDRED SERIES
RAVEN
SWALLOW
CUCKOO
SWIFT
FALCON
FINCH

EXILE
HIDE & SEEK
KISS CHASE

THE EXPLICIT SERIES
EXPLICIT INSTRUCTION
EXPLICIT DETAIL
EXPLICIT MEMORY

THE FORBIDDEN NOVELS
FORBIDDEN DESIRE
FORBIDDEN WANT
FORBIDDEN WISH
FORBIDDEN NEED
FORBIDDEN BOND

WRECK & RUIN
RUIN ME
RUIN HIM

MISTAKE DUET
MISTAKE ME NOT
SLEIGHT MISTAKE

THE BRANDED SERIES
BRANDED
SCARRED
MARKED

TO DIE FOR...
TO DIE FOR TRUTH
TO DIE FOR HONOR
TO DIE FOR VIRTUE
TO DIE FOR DUTY
TO DIE FOR LOVE

RISQUÉ & HARROW INTERTWINED
TAKE A RISK
FIGHTING FATE
RISK IT ALL
FIGHTING BACK
GAME OF RISK

FORBIDDEN PREQUEL DUET
ALL. ONLY.
ONLY YOURS

LOVE AGAINST THE ODDS STANDALONE COLLECTION
SWEET SEAS
HEIR'S AFFAIR
RESCUED
MAESTRO'S MUSE
GETTING TRICKY
THIRTEEN
REMEMBER WHEN...
RELUCTANT SUSPICION
XY FACTOR

LOST & FOUND
LOST
FOUND

ONE

HARLOW SWEETING COULDN'T have dreamed there would ever be a point in her life when the sound of jail would be her normal. Turned out three months was all it took.

The rules weren't so bad. Most of them.

Throughout her childhood, rules were standard. Her parents' rules weren't quite as stringent as those she had to follow in jail. It wasn't like she'd grown up under lock and key or without a scrap of privacy. Although her mom probably would've preferred it that way.

Six of the seven jail units housed male inmates; only one was designated for women. In total, there were around two hundred and fifty inmates meant to abide by the rules. Her included.

This facility was a change of scene. She'd started her tenure in a compound closer to the city where it was dirtier, more crowded, and scarier... Not that she'd ever let on about the last one.

Anyone who said jail wasn't an intimidating place was lying. Living in government accommodations made for a tense experience, especially in the first few days. After a while, the routine became easier. Inmates got used to newcomers over time. Though no one was ever "new" for long; the next batch of fresh meat was always just over the horizon.

Learning how to avoid becoming a target was the priority. Eventually, she formed alliances. Friendships would be too strong a word. No one completely trusted anyone else's story. Being on guard was the only way to ensure staying alive.

After following the line on the floor, she and a bunch of other female inmates waited for the guard to open the visitation room. The familiar jangle of keys and thud of locks was never as optimistic as when she was waiting to get into this room.

Visitation had been a difficult process; more so for those on the outside than her. Lena never came and she understood why. Her little sister wasn't cut out for jail, even the other side of the bars. Her parents visited. Rupert and Clyde as well. Bale never shied from showing up either.

Each inmate was allowed a maximum of two visits a week. Only two people were allowed at any one time. And, yes, conflicts arose. Her crew were the ones most perturbed if they couldn't get in. They were the best at helping her forget. Stories of their antics could erase the chains, for a few minutes anyway.

Everyone wanted an explanation.

Everyone, including the man currently waiting for her in the visitation hall.

When going inside, it never mattered how many of the circular tables were occupied, she always pinpointed Ryske like he was standing alone under a spotlight on a darkened stage. From across the room, they zeroed in on each other. Neither blinked. Striding toward him, she'd pretend they were in a nightclub, or at Floyd's, anywhere except jail. Under his all-consuming scrutiny, she basked in the fantasy for a few seconds. In those fleeting instants, she was a woman going to join a man, nothing else existed.

It never lasted. A noise, a smell, a guard, something would shatter the illusion.

Licking her lips, she anticipated Ryske's hands before they slid onto either side of her face. They carried on into her hair beneath her ears, scooping her mouth up so he could kiss her as thoroughly as was allowed. Maybe a little more thoroughly than was allowed.

She scraped her nails on his shirt, catching the neck to pull it down and make contact with his tattoo.

"Hey!" the guard against the wall five feet away called.

Ryske stepped back and opened his hands at the guy. "Every fucking week."

"Shh," she said, pushing him down onto the bench at his side of the table.

Once seated, they weren't allowed back up again until the end of the visit. The most they could do was hold hands across the wide table. She didn't care the seats were uncomfortable, or that she had to perch in a half crouch just to reach him, she just hated that they were so far apart.

"Bet that guy never gets any from his fucking wife," Ryske muttered over his shoulder.

She squeezed his hands. "Would you please stop starting fights with the guards who get to decide whether or not I get put into solitary?"

"You been a bad girl this week, baby?" he asked, dipping to kiss her knuckles. The guard coughed, Ryske growled in response. "What the hell problem does he have with me kissing your fucking hands? He got a thing for you, baby, huh? I get it. You're the hottest piece of ass in this place, on the fucking planet. He's jealous. Well, she's fucking taken so—"

"Stop swearing, it's not allowed," she said, transferring her hand from inside his to on top to stroke his knuckles.

"It's how I talk. Swearing is how I talk—"

"Crash," she said. "I'll get up and walk out of here if you don't calm down. What's wrong with you today? You haven't been riled like this for weeks." Not since the first visits he'd had to make to her behind bars. "What happened?"

"I talked to Greta," he grumbled.

Ah, her lawyer. "She told you it's going to be at least another six months until the trial," Harlow said, lacing her fingers through his.

"Something about the prosecution gathering evidence. It's fucking nuts. They said they have you on video going in. That's their evidence. That's it. What do they need to gather about that? It's a flimsy fucking case and they know it."

If only she could do more to calm him down. None of the truths they faced were easy.

"My blood is at the scene."

"Because he hit you," he said. She tried to be subtle about sealing her mouth. "Or because it was there from when he held you prisoner?" Curling her lips around her teeth, she hated they were back here again so soon. From the way he groused, he wasn't a fan either. "I don't understand why you won't talk."

It broke her heart to see him so frustrated. "Baby, I've been telling you since the beginning of this…" Looking him square in the eye, she didn't blink. "I'm going to be convicted of murder. You said it yourself, twenty years… That's what we're looking at." She cleared her throat and forced herself to speak. "You have to move on."

"No."

"Ryske, I love you. You know that I do. But I won't let you keep coming here every week and doing this to yourself… It's crazy… Please tell me the guys are saying the same thing. I talked to Dover and—"

"Yeah, stop fucking doing that. It pisses us off."

"Calling the bar?"

"Demanding we abandon you."

Part of her wanted to remind him they hadn't hesitated to do that before. Except she couldn't be cruel when they'd been so kind.

Ryske wasn't a sulker; he didn't pout. He was cocky and wasn't great at hearing what he didn't want to hear. He'd been like that since they met. Nothing about her going to jail had lessened his confidence.

"Bale told me he got his job back," she said, trying to change the subject.

His scowl deepened. "You want to do that? Sit here and shoot the shit like our entire fucking lives aren't circling the drain?"

She widened her smile. "Noon told me about Frida.

She faked a pregnancy?" Harlow laughed. "That's funny… I mean, I guess it's not ha-ha funny, but a girl's got to be desperate to get into the apartment if she goes to those lengths… None of you liked her?"

"Switching off reality isn't so easy for me, Trink," he said. "Guess you've got no fucking clue what it does to me to see you in here." He laid a hand on his chest. "My heart fucking stops every time you walk through that door in that fucking jumpsuit…" He looked away. "It should be me."

"Hey," she said, planting her feet on the floor to rise in a subtle crouch that gave her the reach to touch his face and bring his attention back to her. "That wouldn't change anything… that would just put both of us here. We've talked about this. You can't confess. You can't. You weren't even there."

For a second, he looked into her. "But you were," he said and snatched her hands closer. "Baby, talk to me. Tell me what happened." Shaking her head, she tried to retreat, but he just clung tighter. "What is it? What are you protecting? Who are you protecting? I don't get what the fuck happened that you'd clam up like this. Everything to the cops was 'no comment.' You won't even tell Greta what happened…" No and she'd never shared the reasons why. "She gave me the papers."

That perked her up. "The power of attorney and medical proxy stuff? Did you sign them?" He nodded. "I don't have much in the way of assets, some jewelry, that's about it. There's some money in the bank and—"

"I don't want your fucking money."

"I know that," she said, sinking down to lay her temple on the table. "I know that, baby… Look at me, Crash." Their hands still linked, she lay to the side, her head on the table, her smile spread wide. "I was dreaming about you last night… I woke up wet for you."

She didn't know if the guard heard the whisper, all she cared about was that Ryske did. "I'm supposed to cheer you up."

"You do every night at lights out," she said and sat up to pull their hands in her direction. "Ryske, I wouldn't have gotten through this without you. You don't know what our time together means to me. I'm just sorry I… I'm sorry I wasted so much of it."

His mood a little lighter, he took a turn to be optimistic. "We're going to have plenty of it after you get out of here."

That statement only made her sigh. "I'm not getting out of here, Ryske," she said. "When they sentence me, I could go anywhere. This place is already two hours from Floyd's."

"Forty-five minutes for Noon," he said, and she smiled. "Look, Trink, you can keep telling me to move on and stop visiting. But I don't care if I have to drive cross-country just to turn round and come back again to make it in time for next visiting. I'll keep coming for you." His eyelids sank and his lips curled. "Every time, baby, I come for you every time."

He was flirting with her and it was working.

"I don't think I miss anything more than the taste of you," she whispered. "The other girls talk about good coffee and chocolate cake… All I ever think about is you."

"I'll mail you some in your letters," he said, but couldn't hold in his own laugh.

It got out even before hers did.

"Think you'd start a riot," she said. "We women are pretty sex-starved in here…" Harlow glanced around at the tables surrounding theirs. "They've noticed how many men come visit."

"To visit you?"

She shrugged. "My mom's been the only woman. She only came once. It's too much for her… I understand that."

Sure though she was, a part of her felt shame for disappointing her parents.

"Marlowe still coming?"

She nodded, tracing her fingernail around the star on his wrist. "Less now than he did… I told him he's off the hook for our deal. Don't think it's good for business to be associated with a murderess."

"Said I'd get you one way or another, didn't I?" he asked, gaining her attention. "By default… I'll take it."

"Crash… will you do something for me, baby?"

Narrowing one eye, he was sort of squinting at her, suspicious. "Last time you conned me with that, you told me to let you go. What you want me to do now?"

"Get laid," she said and he groaned. "Maze told me you haven't been with anyone since me. Is that true?"

"I haven't been with anyone except you since we met," he said, pushing her arm up to show her stars. "And I won't be with anyone 'til you're out of here... Well, guess I should be honest, sometimes you're with me in the shower."

"Tease," she said to his wink. "That's the last place we did it."

"Yeah," he said, taking her hand to his mouth. "Boy, am I glad we did."

"Sure, otherwise you might not have had the chance to change my mind about shower sex."

"Told you, baby, you just needed the right guy."

Sliding her hands away from his, she broke contact and tucked them under the table. "And you need to get yourself the right girl... It's not me, Ryske. I wish it could be, but... it's not me." His expression didn't change. "Are you hearing me?"

"No," he said. "I'm not listening to your waffling."

"You're an arrogant prick, you know that?"

Her question fueled his confidence. "Damn right, baby. Just how much do you want me?" He leaned over the table. "Are your panties soaked through right now?"

It was amazing how he could tease her, and use that damn swagger of his to take her right out of this place. "I'm not wearing panties."

The guard coughed at them again. This time, Ryske didn't turn, but his eyes did rise like he was fighting to temper his instinctive desire to lash out or rage. "I don't know how the fuck you deal with this place."

"It's easier when you're not here," she said. "I think you bring out the naughty in me."

"That's the hope, Trink."

Sneaking her hands from beneath the table, she slid them across to his again. "Remember the night we met?" she asked, opening her fingers at the same time he did.

Their palms stayed flat on the table, their digits twined.

"Mm hmm."

"I remember I was nervous to shake Maze's hand after he told me you were criminals… Now all I dream about at night is riding his best friend raw… It's amazing how far we've come, isn't it?"

"As long as you're talking about me, it is. Maze has a few best friends," he said. The joke lingered without getting much of a laugh. Every second they spent together was one closer to saying goodbye. "You know, baby, we haven't talked about this for a couple of weeks, but… If you're gonna keep bringing up the getting laid thing, I'm gonna keep bringing up…"

"We're not getting married," she said, digging her nails into the back of his hand. "My goal is to make you forget about me and have a happy life… I can't fake my death; the best I can do is keep whining at you. Getting married would—"

"We'd get conjugals."

The wiggle of his brows was either meant to tempt or provoke a laugh, probably both. But she had to be realistic and temper his expectations.

"People get married because they love each other and want to spend their lives together. Just so we can have sex is not a reason. Besides, I'm a lifer. Lifers don't get conjugals."

He gritted his teeth in a prologue to the anger that flared his nostrils. "You don't know what you are. You're here waiting for trial and I don't have a fucking clue why you're not causing more shit about being refused bail. You shouldn't even fucking be here!"

The last thing they needed was him being detained and tossed in a cell down the hall from hers.

"Hush," she whispered. "Please, baby, calm down. You know the judge was a friend of Hagan's, that's why he refused me bail."

"That shouldn't be allowed either," he grumped.

"Hagan knew most of the judges and city officials. He had close relationships with all of them," she said. "His charity work wasn't altruistic." Her fingertips traced the shape of his long, broad, incredibly talented fingers. "He deliberately donated to the city and departments within it because he never knew who he'd need in his pocket. It was all about favors, about people owing him. Hence how he got Gina to give me a week off, no questions asked… He had the ear of a lot of people…"

"How do you know all that?" She stopped tracing and talking and froze. "Trinket, how do you know that?"

She'd done so well to keep the details of that night hidden. Since the dramatic arrest outside Floyd's, Ophelia hadn't come to her aid. The murderess hadn't come to her at all. The female Hagan was the only other person who knew what happened on the night of the crime. So far, all of law enforcement's evidence implicated Harlow. She was under no illusions about what the outcome of her trial would be. It seemed futile to drag anyone down with her.

Gathering herself, she attempted to uphold a façade of strength. "He told me."

"He told you that," Ryske said, peering into her. "The night it happened." She nodded. He tightened his hold, probably sensing a crack in her silent resolve. Maybe he saw this as his chance to wedge that crack open. "Harlow, you can tell me anything. You know that, don't you? Anything, Trink. And if you tell me not to tell anyone, I won't, even the guys. You before them."

Harlow didn't open her mouth for fear of saying something else she shouldn't. Her carelessness came from exhaustion. It wasn't easy to sleep in this place. Noise was constant. Sharing with others meant putting up with their habits too. All that was before she even got to how her own thoughts could keep her awake.

Eager hope made him squeeze and shake her hand, coaxing her. "Come on, baby. You were going to tell me. The night you were arrested, you were going to tell me everything."

"I was."

"What changed?"

Offering an explanation seemed like the least she could do. If he'd been this tight-lipped, she would be frustrated as well. It felt right to give him something.

"I didn't know what to say to the cops. I was still trying to figure it out when they told me I'd been identified on the security camera going into the building. I was the only one on camera going to Hagan's apartment that night. One of the cops at the station recognized me. I'd done some work with him when I was in family services… that's why I was arrested so fast. They talked to family services, who revealed I had a connection to Floyd's. They knew that because of how Felipe's case played out."

"Yeah," he said, bobbing his head. "You told me this before."

"They asked me why I went to Hagan's." He nodded, but it took her a minute to answer. "I couldn't tell them… And I thought, if I couldn't tell them that, then I couldn't tell them anything else. I realized if I pulled on one thread that everything would come unraveled… for all of us."

"Wait a minute," he said. "Are you telling me that you're pleading the fifth to protect the crew?"

Licking her lips, she wished she could get closer to him. "If I tell them why I was there, it will open a can of worms."

"You can tell me… You can tell me why you were there."

His frustration was palpable. Ryske was right that she *could* tell him. Except, it didn't matter that her trust in him was absolute. He didn't deserve to shoulder her burden.

Sitting up straight, she considered him. "Crash, I swear, if I ever do get out of here, I will tell you everything. All the time. Always. No lies, just like you said."

Again, his nostrils flared in a show of irritation. "But you're damn sure you won't get out of here… They have the video. They have the blood spot… no fingerprints. No witness." There was a witness, she'd just chosen to remain silent. Thinking about Ophelia always ignited her adrenaline. Not that she could show Ryske that, so she looked to the perimeter of the room instead. "Or not…"

The curious probing of his tone brought her eyes back to him. "What?"

"I said no witness and you turned away… You think I don't know you, Trink? I can read your tells."

"I have no tells."

"You have tells."

Goddamn him. "You should think about the future," she said. The guard pushed away from the wall, a sure sign their time was coming to an end. "You should think about whether or not it's smart to tie yourself to a girl who'll never be in your bed again. I love you, Ryske, but we have no future. You have to do whatever it takes to come to terms with that."

The buzzer rang and she rose in time with her love. They moved closer to each other. Without touching, each appreciated just being in proximity again. She would stand there for the rest of time and be happy with her sentence… if it didn't mean damning him too.

Tipping her head back, drawn to his gaze, she could feel him everywhere when he looked at her this way.

He brought his hand to the side of her head, his thumb tracked across her cheek. "I love you, Trinket… and there's not a damn thing you can do to stop me." He touched her lower lip and she opened to lick the tip of his thumb. "Tease."

Catching it between her teeth, she circled it with her tongue and closed her lips to suck it free. "You remember what it feels like on your cock?"

The sly ascent of his lips gave him a feral air. "I sure do, baby. Not something a guy forgets in a hurry."

The back of her hand drifted forward, brushing her fingers across his fly.

"Sweeting!" a guard barked, startling her.

Ryske growled and caught her shoulders.

"I have to go, Crash," she said, grabbing him to pull him down for a kiss. "I love you."

Turning to hurry back to the line with the others, she fell into her place in their ranks. For as long as she could, she watched him. He stayed put. Standing there. Watching her right back.

Other visitors were leaving, ignoring their inmates, but not her Crash.

Ryske's eyes stayed on her until the last second. Just before she disappeared back into the corridor, he winked.

She could be holding him back; his life was on pause because of her. But she couldn't stop reacting to him, couldn't stop loving him, and she feared that would undo them both.

TWO

THREE DAYS LATER, just moments before the phones were turned on, a guard pulled her out of the hall. The timing couldn't have been worse, calling Ryske was the highlight of her day. He'd always pick up within three rings. It gave her a thrill to tease him for being so needy.

It was just a tease though. It flattered her how open he was about his feelings for her. He didn't apologize to anyone for them either.

Within days of her being incarcerated, he'd handed over a number for the cellphone he'd bought. Only she had the number, no one else. It was a burner, nothing fancy, but he needed that link to her, and she wasn't averse to having her own dedicated line to him. For everyone else, he still used the usual Maze-created answering service.

The guard led her down the sterile gray corridor to one of the private interview rooms; somewhere she'd only been once during her time in this location. He opened the door and stepped back to let her inside.

Her lawyer was seated at the central table. She paused, unsure whether to feel dread or relief. The visit was unexpected, which could spell bad news… Good news was unlikely; there wasn't much of that these days. During the fight to get her moved, the two of them had seen each other often. Usually there was a call first. It was unlike Greta to just show up.

Greta Mann was a good lawyer. For the most part, she was thorough and personable. Though, Harlow had no idea how well the woman would stand up in court fighting a trial stacked against them. Defending a client who refused to provide any information posed many challenges. The lawyer's record was good, but Harlow valued killer instinct more. Given the lack of reasonable doubt, the only way they'd catch a break was if they played dirty.

"Harlow," Greta said, standing up and gesturing to the opposite chair.

There was nowhere else to sit and the chair was fixed to the ground, so she didn't really have a choice about where to park her butt. Since being arrested, she'd noticed there were a lot of pleasantries put on for show or to alleviate awkward moments. Pleasantries that were actually obligations, not suggestions.

"What's going on?" she asked, lowering herself into the chair.

"Something happened," Greta said.

Obviously, or else the lawyer wouldn't be there. Concern spiked. Her father and Rupert were supposed to be visiting that afternoon. What if Greta told her something had happened to one of them?

"What? What happened?"

"It's… We went to court this morning. I called for an emergency session and submitted a motion to dismiss. Two days ago, there was a robbery. An evidence locker was ransacked, they think it was kids; there was a lot of graffiti and criminal damage. One officer was seriously injured. Evidence in a few cases was taken or destroyed. Chain of custody is going to be questionable in all of them now. We didn't know for sure at first, but one of the cases missing evidence was yours."

This was a lot to take in. Greta was good at relaying information; she just struggled to keep up. Wow, this was… uh…

"What does that mean?" she asked to be sure.

Greta smiled. "I think the whole case against you will be thrown out. There's no witness or confession, the video and the blood were all they had. Without them, there's no case…" Her smile widened. "Your silence has helped us. They don't even have a statement from you placing you at the scene."

"So, wait…" she said. "They're throwing the case out?"

"No," Greta said, losing her smile. "Because of the break-in, there are a dozen cases that need to be reviewed as a matter of urgency. It's all very embarrassing; they want to keep it as quiet as possible. The judge is going to hear petitions on each case individually after the State's Attorney reviews them. He's been given six weeks to decide which cases he wants to pursue. He'll have to persuade the judge there's compelling enough evidence for conviction. Pending the review, the judge has agreed to release you on an ankle monitor. You'll have to stay at your parents and only leave there for court. But, providing no other evidence surfaces, I have complete faith that the judge will grant my motion to dismiss."

What did…? She didn't know what to… how to… this was unbelievable. "You're saying… I can be free?"

"They'll release you today, right now," Greta said, standing up. "I'm going to be with you while it's worked out. They're getting the papers now. You'll be transported to your parents' home and fitted with an ankle monitor."

She couldn't absorb it. Her sentence just dropped from twenty years to twenty minutes. For the time being at least.

Ryske.

"Wait, who knows about this?"

Greta smiled. "I haven't called Ryske. Only your parents… I don't think the State's Attorney will be spreading this around." Neither would her parents. A potential felon in their house? What a scandal! "The State's Attorney's office may have notified the victim's next of kin."

This was unbelievable. There were moments of

serendipity in life, but this was almost too much to comprehend. Even if she ended up being convicted, this interim reprieve was a gift. Just being granted a short time away from this place, breathing clean air again, was something many inmates wouldn't experience.

Being in a stupor over how it had come about didn't mean she'd snub the opportunity.

She was going home.

***

GETTING OUT OF JAIL was a blur. Harlow wasn't allowed much time to grab her stuff and tell the girls she'd been switched to house arrest. They had a dozen questions she couldn't answer, she had all the same ones herself.

Her release involved a lot of paperwork and shuffling from here to there. At her request, Greta agreed not to call Ryske. She wanted to tell him herself. Revealing her freedom would be fun. The interrogation after wouldn't be. Especially given she had no idea how they'd struck it lucky.

Regardless of the confusion, he'd be over the moon. Thrilled that she wasn't in jail anymore and that he'd been right.

The only downside to her freedom was the awkward dilemma it posed. She'd promised Ryske if she got out, she'd tell him everything. They both wanted her out of jail. Only one of them wanted to talk about how she'd ended up there in the first place.

Staying at her parents' house might be tricky.

Until she started to recognize the streets they drove through, she hadn't given that situation a lot of consideration. Only when landmarks became familiar did it hit her that this was real. Ryske wouldn't be the only one with questions… her family would have them too. They knew even less than her lover.

Freedom wasn't as simple as getting out of the police car and returning to normality. Her life would never be what it had been. Not that there was any kind of normality for her before jail.

While mourning Ryske, her childhood bedroom had been a sanctuary. After his resurrection, it was a base for them to make love.

As for her parents, they still didn't know anything about her life in the city… or the money Rupert gave her either. They certainly didn't know about her relationship with Ryske, or even that he was connected to her beyond their phony introduction at the Sweeting dinner table.

The Floyd's crew and her parents never overlapped. Her bail hearing happened before her parents knew she'd been arrested. Only after bail was refused did Harlow decide to tell them where she was, and boy that had been a call.

On her instruction, Greta hadn't notified anyone of hearing dates, neither her family nor her crew. Most were procedural, some she didn't attend either. She hadn't gotten as far as thinking about what she'd do when the trial rolled around.

Just being out of jail was strange. The sight of people going about their banal lives kept pulling her attention away from her concerns. For her transport between jails, she'd been in a van that provided no view of the outside world. This time, in a police car, she got a glimpse of the world again, and how oblivious people were to the dangers around them every minute.

Eventually, they pulled into her parents' driveway. No one came out from inside while the officer took her from the car and escorted her into the building. Her mother and sister, Lena, were in the living room waiting. Both seemed nervous; Lena did a worse job of hiding it.

The officer was explaining the terms of her release to a rather blank-faced Jean Sweeting when Harlow's father, Brysen, came in with Rupert. The men had gone to visit her in jail. With all the activity, it hadn't occurred to her, or Greta, to call them. On their arrival at the jail, they'd been told that she'd already been released to house arrest.

Her father knew about the agreement; he'd had to approve it after Greta was in court. But he hadn't expected it to happen so quickly. From his tone, she couldn't tell if he meant she wasn't welcome, or just that no one was ready for her to be there.

Her ankle monitor was fitted and she was given care instructions. With it on, she could shower, but had to avoid submerging the device. She had to stay inside her parents' property line, but could go into the yard or onto the driveway.

In contrast to the rules and procedures in jail, the new ones would be a breeze. The officers left in a flurry of activity, and then suddenly, they were alone in her parents' front room.

"Well," Rupert said, trying to break the tension of the awkward silence. "How does it feel to be free?"

"Surreal." Harlow touched her hair. "I need to shower and change my clothes. Maybe after that I'll feel normal again…" Though she doubted it. "This still feels like a dream I might wake up from."

"That's understandable," Rupert said, moving aside when she stood up.

Everyone seemed to be giving her a wide berth. Especially her sister who darted away from the doorway when Harlow started toward it.

"Did you do it?" Lena called out, stopping her. "Did you really kill that guy?"

They had questions, everybody did. There was an irony in sweet, innocent Lena being the first to ask such an important one. Her little sister would be the last person she'd burden with details of the night Hagan lost his life.

"Lena," their mother whispered.

"Uh," Harlow said, forcing a smile as she faced the room. "I'm going to make a couple of quick calls first. Excuse me."

Quick call was right. She ran up the stairs and grabbed the handset from her nightstand to dial as fast as possible. Ryske would've been expecting a call from her hours ago. She just hoped he hadn't called the jail in a panic.

The number that flashed up on his cellphone would be unknown to him, which meant he might not answer. She was still worrying about being diverted when the ringing in her ear stopped.

"Who is this?" Ryske snapped down the line.

Relief, he'd answered. Though he wasn't in a great

mood. Either he was worried someone got the number from her under duress, or that telemarketers were angling to con him. Good luck to anyone who tried that.

Her mouth opened, but she didn't know what to say.

After a few seconds of nothing, a sly smile curled her lips. "A very horny, very naughty girl."

Silence came before he groaned. "You feeling frisky, baby? In a new pod?"

Kicking off her shoes, she pushed herself to the middle of her bed. "I'm sitting in the spot where we first made love."

An exhale of disbelief and relief reverberated to her ear. "House arrest?"

"That's right," she said. Peculiar. How had he come to that conclusion so fast? "How did you—"

"I'm on my way, Trinket. Don't go anywhere."

She couldn't go anywhere even if she wanted to. The line went dead before she could ask questions.

Shaking herself from her daze, she'd call Ryske on his quick thinking when he arrived, which shouldn't take too long.

Clyde got a call next. Getting him off the phone was hard work. Her persistent friend wanted details on how she'd ended up at her parents' home. More details than Ryske, who she'd expected would want to know everything. Except, he'd had no questions. It seemed like her love had expected it. Like he'd anticipated it.

How had he anticipated it?

THREE

HER SUSPICIONS ABOUT Ryske's quick conclusion stuck with her in the shower. Having time, and privacy, under the jets of warm water was a welcome novelty. More than once, she reminded herself no one was looking over her shoulder.

Though there was no doubt she spent more time getting ready in the bathroom than she had on any one occasion during her stay in jail, she didn't procrastinate too long. If Noon was driving, Ryske would already be in town. His appearance at the Sweeting house would be unexpected, as would that of his driver, if Ryske brought Noon inside. Leaving the pair alone to explain why they'd showed up wouldn't be fair. So she sped through her old post-shower routine to ensure her presence when they arrived.

Doing her hair and putting on a dress felt odd. For the last three months, her wardrobe consisted of a jumpsuit and a cheap hair tie. Nothing more, nothing less. Being herself again was liberating. Just for kicks, she dug out her makeup and added a little eyeliner and gloss to her look. What a rebel.

For the first time in months, she recognized the woman looking back at her in the mirror. Not because of the hair and makeup, they were peripheral. Familiarity came in the color in her cheeks and the smile on her face. One that didn't have to be followed by a frown.

Ryske was coming.

She'd be able to put her arms all the way around him and hold him close without a guard telling them to break it up. She'd be able to taste his tongue, to feel his hands… Her senses were free to be overloaded by whatever she chose to do with any part of his body. And her plan was to play with every single inch of it… several times.

The doorbell propelled her from the vanity stool. Oh, it was nuts to be as excited as a virgin on prom night. They'd seen each other three days ago and had enjoyed each other before. Maybe not as much as she'd have liked, but she only had herself to blame for that oversight.

Running from her bedroom, she swung herself around the mid-landing banister and hurried down the second flight just in time to see her mother and Rupert going toward the entryway.

A pang of disappointment struck. Stupid. Greeting Ryske herself would be dangerous given the high likelihood they'd mount each other right there on the front steps. What a show for the neighbors that would be.

Almost self-conscious, she ran a hand over her hair and down her dress, trying to sweep away the fizzing energy of anticipation.

Jean opened the Sweetings' front door. Rupert stood just behind her, probably acting as security. They didn't know who was on the other side and with a suspected murderess in the house, vigilance was appropriate.

Patient, just be patient.

Except, huh, if a visitor intended to start a fight, she'd be best equipped to handle it. Costello's tricks had come in handy more than once in jail. Maybe she should be answering the door. In the ranks of fighters present in the house right then, she would be top of the list to combat anyone vicious.

Shame it didn't take long to be reminded vicious came in many forms.

"Oh," Jean said, her voice strained and surprised. "Oh, we didn't expect…"

Surprise *was* to be expected. But why would her mom

be so awkward about finding Ryske at the door?

The reason became all too clear when Rupert stepped aside to reveal Ryske wasn't the one on the doorstep at all.

The unanticipated guest spotted her standing dumbfounded at the bottom of the stairs and extended her arms to rush in, squeezing between Jean and Rupert.

"Harlow!"

In shock, she didn't have the wherewithal to object to the perfumed embrace. "O… Ophelia," Harlow said, trying to relax enough to pat the woman on the back. "What…? What are you doing here?"

Clutching her upper arms, Ophelia put a little distance between them to look her in the eye. "Oh, I knew it was nonsense. Of course, it was nonsense."

Turning to Jean and Rupert, still in the entryway, Ophelia put a tight arm around her.

"Miss Hagan," Rupert said, looking at Jean and then at her. "We were very sorry to hear about your brother."

Jean closed the front door, lingering there to gather herself. Despite a valiant effort, it failed. Still, her mother was good at faking it.

"Yes," Ophelia said. "Yes, it was awful… I couldn't believe it when I heard of Harlow's arrest. I was appalled. There's no way she could be responsible for this. I'd known for months that she and my brother were involved. They had real feelings for each other, you understand."

Real feelings? What the hell was Ophelia doing? What in the…? Why would the woman appear here now after being nowhere for three months? And why in the hell was she insinuating a relationship where none existed?

"You were… involved with him?" her mother asked.

Rupert frowned too. He had more reason than most to be confused, even angry. Why? Because she'd implied they'd get back together, oh, and had flat denied being involved with Jarvis Hagan.

She hadn't come up with anything close to an answer for her mother before their guest spoke again.

"As soon as they called to tell me about Harlow's case, and this wonderful development…" Ophelia grinned. "I just had to come and show my support… You don't mind if I spend some time with Harlow, do you?"

"Uh, no," her mother said. "We were about to have dinner. We'd be thrilled if you would join us."

"Perfect!" Ophelia said, keeping Harlow tight against her side. "Where's the dining room?"

Her mother directed Ophelia to the opposite corner of the square foyer. Only then did Ophelia let her go to follow.

Rupert caught Harlow's arm before she could go after them. "You were sleeping with him?" Rupert asked. "Is that why you killed him?"

Hmm, her former fiancé hadn't picked the best moment to push her buttons. Harlow was already struggling to figure out what Ophelia was up to. She didn't also need it sky-written that her whole family assumed she was guilty of homicide.

The front door opened, making her and Rupert turn. Ryske came striding in and stopped short when he found them in the foyer. For a second, the three of them examined each other.

"Mr. Ryske," Rupert said. "What are you…?"

No prizes for guessing Rupert might struggle to figure out why this particular man appeared. Ryske didn't seem to care; he zeroed in on her, smile emerging, yes, he was pleased to see her. Poor guy didn't know what he'd walked into. Raising a finger, still trying to think of something neutral to say, the decision was made for her.

"Baby," Ryske said.

He'd been talking to her, she knew that. Except she wasn't the one to respond.

"Sweetheart!" Ophelia exclaimed, startling them all, though none more than Ryske.

Ophelia rushed across the foyer, breaking between her and Rupert, much as she'd burst into the house. This time, she captured Ryske's face to pull him down for a kiss.

Rupert turned to the dining room, no doubt to give the couple privacy and to have some sort of silent conversation with whoever was loitering in the doorway behind her. Harlow, on the other hand, couldn't take her attention away from the amorous couple.

Amorous was overstating it. Ophelia gave the kiss her all, really her all; Ryske didn't even close his eyes. Her love sought her out, obviously expecting some kind of explanation. When he didn't get one, he broke the kiss, pushing Ophelia away with more force than the woman would appreciate.

To her credit, Ophelia took it in stride. "My Ryske was so worried about my decision to come here," Ophelia said, slipping an arm around his waist to tuck herself against him. "I can't say I was surprised when Lena spotted him from the dining room. I thought he might be close by. My fiancé is very protective."

"Your—"

"Makes sense," Harlow said, cutting Ryske off. "Makes perfect sense."

Her family discussed Ryske's engagement to Ophelia during his last visit to the Sweeting house. Lena must have seen Ryske storming into the house and pointed out Ophelia's "fiancé."

"I assure you, Mr. Ryske, there will be no trouble for your fiancée here," Rupert said, stepping in front of Harlow. "You are free to take her home, or both of you may stay for dinner, whichever you think is best."

This wasn't Rupert's house, but he'd been part of the Sweeting family a long time. It wasn't unusual for him to extend a dinner invitation to someone if the moment called for it. In many ways, he was the son of the family. Brysen's heir.

Given her own experience of being with Rupert, it didn't surprise her that he assumed Ryske would make the decisions for both him and Ophelia. That was how Rupert thought a relationship should be.

Her gaze fell to Ophelia's hand. The woman was wearing *the* engagement ring… The one Rupert gave her. Oh, shit, shit, shit. Harlow had re-gifted it to her crew. Should she panic? The design wasn't unusual; it wasn't custom. Maybe if Rupert only glanced at it in passing, he'd assume the women had similar tastes. He wouldn't conclude it was the same ring he'd purchased… right?

Closing her eyes, she cursed the gods for blessing her with freedom. She hadn't been home for two whole hours and already she was embroiled in another con.

"Oh no, we want to stay," Ophelia said. "Don't we, sweetheart? We want the Sweetings to know that we bear Harlow no ill will."

And that was the kicker. Ryske couldn't now usher Ophelia out of the Sweeting house without implying he did bear her ill will.

"Yes," Ryske said, his voice low in his throat. "We'll stay."

"Good," Rupert said. "You know where the dining room is."

Stepping backwards, Rupert almost crashed into her, so she put her hands up to remind him that she was there. Yep, the felon still existed. Ryske managed to sneak a quick glare her way before passing Rupert.

That was rich, what did he have to be mad about? She was the one who'd just witnessed him kissing another woman… and a murderess at that.

FOUR

EVERYONE SHUFFLED INTO the dining room and seated themselves. Ophelia took Harlow's former place between Rupert and Ryske. Ankle monitors apparently meant demotion to the end of the table. Bottom rung. No one wanted to sit beside the suspected felon, so Harlow was propped there like the court exhibit on display.

Dinner was served and everyone was polite while eating. Regardless, manners could only take them so far, the awkward tension in the air needed a vent.

"What's prison like?" Lena asked.

Well, at least her sister was cutting through the crap. "Worse than jail," Harlow answered, picking up her water. "Which is where I was." Lena shifted in a squirm mirrored by most others at the table. Her answer was intended to relax the mood. Instead it came off as passive aggressive. The trouble was, Harlow wasn't relaxed enough to relax anyone else. "Sorry, Le… uh, it was… noisy. It wasn't so bad. Our cells were arranged on two tiers around a common day room. It was medium security, so it could've been worse."

"I would've just died," Lena said. "I mean dropped down dead."

"Lena," Jean murmured in a soothing, yet warning,

tone. "We don't want to talk about that… not now… not in front of our guests."

Perpendicular to her left, Jean sat next to her husband who had Lena on his other side.

"Have we forgotten the wine?" Brysen asked, probably as a way to redirect the conversation.

"Oh, yes, I'm sorry," Jean said and leaped to her feet to retrieve a bottle of wine.

Keeping her attention on her food, Harlow didn't even want to know if Ryske was looking at her. She feared eye contact would betray them to everyone. Just being in a room with him was driving her crazy… and not in a good way.

Discomfort faded to disgust as soon as her mother poured the wine. Harlow got a whiff of it and scowled. The smell made her feel so sick that she picked it up to hand it off to Rupert.

"Can you move that away from me, please?"

Rupert handed the glass down the table to Ryske who put it next to his own. "Are you okay?" Rupert asked, picking up her hand.

"I'd have thought you'd be desperate to get blitzed after three months in prison," Lena said.

Harlow didn't feel like correcting her sister again. "Blitzed, maybe," she said, wrinkling her nose at the bottle. "Wine, no thanks."

"You're not…" Jean started speaking with what could almost be deciphered as fear. "You're not pregnant, are you?"

Ryske's fork clattering onto his plate wouldn't be significant to anyone except her. The shock served him right after the way he'd joked about her potential pregnancy the last time he stayed at her family home. Ha! It was all shits and giggles before they'd had sex. Now, the accusation had the real potential to be true.

Everyone else at the table waited for an answer.

"She's been in prison for three months," Lena said. "That stuff about inmates sleeping with guards isn't true." She gasped. "Is it, Har? Did you sleep with the guards?"

"No, Lena, I didn't sleep with the guards."

"She did have relationships before being arrested," Rupert said for no good reason.

Rolling her head in his direction, she closed her eyes in a lazy blink. They'd had this conversation before. Just because he was pissed about what Ophelia said in the hall, didn't mean they should resort to backbiting.

"I'm not pregnant."

"How can you be sure?" Jean asked. "Oh my God, that would be the cherry on the cake, wouldn't it?" Jean was less subtle about dropping her fork after her sarcastic bark, something she would usually keep in check in front of guests. "Honestly, Harlow, I don't know what happened to you. Since you and Rupert broke up, you've never been the same."

Inhaling, Harlow conceded her mother was right. Though the two of them had opposing opinions on the virtue of her metamorphosis.

"You can rest easy, Mom. I had a full physical when I switched jails. A pregnancy test is part of that. As is a full STD panel... I am clean."

Stating that for everyone, she made eye contact with Rupert and each member of her family before sitting back and folding her arms. That declaration should satisfy their curiosity though it grated on her. No one else at the table would be expected to provide such an explicit announcement.

"It must be awful to have a baby in prison," Lena said, her gaze drifting toward the French doors behind Ryske and Ophelia. "You go through the trauma of birth and then they just whisk your child away to be lost in the system."

Uh, excuse her? That brought Harlow up short. Her fingertips had been en route to her fork, but her sister's comment was so offensive she forgot about the flatware and the food.

"The system?" Harlow asked. "Why would my child be lost in the system?"

Lena jolted back from her daydream. Her attention darted around the table as though she expected someone to save her. No, nope, wouldn't be that easy. Harlow fixed on her little sister, ready to wait there all night for clarification, if that's what it took.

"Well, I…" Lena started. "I just assumed if you're away for twenty years—"

"My child would live with its father," she said.

Jean was taken aback. "His father?"

"Yes, Mom," she hissed. "Contrary to popular opinion…" Harlow cast a quick glare at Ophelia before returning her focus to her mom. "I wasn't opening my legs for every man who passed my way… I know who I had unprotected sex with."

"Oh my God," Jean said, clutching her husband's hand. "Harlow, must you?"

"I wasn't the one who brought it up."

"Unprotected?" Rupert asked.

It was difficult not to roll her eyes, and even harder not to look at Ryske; he'd be loving every single second of this.

"Yes, Rupert, unprotected," she said, twisting toward him. "You know what else I like now? Shower sex… And I learned that before jail before anyone makes any girl-on-girl assumptions." She put a hand over Rupert's and tilted her head. "Turns out, you make it far more complicated than it has to be."

Withdrawing his hand, Rupert cleared his throat. "Harlow," he murmured.

"Is he the kind of guy that you could… trust to raise your child?" Lena asked.

"Well, I don't know, Lena, but given that the child's mother would be a convicted murderess, I guess whatever Daddy is, it would be a step up from there," she said, fed up with the assumptions and accusations.

"But to do it alone—"

"He wouldn't be alone," Harlow said. "He has a network of incredibly loyal friends I consider family… All of them would support my child. All of them… Maybe he wouldn't have a big house in the suburbs, but he'd be loved every day, and he'd know it. He'd learn about loyalty and passion and he'd always get As because he'd charm the pants off every teacher."

"What if it was a girl?" Lena asked.

Harlow smiled. "Then God help her boyfriends," she said. "She'd probably be a virgin until after her Daddy and overly protective uncles died… but she'd be a badass. No one would take advantage of her, not ever. She'd be smart and quick and wrap men around her little finger… especially her Daddy."

"Just like her mom."

Ryske's voice caught her gaze. Neither had to say anything else. She could feel his pride… and his desire, pulsing through the air. Oh, and damn her, she sent it right back.

If there was one thing in this world she could have complete faith in, it was Ryske. The depth of that conviction only grew the longer they looked at each other. Fierce and sure, she would be adamant about him caring for any child she had in prison, if that was the way life went. Ryske wouldn't deny their child, and he wouldn't let her down.

Something about the lost possibility pricked moisture in the corner of her eye. She'd never carry another man's child. Never. If she couldn't bear children for Ryske, she wouldn't bear them for anyone.

"What if he didn't want the child?" Lena asked, as oblivious as the rest of the table to the moment passing between them.

"Why wouldn't he?" Ryske asked with a thread of offense.

The doorbell interrupted. Probably a blessing… or that's what she thought until her hope landed on a frowning Ryske. What was with that look? With wide eyes, she asked him without words if any of the guys could be on the doorstep. Somehow, he heard her question because he shook his head once in response.

Still, given her conclusions before dinner, before she knew Ophelia was the one a-knocking, Harlow prepared to answer the door to friend or foe. If things got hairy, Ryske was there to have her back.

"I'll get it," she said, pushing her chair out and leaving the dining room.

Not like she wanted to be in there anyway. In jail, the inmates fantasized about food they'd eat if they were on the outside. Now free, it didn't taste as good as she remembered.

Crossing to the front door, she took advantage of the few seconds alone to breathe. When she opened it, her day got a lot brighter.

A scream of joy burst out. "Oh my God, Clyde," she said, grabbing for him to pull him into a hug.

A friend! Just a friend. One without complications… Well, other than that one little moment of insanity.

Throwing his arms around her waist, he picked her up and smacked a kiss to her forehead. "You look amazing," he said, setting her on her feet to check her out. "Not at all like a crazed murderer, not one bit." She scrunched her nose. "Too soon?"

Slapping a hand to each side of his face, she squeezed him. "I missed you," she hissed through clenched teeth.

"Good, because I brought you something."

"Me?" she asked. "A present? You brought me a present?"

He nodded. She could already see her suitcase on the step beside him, but that obviously wasn't the gift because he crouched down to retrieve something from behind it. At the sight of the brown paper bag, she gasped and slapped both hands over her mouth.

Opening up the bag, Clyde was careful about showing her what was inside like it was a secret.

A huge bottle of hard liquor. She squealed. "I knew there was a reason you were my favorite," she said, snatching the neck of the bottle through the paper bag, and Clyde's hand to pull him inside.

Everyone from the dining room was squeezed in the doorway, probably wondering why she'd been screaming. Clyde fought with the suitcase to get it through the entryway. Inside, for her, dinner was over. Instead she pulled her friend toward the stairs.

"We're going upstairs," she said like back in high school when her buddies came over. "Dinner was great, Mom. But, you know…" She faked a yawn. "Tiring day."

Jean blinked at Brysen, at a loss for words. Rupert was more expressive, though he wasn't vocal. He curled a protective arm around Lena's shoulders. Yep, he disapproved. What a surprise. With murder, jail, and all that jazz, it was on them if they didn't expect her to disappoint them.

Dragging Clyde upstairs, she herded him into her bedroom and kicked off her shoes.

Next thing was opening the liquor. "Put the case up on the other side of the bed for me, will you, please?"

Clyde did as she asked, then backed up to sit on the window seat. Harlow gulped down some JD while tugging at the zipper on her dress.

"Was that Ryske downstairs?" Clyde asked.

Harlow thrust the open bottle at him and slid the straps of her dress off her shoulders to wriggle out of the material. Unzipping her case, she threw open the top and raked around in the clothes inside. The smell hit her hard and she groaned as her head fell back.

"You smell that?" she asked, grabbing handfuls of the clothes to bury her face in them. "Floyd's."

"You're a strange woman."

Throwing him a smile over her shoulder, she dropped the clothes and nodded at the alcohol. "Drink with me."

"I have to get home tonight, and it's not a short journey."

"Stay the night," she said, picking out a skirt from the case. "We have two guest bedrooms."

"You think Ryske will be okay with that?" he asked, taking a drink. "Things haven't exactly been great between us... What is he doing here?"

"Him being here isn't the shocking part," she said. "The woman he's with is Ophelia Hagan..." She paused to look him in the eye. "You know? Jarvis Hagan's sister."

The bottle dropped from his lips to land on his knee. "Oh my God, his sister?"

"Yep," she said, lunging over to snag the bottle and enjoy another slug.

Holding it up to the window, she offered a silent toast to the man she'd gone to jail for killing.

"Is he dating her?"

"They're engaged," she said, appreciating another

slurp, then handing back the bottle.

"Wait, wait, wait," Clyde said, propping the bottle on his knee again. "I thought that was a scam to piss off her brother." Harlow nodded while organizing clothes. "But… her brother is dead."

Smiling, she looked at him again. "Honey, you don't gotta tell me that."

FIVE

HER BEDROOM DOOR OPENED, and boom, the moment changed. In only her underwear, the intrusion was unexpected. Right until Ryske came in and closed the door behind him. She relaxed. Her man had seen her in far less than underwear.

Even the scowl on Ryske's face wasn't enough to discourage electrified carnal craving zapping her blood.

Harlow squinted over her shoulder at Clyde. "I'm so sorry," she said to her friend.

"For what?" he asked, confused.

For what she was about to do. Three months had been too long. All her pent-up need and desire gathered to critical mass until she just couldn't contain it anymore.

Dumping the clothes, she ran around the end of the bed and launched herself into Ryske's arms. Their mouths locked before her legs coiled all the way around him.

"Oh, baby," she murmured, pushing his jacket off his shoulders. "Kiss me."

Ryske's hands dug into her ass, holding her to him, rocking her pelvis up and down over the ridge in his slacks. The motion made maintaining the contact of their mouths more difficult, but it felt too good to object. Anyway, their tongues were practiced enough to delve deep.

Yanking at his tie to jerk it free, she wanted to break all the rules they'd been forced to adhere to in jail. Even though mussing his clothes was a bad idea, given he'd have to go back downstairs at some point, all she could think about was tasting him. She pulled his shirt buttons open to duck and press her lips to his tattoo.

With a pointed tongue, she traced its shape. "Let me down, baby," she hissed, dragging her teeth up to his throat. "I want you inside me."

Wrapping her arms around his head, she tried to force their mouths together again.

"In front of the sap?"

Relaxing her kiss, she spoke against him. "What if this is our last chance?" she murmured, licking the seam of his lips. "What if there's never another chance to have me?"

The question was a tease, though there was an element of truth in it. They'd lived without each other for months.

With her arms and legs locked around his neck and torso, he loosened his embrace. Though that didn't disconnect her from his body; she clung to him while he wrestled off his shirt to toss it aside.

Collapsing onto the bed, Ryske scooped her legs higher around him, grinding himself down harder. In a feigned attempt to fight, she pushed back, matching his vigor.

Harlow whimpered. "Oh, fuck, Crash," she gasped.

Seizing her throat, Ryske rose up exuding manic need.

Clyde must have felt the tension jump a few notches because he squawked. "Oh, hey," he said, probably worried about Ryske's intention.

The last thing she wanted was freedom from Ryske's grip, even in spite of her friend's concern. Unfortunately, she wasn't about to make it easier. An instinctual growl of need vibrated through her chest.

"Tighter," she said and yelped when Ryske's fingers strengthened.

This was foreplay, which her friend seemed to figure out.

"I've gotta get out of here," Clyde said.

If he hadn't known what was coming next already, he couldn't deny it anymore. The polite thing to do would be to stop and apologize. The trouble with that? The overwhelming drive of their urgency to be joined. Containing themselves was impossible.

Clyde was tiptoeing toward the bedroom door when it opened, which inspired enough terror to rip her gaze from Ryske's. If her family or Rupert found them like this, there would be no upholding the façade.

In contrast to earlier in the day, seeing Ophelia enter was kind of a relief.

"What the hell are you doing?" Ophelia hissed, closing the door, casting a disapproving eye over Clyde, then landing her hands on her hips. "I don't know you."

"Ophelia Hagan, meet Clyde Flaxman," Ryske grumbled, though he hadn't taken his attention from the woman beneath him. Running a hand from her jaw to her cleavage, his fingertips slid over the mound of each of her breasts. "Now both of you fuck off."

"Fuck off?" Ophelia snapped.

Breathing out, Harlow's heavy body sank into the mattress. "They can't," she admitted.

His fingertips felt so good. Skimming the edges of her bra cups, they ascended to her lips. Harlow kissed them, sucked and nibbled on them, relishing their freedom.

"Then they can watch," Ryske said, stealing his touch from her lips to reach for his belt. "I need you, Trink."

The almost pained confession only made it harder to stall him.

"Crash," she whispered, curling her fingers around his wrist to pry his grip from her throat.

Although he resisted for a second, he allowed her to ease them apart to sit up. Ryske went so far as to sit with his feet on the floor. Still between her legs, mind you, so one of her legs stayed hooked over his lap.

"What the hell is going on here?" Ophelia asked.

The question was enough to erase some of Ryske's desire. His head snapped around so fast she guessed Ophelia wasn't being treated to one of his panty-melting smiles.

"What the hell is going on here?" Ryske repeated the question. "What the hell are *you* doing here, Fifi?"

"Me?" Ophelia asked. "I got a call from the State's Attorney that the woman responsible for my brother's murder was being released to house arrest. Why shouldn't I be here?"

"Wait a second," Clyde said, stepping backwards to get closer to the end of the bed. He watched her drape her linked fingers over Ryske's shoulder. "This will be a conditional release… Are you allowed to be this close to a member of the victim's family?"

Nothing explicit was said about that at jail or by Greta… that she heard. The question was alarming enough to send Ryske to his feet.

"Get the fuck out of here," he said to Ophelia, no wiggle room in that demand.

Mmm… His clear, firm tone turned up the heat in Harlow's hormones again… Three months was too long.

Ophelia sighed and folded her arms. "I signed a waiver. I'm not afraid of Harlow. I signed a release so we can maintain our friendship."

"Our friendship," Harlow muttered, picking a top out of the suitcase to pull it on over her head. "Crash, you should put your clothes back on… Clyde, can you pass me that skirt over there?"

Clyde went around the bed to pick up the skirt she'd dropped. He handed it over at the same time Ryske retrieved his shirt from the floor. He tucked it in and buttoned it while Harlow wriggled into her skirt.

"I think we should sit down and talk about this," Ophelia said, crouching down to pick up Ryske's tie. He tensed when she sashayed over and lifted his collar to hook the tie around his neck. "Are we really going to let Harlow go to prison for murder?"

"You haven't cared about where she's been for three months," Clyde said.

Sitting cross-legged on her bed, Harlow started to fold the clothes heaped in the suitcase.

"I have cared," Ophelia said. "What was I supposed to do? I couldn't visit a place like that."

Once Ryske's tie was done, better than Harlow would have done it, Ophelia smoothed her fingers through his hair to right it. She just couldn't resist taking the opportunity to touch the man, even though he didn't belong to her.

"You could've written her a letter," Clyde said. "Made a call."

"Clyde," Harlow whispered, and shook her head once.

"No," Ophelia said, stepping to the side. "If he has something to say, he should say it."

"He has nothing to say," Harlow said. "This is my first night home, I don't want a fight." Ophelia still had her chin hitched high. "Ophe."

Drawing the woman's attention, Harlow made it clear by the way she narrowed her eyes that Ophelia shouldn't forget the distribution of power. Ophelia might go around telling people that Harlow had been sleeping with Jarvis, but both of them knew that wasn't true.

Coming forward, Ophelia sat on the bottom corner of the mattress, and leaned against the metal frame at the foot of the bed. "I think we should talk," Ophelia said.

The wide, wet eyes thing didn't work with her. Harlow reached for another top to fold it into the case. "I don't think we should."

"We have to talk, Harlow," Ophelia said. "We have an opportunity. If I can help you, I will." That claim was hilarious. "I will... Tell me what you need me to do."

Opening her mouth, she looked at Ophelia, ready to say something. Except she caught a glimpse of Ryske. They weren't alone. So Harlow went back to folding without a word.

"Don't stop on my account," Ryske said. The polite act was snide. It only lasted a second before he became more demanding. "What the fuck is going on?"

"You didn't tell him," Ophelia stated.

Harlow stopped folding to set her narrow gaze on the heiress again. "No," she said. "I didn't tell him."

Tension prickled through Ryske. No amount of distraction could hide how his body grew rigid.

"Oh…" he breathed out the word in a long exhale, "my… God…"

That wasn't an encouraging tone of clarity.

"Oh my God, what?" Clyde asked.

"Nothing," Harlow said, slapping the lid of the suitcase closed and springing to her knees to zip it up again. "We are not talking about this. None of it. Not tonight."

Getting off the bed, she threw her head forward and drove her fingers into her hair to give it more volume. Once satisfied, she went to Ryske and bounced onto her tiptoes to drag him down for another kiss. Busying him with her mouth, she robbed him of the bracelet on his wrist. Slipping her fingers under the leather, she pushed it off over his hand.

"What are you doing?" Ophelia asked, rising from the bed to watch Harlow loop the accessory onto her own wrist.

The bracelet had been tucked up under Ryske's shirt cuff during dinner. In front of anyone else, it wouldn't matter which of them was wearing it. But her family knew it as hers. Explaining why Ryske was wearing her bracelet might create confusion they could do without.

She wiped her smudged gloss from his mouth and retrieved the JD from the window seat where Clyde left it. Having processed whatever he thought he'd figured out, Ryske turned to Ophelia. What conclusions had he drawn? They didn't seem to be in Ophelia's favor given the glare on his face.

"This is a con," Ryske growled at her. "Go with it or don't. You're a cover, that's it."

The beauty stuttered. "Ryske, I don't—"

"I belong to Harlow," he said and bowed to get closer to Ophelia's face. "Don't forget that for a fucking second… One word from her and I go to heel."

Ophelia blinked. The confusion and affront on her expression soon swung her way. Harlow couldn't refute what Ryske said and wouldn't contradict him, not in a setting like this. In her bedroom, where all parties knew the truth of their relationship, they could be them.

"I want a minute alone," Ophelia said, shrugging off her hurt to hitch her chin high again.

"With me?" Harlow asked and shook her head. "There are only two things in the world I'm interested in being alone with right now." She held the bottle aloft. "This bottle." She pointed at Ryske. "And his cock… Unfortunately, I can't have that right now." Hugging the bottle to her chest, she started across the room. "So, I'll have to stick with my friend Jack." Harlow took Clyde's hand. "Come downstairs and meet everyone."

Leading her friend to the bedroom door, she imagined her family confused. Though the people downstairs probably had fewer questions than those in her bedroom. Her included.

Guiding Clyde downstairs, she introduced him to her family. It was a relief to be honest about how they'd met and the nature of their relationship. Though the Sweetings may not have bought it. She doubted they'd ever return to a time when her family took her word at face value. Given just how much she was withholding, she couldn't blame them.

SIX

RYSKE AND OPHELIA had come downstairs just a couple of minutes after her and Clyde.

The sight of them together might turn her stomach, but she couldn't deny they projected a realistic image of being a couple. With his arm around Ophelia's shoulders, Ryske was kind of draped against the beauty like the position was an everyday occurrence.

Though she could sense tension between the pair, it only helped sell their relationship. Her family seemed to have assumed that Ryske didn't think it was a good idea for Ophelia to be in the Sweeting house. If Ophelia really had come to visit the woman accused of murdering her brother, Harlow would probably agree with him.

Everyone was seated in the living room. The air lighter now they were spread out and in comfortable seats. No doubt it helped that everyone had a drink in their hand.

Her mother kept trying to offer her a glass. Harlow found comfort in her bottle and didn't feel the need to pour a measure when she could keep hold of her private hoard of liquor.

"The garden party was supposed to be tomorrow night," Jean said, going around the room topping off everyone else's wine glasses. "We'll have to cancel now."

"Why?" Harlow asked, taking her mouth away from her bottle. "Because your felon daughter came home? You should've told them to keep me in jail another couple of nights." Nobody else smiled when she did. "No one has a sense of humor anymore… I think you should have your anniversary party and go on your vacation. You do it every year."

"We can't do that," Jean said, taking her seat in front of the window again. Jean and Brysen had identical chairs, side by side with a small table between them. "A hundred people were invited to the party. We hired an event planner, caterers—"

"It's your one big party of the year," she said. "We don't really do birthdays and Christmas is always a bust… You deserve a little fun… I promise to stay in my bedroom."

That cheered her mother. "You… you wouldn't attend?"

Whenever she had to be in public with Ryske, it thrilled Harlow to show as much skin as possible. Pointing her toes to present the ankle monitor on her bare leg, she discovered another advantage to wearing a short skirt. One that didn't involve tormenting her lover, but did involve a clear view of her manacle. Wearing the device with pride served as a reminder to all that she was tethered.

"I just don't have anything that goes with this shade of gray," Harlow said.

Jean smiled and reached for Brysen. "I suppose we could… Everyone has RSVP'd and the food has been ordered."

"It's your decision," Brysen said, guiding Jean's hand to his mouth.

Her parents weren't often affectionate. It was nice to have presented them an excuse to share some fondness.

Picking up Ryske's arm, Ophelia tucked herself against him, snuggling in closer. "I love a party," she said. "I think it's an excellent idea to celebrate your love."

"You should stay," Jean said. "Come to the party."

"Oh, I don't know," Ophelia said, doing an

unconvincing job of being opposed to the idea. "We wouldn't want to intrude."

"It's no intrusion," Jean said. "Your fiancé has stayed here in the past."

"He has?"

"Yes, during his business dealings with Sweeting Securities. Before your friend was taken ill… were they okay?"

Ophelia blinked at Ryske and glanced at her too, but quickly smiled. "Oh, yes. Thank you."

Harlow hoped Ophelia didn't expect any brownie points for going along with the lie. Changing the subject seemed the safest course of action.

"I already asked Clyde to stay," Harlow declared to the room.

"In your room?" Lena asked.

"No," she said. "In the second guest room."

"That's fine," Jean said, wearing a rigid smile.

Harlow wasn't the only one to notice, Clyde squirmed. Copying Ophelia's earlier maneuver, she picked up Clyde's arm to wrap it around her, as a comfort for him not her. Clyde was her friend; he'd been there for her. It wasn't right he should be uncomfortable.

"We will have to cancel the vacation," her father said.

"Why?" Sitting up straight, Harlow was too shocked to react to Clyde's arm slipping off her shoulders. "You won't get a refund if you cancel now."

"We can't leave Lena here," he said, nodding to his youngest daughter.

Her spine lost some of its starch. "You mean, you can't leave Lena with me," Harlow said and scratched her temple. "You know, if you're going to leave her anywhere, with an alleged murderess is probably the safest place. Especially when that murderess loves her dearly and would protect her with her life… You don't think I would hurt her, do you?"

"He didn't say that," Jean said.

"No," Harlow said, slipping to the front of the couch. "God forbid anyone say what they actually mean in this family." Rising to her feet, she curtsied. "Excuse me a minute.”

Slurping from her liquor bottle, still wrapped in brown paper, she didn’t look at anyone as she left. Vaulting up the stairs to reach her bedroom, she shoved the suitcase onto the floor, without caring it landed with a thud.

Slumping on the bed, she dumped the liquor bottle on the nightstand and picked up the phone to dial. While listening to it ring, she flopped onto her side, curling into the fetal position, facing the window.

“S’up?” came the male voice on the line.

“I’m losing my mind,” she muttered and let her eyes close.

“Hey, Nightingale!”

It was a comfort that someone could sound so happy. The ambient hum from Floyd’s comforted her too, though the background noise didn’t last. It ebbed until it was indecipherable, so she guessed he’d slipped into the den.

“Did you hear me, Dover? I’m losing my mind. I’m going insane.”

He laughed. “Babe, we’ve known you weren’t right in the head since you fell for that creep you’re with.”

“He’s not here,” she said, tucking the phone between her ear and the pillow. Her arm actually reached behind her, seeking him out, just in case. Her fingers were disappointed. Bringing her arm back, she rested a fist on her cleavage. “I want to come home, Dover… Tell me I can come home.”

“Any time,” he said. “Just let us know in advance if S.W.A.T. is gonna come looking for you again… You know, so we can stash you in the new hidey hole we’ve had built in the cellar.”

Okay, she smiled, S.W.A.T. was a bit of an overstatement, but she wouldn’t mind a secret room for her private use. “Does it come with leashes and chains?”

“Nah,” he said. “We limited Ryske’s design input.”

Laughing, a weight lifted from her. “Thank you.”

“For what?”

“Talking to me like I’m a human being. Not asking anything from me.”

“We ask one thing,” he said. “That you be you every

minute you can."

A tear warmed her lashes. She swiped it away. "I want this to be over."

"I know," he murmured. "I know you do, darlin', it's what we all want… But, hey, house arrest, that's better than jail, right?"

"Was it you?" she asked. "The robbery… Ryske knows more than he's had a chance to tell me."

"He's there? I mean, he's at your parents."

"Yeah," she said. "Ophelia showed up too, and my parents think they're engaged. It makes sense for him to play the role given that she's here, but… I don't know. I think I was ready to just do it, you know?"

He clucked his tongue. "You two have no problems when it comes to doing it. But if you mean telling your parents about your relationship, tell them. Ryske won't deny it. He sure won't deny it for the sake of Ophelia."

"Who is that?" Another male voice traveled down the phone line, quieter, implying someone had come up behind Dover.

Something beeped. When he spoke again, the line echoed like she was on speaker. "It's Nightingale," Dover said.

"Oh, hey," Maze said.

"We just gave your guy a ride," Noon said, his voice louder than the others.

"Shit, boy, you don't have to shout," Dover said. "It's on speakerphone."

Despite it being impossible, she was sure she heard one of them shove another. It was nice to be a part of their playing, even from afar.

"You brought him here, but you didn't come to see me?" she asked, pushing out her lower lip in a faux pout.

"Ryske wanted to get a lay of the land first," Maze said.

"Yeah, or just a lay," Noon muttered.

Sounded like Maze gave him another shove. "We'll come over whenever you're ready."

"My parents were supposed to be going on vacation

day after tomorrow," she explained, thinking that would've given the guys the perfect opportunity to visit. "My dad said they want to cancel… I think they're afraid to leave me with my sister. You know, given my murderous tendencies and all."

Silence reigned on the line. Oh, God, were they doing the awkward thing she relied on them avoiding?

"Is she hot?" Maze asked. "Your sister can come stay here… We'll protect her from you."

Another tear slipped from her eye. She wiped it away. They weren't being awkward; they were waiting for the optimum moment to start joking. Comedy: tragedy with timing.

"Like you could," she said, trying to prevent sentiment seeping into her voice. As much as Harlow liked them to believe in her strength, she also trusted her guys not to comment on her weakness when it snuck out. "I could take you down in a minute."

Noon laughed. "I think she could."

"Oh, yeah?" Maze asked. "Think I'm afraid of you, little girl?"

Sitting up, she tucked her heels on the edge of the bed. "I think you should be, tough guy. Just because I'm wearing your mark doesn't mean I'll go easy on you… I don't know the meaning of soft."

His voice became comically seductive. "Neither do I," Maze said and everyone laughed.

"Anyone else want to take a shot?" she asked. "It's been three months since y'all had a chance to get dirty with me… I can take you all at once. Three on one."

"Three guys, one girl," Noon said.

"Listen to that," Maze said. "This one's got a high opinion of herself, doesn't she?"

His teasing just encouraged her. "I guarantee I'd be the only one left standing at the end of that session. Bet you'd all be spent and begging for mercy before I even break a sweat."

Maze spat out a disagreeing laugh. "Ha, no fucking way. You've been playing lesbian for the last quarter. Do you remember what to do with a guy?"

"Oh, we're talking about sex?" she feigned surprise. "I don't know, baby, why don't you ask your best friend's cock how good I am? It jumps to attention every time I walk in the room."

The guys laughed again.

"Always fucking did for you," Dover said.

Harlow loved the teasing, the playing, the normalcy, and the lack of judgment. She'd missed it. She could say anything to them and them to her. Their interactions were the very definition of a safe space; they were exactly what she needed.

A creak at the other side of the bedroom brought her around fast. Rupert, standing in the bedroom doorway, was a surprise. The frown he wore was less unexpected.

"Guys, I've gotta go," she said, her attention staying on Rupert. "Stick by the phone, I'll call later. I love you."

Hanging up on their farewells, she put the phone back on its base and stood up to face the judgmental silhouette in her doorway.

SEVEN

IT DIDN'T TAKE HER EX long to get to the point. "Who were you talking to?" Rupert asked.

Harlow used her foot to push the suitcase under her bed. "Friends," she said, smoothing her skirt and starting around the bed when he began to walk deeper into the room.

"Harlow," he said and tried to reach for her, but she swerved out of the way of his arm.

Leaving the room was supposed to be her reprieve; an escape from the pending conversation. It didn't work. At the top of the stairs, he caught her and turned her to face him.

"Let me go, Rupert," she said, trying to pull her arm away.

"Who were those friends? Why were you talking about…"

If they were going to have this conversation, she wasn't going to apologize.

Lifting her chin, Harlow met his eye. "Cocks?" she asked, crooking a brow and shaking her hair down her back. "Because it's what I do now, Rupert." Though he still had her arm, she raised both in a proud shrug. "I'm free, Rupert, and I'm not talking about being free from jail… I'm free from society. I don't care about talking properly or impressing the neighbors. I'm free to be me and that's what I want to do. I want to be me."

"And that involves being intimate with three men? That is what you were talking about, wasn't it…?" He shook his head, disapproval written all over his face. "I don't know what happened to you… I don't know why you feel you have to act this way."

Widening her smile, she inhaled a cleansing breath. "This me isn't an act. Everything before, everything when I was with you… that was the act. I was never that person."

Startled, he blinked and recoiled a few inches to get a wider view. "You were never the person I fell in love with… Is that what you're saying?"

The last thing she wanted to do was hurt him. "No," she said, "that's not it…" Explaining her meaning was complicated. "You remember when we got together, what it was like? How we used to laugh all the time? How we used to talk about… everything?"

"Yes."

Narrowing her eyes, she looked into him. Could he understand? Didn't he get it? "What happened to that? When did we turn into our parents? That's what we did. Both of us. We started caring so much about what our mothers thought that we forgot to be ourselves." He relaxed, maybe beginning to understand. Stepping closer, she rested her hands on his waist. "Remember when we had sex in the courtyard of that hotel at your cousin's wedding? We had a room right upstairs, but we couldn't contain ourselves that long… No, it wasn't that we couldn't contain ourselves, it was that… we wanted to do it there. We didn't care about being irresponsible or being caught."

"We were kids."

"Were we?" she asked. "Is that what it was? When did your clients' perception of us become more important than us?" His frown returned. Harlow smiled and laid a hand on his cheek. "I'm not blaming you, it was me too. And maybe this is who you're supposed to be. Maybe this is a life that makes you happy… but it doesn't make me happy… I'm still the girl who took you by the hand and led you out to that courtyard… I didn't care we were twenty feet from five hundred guests… I didn't care there were rooms overlooking us and our only protection was that spikey plant thing…"

She grinned. When he mirrored her expression, it seemed he was reliving the same memory playing in her mind.

His mouth loosened to release a nostalgic laugh. "You cut your palm on that thing."

Which was how she remembered it so well. Opening her hand, Harlow showed him the two short white lines in the middle. "I still carry the scars."

Breathing out, his hand floated toward her hair. "We were insane back then."

"We were in love," she said. "And it was real… It was, Rupe. I did love you. I do love you. You were my first love. There will always be a part of me that belongs to those memories. We share something with each other that we can't share with anyone else… we grew up together…"

His fingers drifted into her locks. "You've outgrown that now."

"Rupert, I'm insane. You shouldn't be with me even if you wanted to be… I could go to prison for decades. My life is already over. Yours shouldn't be put on hold… I'm never going to be yours again… not like I was in those days."

"This man, the one who you… who you were talking about at dinner?"

"Yes," she said, open to his questions.

His curiosity was natural and she had nothing to hide… except the identity of her lover.

"You love him? You're in love with him?"

"Yes," she said. "That doesn't mean I didn't say the same thing to him. I did. I don't want his life on hold either. House arrest might seem like a reprieve, but when you've had your freedom taken away in a snap like I did, you're always waiting for the moment it will happen again."

"You think you'll be convicted?"

Harlow didn't know how much he knew about the evidence trail or the crime that led to her arrest. "I think that until a judge dismisses the case, I will keep the mind-set that I am going to be sent to prison for a long time. Better to plan for tragedy and welcome comedy."

"That's rather pessimistic, isn't it? You were never a pessimist."

There was a reason for her attitude, one she hadn't shared with anyone. "If I waver," she murmured. "He'll think there's hope."

Rupert peered closer. "You want him to move on," he said. She nodded. "You've told him to leave you."

"I've told him we're over. He doesn't listen."

Still, Rupert didn't completely understand. "Ophelia Hagan, she said you'd been intimate with her brother… and those men on the phone… you were talking about sleeping with three separate men. You were always faithful to me, weren't you?"

Somehow, she knew that the question wasn't really about their relationship. "Yes," she said. "You know I was faithful to you."

"If you love this other man, how could you be unfaithful to him? Is it your attempt to push him away?"

Telling him that truth could mean revealing more of her crew than she wanted to share. Until she figured out Ophelia's game, she wouldn't contradict the woman either. Trying to disguise her discomfort, she slid her toes up the back of her smooth calf.

Teasing was probably the best way to divert Rupert's attention. "Pisses him off," she murmured and leaned in close. "I like pissing him off."

Seeing how that confession startled Rupert was such a contrast to how Ryske would react. Her Crash would smile and do something outrageous.

Just at that, the restroom door opened farther along the hall. The upstairs family bathroom was often used if the downstairs washroom was occupied. Ryske came out, and paused to look between them like he hadn't expected there to be people in the hallway.

What a con. Ryske would've heard their conversation. There was no way she'd believe he was surprised to see them, no matter how well he sold his astonishment. Her head fell to the side in expectation of an admission. He should give her some signal of apology for eavesdropping. But this was Ryske. He didn't apologize for being him or taking advantage of a situation.

Rupert cleared his throat and tried to put an arm around her. "Should we go back downstairs?"

She pointed her thumb over her shoulder. "You go on. I have to get my bottle… I forgot to bring it from the bedroom."

"Of course," Rupert said, glancing at Ryske, who he probably expected to join him.

Ryske didn't move, which left Rupert no option except to frown and go alone. Anyone else would expect Ryske to go downstairs to join his fiancée. Harlow knew better.

Spinning on the spot, she flounced into her bedroom and rounded the bed to reach her bottle on the nightstand. She hadn't got to it by the time the bedroom door closed.

"It pisses me off?"

Picking up the bottle, she used it to hide her smirk and tried to keep her gaze innocent. "Are you denying it would piss you off if I slept with other men?"

Ryske approached, confident in his slow steps across the room. "You've been sleeping with other women for weeks."

"Other women, yes," she said, letting him take the bottle to put it back on the nightstand. "Sleeping, yes." She wrinkled her nose. "Sex? No… No, I don't believe I've had that for quite a while."

Grabbing her hips, he whirled her around and tossed her face down onto the bed to thrust up the hem of her skirt and pull down her panties. "I hate it when you wear underwear."

"Noted," she said.

When she peeked over her shoulder, he wasn't looking at her face. His fascination stuck on the salacious sight he'd exposed. Bowing down, he used his strength to part her legs and drove his tongue into her, burying his head between her thighs. Squeezing her lips together, she struggled to contain the sound of need that ached to burst free.

"I've missed you," he whispered, his fingers exploring the creases of her body, stimulating her juices.

"Are you talking to me or my pussy?"

"Definitely your pussy," he said and dipped lower to suck her clit hard. "I haven't missed that goddamn mouth."

Sitting up, she forced his tongue away from her center and reached for his belt to unfasten his pants. "Yes, you have," she said, grinning at him. "You've missed it being occupied."

Taking his cock in both hands, she opened wide to suck him into her throat. His groan was an enlivening incentive to keep going. Even when he snatched her hair in his fist to try pulling her away, she fought to keep going.

"I'm gonna fuck you," he growled. "Fuck, Trink!"

Unwilling to relinquish her control, Harlow sucked him harder, then pushed him into her cheek. Blinking up at him while she rubbed her cheek, stimulating the head of his dick from the outside of her mouth while her tongue played on his shaft.

When he gritted his teeth, she smiled and let both hands rise to fondle his balls. "You are fucking me," she whispered, his cock resting on her lips. "I want you to fuck my skull, right here, like this, until you can't take it anymore, until you fire your spunk into my throat." Leaning back, supporting her weight on one arm, she drew a nail down the center of her chest over her cleavage. "So, it can trickle down, all the way down inside me…" She rubbed her stomach. "I want you everywhere in me, Crash…" Sitting up again, she snatched his cock in her sure fist and pulled him back to her mouth. "Fuck me, Crash. Fuck me right here."

With her lips tight around her teeth, she let him push into her mouth and breathed out her pleasure in a moan that vibrated through him, making him throb on her tongue.

Determination surged through him. He grabbed her hair in his fists to thrust hard into her mouth. Feeling the stretch of her throat and the intensity of his need, she did her best to suck even when he was pulling out.

Their rhythm was natural. This kind of intimacy was where they started. Harlow knew when to breathe, how to pleasure him. Everything she did seemed to work. Blinking up, she recognized him climbing toward climax. The best way to get him there was to meet his eye.

The moment she did, he hissed and cursed. Granting her wish, he came in her mouth, spilling himself deep. After she'd swallowed him down, she leaned back, though his fingers were so tangled in her hair that it took a few seconds to extricate themselves.

"Now, what are we going to give you?" he asked, touching her temple.

Harlow pounced to her feet. "I told you in visiting that was what I missed most… So thank you, baby," she said, going to the mirror on her vanity to check her appearance. Grabbing a comb, she did her best to fix her hair. "You better get downstairs before Ophelia misses you."

Having done the best she could with the comb, she bent over to apply some new gloss to her lips. In the same moment Ryske's reflection created movement in the mirror, her skirt was lifted again.

His hand skimmed over her ass and then he smacked her hard. "When will this be mine?" he murmured.

Her? Or her ass?

Smiling, she put on another layer of gloss and lingered over screwing on the lid of the tube. Even after she put it back on the vanity, she didn't straighten. Those hands on her ass, on her skin, God, she wouldn't take them for granted.

"You're going to give me a complex," she said, undulating with his caress. "You keep talking to parts of my body, but never direct to me."

"Because you waffle," he said, using both hands to stroke her ass, up over her hips and around to her stomach. Flattening them on her abdomen, he slid them higher to cup and squeeze her breasts. "Mm, there they are."

When she stood up, his hands stayed under her top on her chest. "You know I've been accused of murdering your fiancée's brother," she said. "Rupert just caught me talking to my crew about their dicks and I just sucked the spunk from yours."

"Yeah," he said, crouching to kiss her neck without

moving his hands from her chest.

Nice as they felt, she couldn't be seduced into existing in him. Not here, not now. She pulled his hands out of her top and turned around to lay her palms on his chest, stacking them over his heart.

"I told Dover I want to go home," she said, enjoying the contentment that spread through him. "Nothing would make me happier than to strip off and climb into that bed with you." When he began to descend for a kiss, she leaned away and increased the pressure on her hands to hold him back. "But if my family find me stealing her fiancé too…"

Offense ticked his jaw. "I'm not her fiancé… Trink, if you keep pushing this, I'll go down there and tell them myself."

"They think I killed her brother… and you are the man she loves… I'm one hell of a temptress. Ophelia told my mother I was sleeping with Jarvis." She touched his lips. "Which I know you know I wasn't, she knows it too. So they think I slept with him and murdered him. Then, you come here with your fiancée, I tempt you away from the woman you proposed to, and screw you while she's in the same house… What am I going to do to you next?"

His swagger increased in time with his hands slithering around her body. "Whatever you goddamn like, any time you want."

"The black cloud isn't gone yet. Until then, we have to prepare for the worst."

"You told Marlowe you don't want me to hope."

She sighed and let her head fall to his chest. "I wish you hadn't overheard that."

"Me too," he said. "I don't want to hear about you having sex with other guys. Don't talk to other guys about sex."

She snorted. "Guess that's my relationship with Maze and Noon over."

"Three on one?" he asked. "Think I'll have to talk to the guys about how they talk to my girl."

Inhaling him, she closed her eyes and sank into his embrace. "I like the way they talk to me… My crew ground me. They give me something to lean on when the world is falling apart."

Easing her back, he kissed her. "Okay, baby, I'll trust you."

Linking their fingers, she led him to the door where she had to release her grip. Still, some contact was better than nothing. With jail on the horizon, nothing could soon be all they had.

"Let's get downstairs and convince my parents they can go on vacation. If they go, we can have a real party." Smacking her ass, he tried to push her out the bedroom door. Spinning around, she stole another kiss. "You go first," she said. "I forgot my bottle again."

"I'll wait."

"Don't," she said, scampering around him to dart back to her JD. "We can't go downstairs together anyway. Just tell them I was talking to you about my wholesome childhood or something. Go back to Ophelia."

He groaned his disapproval but surrendered to her request and went.

Ryske could make excuses about them chatting. She trusted him to cover for them no matter the situation.

The negative connotations of them showing up together was only part of the reason she'd sent him on ahead. Harlow hadn't spoken to Bale since her release. She didn't want to leave anyone out… especially the sensible honorary crew member. So, after another drink, she lay down on the bed and got ready to spill her guts to the doctor.

EIGHT

FOR MOST OF THE NIGHT, Harlow struggled to sleep. Wasn't easy to forget Ryske and Ophelia in the next room. Their headboards shared a wall. Her love was right there, inches away… with another woman.

Her fear wasn't the headboard banging. Ryske didn't want to be intimate with his fake fiancée; Harlow was positive of that. The pair were alone, in private, with the ability to speak. That was the problem. Any information they shared, any conversation they had, could blow everything up.

She wanted to be the one to tell him the truth of what happened the night Hagan died. Being stuck in her bedroom, with him so near, yet out of reach, left her helpless.

At around two thirty, voices carried through from the adjacent room. It was impossible to decipher specifics, but the tones were obvious. Ryske was unhappy while Ophelia was more subdued. At first anyway. Soon the aggravation increased in volume and urgency. Then there was silence.

A few tense moments of indecision almost brought her out of bed. To go through or not to go through? Yes, she'd get answers with the former, but her presence would add fuel to the fire. One which would spread fast. Everyone would wake up… Secrets would out… She stayed put.

In the morning, she woke before anyone else. For longer than was decent, she considered sneaking in to violate Ryske. Ophelia wouldn't thank her for the intrusion, fire, spread, secrets… she went downstairs to put on coffee instead.

Breakfast was going to be awkward if last night was a measure of how things would be.

Standing in the kitchen, pouring coffee, thinking about what she'd tell Ryske, her mother appeared. Lena wasn't far behind. Both took coffee but did little in the way of including her in their discussion about the day's itinerary.

Having guests gave Jean a needed distraction. In a manifestation of the anxiety level in the house, Jean prepared breakfast with more gusto than she'd ever seen from her mother.

On top of everything else, the annual anniversary party always caused her mother stress. Under normal circumstances, Jean loved being the center of attention. With a felon of a daughter in the house, this year the stress level was far higher than normal.

Leaving the women to make breakfast, Harlow went back to bed to get more sleep.

Even after she woke again, staying in bed appealed. That was until noise from downstairs betrayed the house was awake. Knowing who she'd see at the breakfast table gave her a reason to get up and go down to the dining room.

Everyone was finished eating, but they were all still there, with Clyde in Rupert's usual seat.

Darkening the doorway of the dining room, Harlow ran a hand into her hair and yawned. "Good morning."

"Morning?" Jean said. "It's almost the afternoon." That was an exaggeration. It was only ten thirty. "Couldn't you have put some clothes on?"

She was wearing a shirt, Ryske's shirt incidentally. It had ended up in her suitcase, so she figured that made it hers.

"Am I offending someone?" she asked. No one responded. "I didn't want to dress without having a shower… but I came on the hunt for more coffee. Seems everyone's getting along. What are we talking about?"

"The longevity of love," Ophelia said, curling a hand around Ryske's arm and angling to lean on him.

The conversation choice was relevant, given that the party tonight was for her parents' anniversary. Everyone was getting along. It was nice. Just a shame she had to be absent in order for them to relax.

"Yes, it should be celebrated while it lasts. Love can be fickle," she said and yawned again. "Oh, I feel good this morning. It was nice to make decisions for myself for a change. Going back to bed was a fuck you to jail."

"Harlow," Jean hissed, getting up to push her eldest daughter into the chair at the end of the table. "Your father is going to take Lena and me to the mall. Your friend Clyde was kind enough to offer to clean up."

Clyde gave a wave. Sometimes he came across as so cute and innocent.

"You're in good hands. You should see his apartment, it's spotless," Harlow said. "He's a real ball buster. He always remakes the bed after I've done it."

"You do the pillows wrong," Clyde said and they shared a smile.

Ophelia squeezed herself closer to Ryske. "I didn't know they were in a relationship, did you, honey?"

If that was an attempt to aggravate anyone at the table, it failed.

"They're friends," Ryske said.

"Yes," Harlow agreed. "Just friends."

"I feel bad leaving you with the clean up when you're our guests," Jean said, scanning the remnants of breakfast. "It seems inappropriate."

Brysen and Lena were rising from the table. "If you want to stay home, Mom, we can," Lena said. "You only wanted to go out for vacation stuff. It's not like you need anything for tonight. We planned your outfit weeks ago."

"We'll be fine, Mrs. Sweeting," Clyde said, leaving the table. "Ryske and I will handle it."

The way Ryske's head rose forced her to stifle a laugh. Clearly being volunteered for cleanup duty came as news to him.

Harlow folded her arms. "Ha, Ryske doesn't clean up in his own place. Dishes aren't his forte and I don't think he's ever made a bed in his life. Why do you think he only uses a sheet as a cover?" All eyes in the room slid around to her. Oops. Her mouth had run away before her mind could catch up. Trying her best to stay loose, she wiped sleep from her eye. "That's what Ophelia says anyway," she said and stretched. "Is there still coffee?"

Her quick diversion seemed to work. Her parents and Lena went back to talking about the day as they filtered out of the dining room.

Harlow picked at the food left on the table for a minute before peeking up at Ryske. "I'm sorry," she mouthed to him.

"Love you," he mouthed back.

"We'll only be an hour," Jean called from the foyer. "Everyone behave."

"That'd be a first," Ryske muttered.

Amused by her love, she didn't need to look at anyone else. Just to be sure there were no delays or backtracking, Harlow went after her parents to see them and Lena out. Her mother took the opportunity to remind her about five times that she wasn't allowed to leave the house. With the ankle bracelet weighing her down, it wasn't like she could forget.

She watched her father pull out of the drive and waved them off. As if the monitor on her leg wasn't enough of a scandal, Harlow guessed her choice of apparel would shock any nosey neighbors peeking around their drapes. After everything she'd endured, Harlow had learned there were worse things in life than offending snooty neighbors.

Closing the front door, she turned the key in the lock and then immediately changed her mind and unlocked it again. While existing behind an unlocked door was still an option open to her, she'd take advantage of it.

Clyde was already gathering dishes when she returned to the dining room. "You're doing a good job," she said, keeping one eye on Clyde while she moved around the table. "You and Ophelia can handle it, right?"

"Me?" Ophelia asked. "Why should I clean up? Ryske is capable."

Pushing his shoulders, Harlow forced Ryske to lean back in his seat and lifted her foot over his lap to straddle him.

Ophelia was still draped against him. At least, she was until Ryske extricated his arm and curved it around to hold the ass of the woman rocking her pelvis over his.

"Ryske needs a shower," Harlow said, coiling her arms around his neck and pulling him to her for a kiss.

"Ryske has had a shower," Ophelia said. "We have all showered."

Letting her lips curl, Harlow pressed her face to his. "I know, but I'm going to make him dirty."

Standing up with her still wrapped around him, Ryske pushed his chair away and started around the table. "I feel dirty already," he said, carrying her up the stairs and into the shower.

***

ALTHOUGH THE WARM WATER cascaded over her body and through her hair, it was the man pinning her to the wall, teasing her body, who infused her with energy.

His finger trailed downwards, seeking her pussy. "We can't have sex," she whispered.

Taking his mouth from her neck to look her in the eye, he squinted. "Trinket?"

After getting naked and slippery with him, it was no wonder he was confused by her hitting the brakes. Playing it coy like she had in their early days would be a massive step backwards. They'd gone beyond flirting or playing hard to get. Sex was the only thing on his mind. Hers too. Still, frustrating as it might be, one of them had to be sensible and live in the real world.

"I'm not on birth control," she said. His concern bled away to a smile that revealed he was living in Fantasyland. "Don't look at me like that, we're not having babies."

"That's not why I'm smiling," he said without elaborating.

All he did was step back to put space between them and pick up the soap. He lathered the bar in his hands and ran them over her body. Bracing a hand to either side of the small cubicle, she let him wash her all over. The stall wasn't much bigger than the one in jail and was a quarter of the size of the Floyd's shower they were used to sharing.

But she stood there wearing a smile, experiencing him soaping each crevice of her body. He crouched at her feet to pamper every inch.

When he stood again, he noticed her smile and kissed her. "Happy?"

"Happier than I have been in a long time," she murmured. "I love it when you run your hands over my body."

"That's why I love washing you," he said, crouching to suck each of her nipples to points.

Snagging the soap from the shelf while he played with her breasts, she worked up a lather on her own hands and was pleased to find his cock filled and ready for her.

Working him in both slippery hands, she was about to drop to her knees when he spun her around to rinse the soap from her back. Once he was done, he shut off the water and led her out of the stall to wrap her up in a big fluffy towel from the shelf.

That wasn't enough.

What they'd done in the shower barely scratched the surface of what she needed. The want had been building in her for three months. Sure, they couldn't go all the way, but they could relieve each other's desire.

"Baby," she said, reaching for him, but he ducked to swipe up their clothes from the floor. "I want more."

The grin on his face intrigued her. "Oh, and you're gonna get it, Trink."

He was naked, save for the clothes he had bundled in one arm. The lack of apparel didn't stop him grabbing her hand to pull her out of the bathroom. In Floyd's, he walked around naked all the time. But there was something extra naughty about him doing it at her parents' house.

He closed the bedroom door behind them and rushed

her toward the bed, releasing their clothes from his arms. In the midst of a laugh, Harlow dropped her towel and fell forward onto the mattress. Crawling to the middle, then flipping onto her back, she noticed he was pulling something from his suit jacket pocket.

"Flaxman wasn't the only one to bring you a gift," he said and tossed whatever it was to the bed.

Sitting up to investigate, she discovered a bumper box of condoms. "Only twelve? Crash, you disappoint me," she teased, opening the box to take one out and open the foil. "Come here."

Going to the edge of the bed, he let her roll it on and then tumbled down on top of her.

He kissed her as she splayed her fingers on his shoulders. "I asked Bale to write me a prescription," she whispered in his ear, his lips descending to her jaw and neck. Harlow stroked every part of him she could reach. "I said you'd meet him somewhere to get it. I can't leave the house. We'll have to use rubbers for seven days."

From her throat, he rose to kiss her lips. "Or we don't use rubbers."

Rolling her head side to side in a shake, she chose to believe he was kidding. "No baby."

He angled his chin. "Was that 'no baby' or 'no, baby.' Are you saying we'll never have kids?"

Running her fingertips over his jaw, she enjoyed the rasp of his stubble. "I'm telling you we're not discussing it with jail hanging over our heads."

"You were okay with it last night at dinner."

Trust him to catalog every detail. "If it had happened…" she said. "We would've dealt with it. I would never have an abortion."

Kissing her cheek and ear, he pushed her damp hair from her temple. "With my kid or any guy's kid?"

Using her shoulder, she pushed him back to look at him. "Are you trying to make me discuss this?" The air of mischief dancing around him said it all. "Don't do your little conman, double-talk thing with me during foreplay."

He kissed her. "No? When should I do it?"

Digging her nails into his tattoo, she was rougher than normal. "How many women have spilled their secrets to you in the throes of passion?"

"Dozens," he said without shame. "But you're the only one I've spilled my secrets to."

"Smooth," she whispered and gave him a shove. "I want to ride, lay on your back."

Ryske didn't fight her and rolled over, lifting her body onto his to let her take control of their union.

She started to slide herself onto his cock but stopped midway. Before she could do this, before she got carried away with him, there was something plaguing her mind.

Spreading her hands on his ribs, she balanced her weight on the anchor points of his body. "Crash," she murmured, aching with need for him.

"Trinket?" he asked, scooping his hands over her breasts to fondle her. Given the trajectory of their passion, he was allowed to be distracted by her figure. It took him another few seconds to figure out she'd stalled for a reason. "Trink, what's wrong?"

"Why did you never ask me?"

His expression didn't change. "I'm asking now."

Suspicion tilted her head. "So, ask me."

He smiled and breathed out a laugh. "I have no goddamn idea what you're talking about. If there's something you want to tell me, tell me."

"You never asked me if I did it."

His mood changed. When he was relaxed like this, it didn't take long for his expression to betray his feelings.

Catching the curtain of her hair, he held it to the side of her head in his curved hand. "Trink, I didn't need to ask."

"You think I'm incapable?"

"I think you're capable of anything you set your mind to, baby. But you told me and the guys that you did nothing. You said the gun I gave you wasn't used in a crime. That's all we needed to hear."

"Really?" she whispered.

His curiosity piqued. "Did you think we doubted your word? All this time you... Shit, Trink..."

His frustration was almost offense. But she'd heard what she needed to hear. In this precious alone time, she had no intention of sitting up or moving away to talk more about it. His truth suffused her blood with heated arousal. Sliding down onto his cock, she exhaled a satisfied breath that mirrored her sense of relief. His confidence gave her a release that went far deeper than the physical.

Rocking her hips, she pushed forward and back, feeling how he occupied the space inside her sculpted to fit him and him alone.

His grip settled on her hips, steadying her as she moved. "Wouldn't have mattered anyway," he mumbled.

She stopped. "What?"

Blinking from her body up to her face, he seemed taken aback she'd stopped. "I said it wouldn't have mattered," he said and cursed at himself, probably for speaking at all. "Shit, baby, we told you to be yourself and baggage didn't matter. Do you think I would love you any less if you'd slaughtered an army of guys? Do what the hell you like… All I want is what you've already given me, your fucking loyalty."

Acceptance. Pure, unadulterated acceptance. Even in their advanced state of sexual limbo, that required a breath and a kiss. On pause, with their bodies still linked, she held his face in both hands and forced her tongue into his mouth. Wishing she could give him even a quarter of the security he provided, she could only feel complete with him.

Whether they were together or not, whether they had a future or not, she'd always be in his heart. Nothing would change that.

Sometime during that kiss, her hips started up again. Being occupied by him felt right. He took her to a bliss of oblivion she needed now more than ever.

Instinct moved them in sync until Ryske flipped her onto her back and took control. He liked to be in control; she liked him in control too. Her Ryske never failed to deliver. He worked hard for her, for them, and didn't stop until both hit their climax.

NINE

THEY WERE STILL PANTING when their bodies parted.

"I hate using condoms with you," Ryske said, shifting to kiss her quick before vaulting off the bed. "Wait here."

Propping herself on her elbows, Harlow called, "Use the towel." He was already reaching for the door handle. The sudden request stopped him and he glanced back, a question creasing his brow. Ryske wasn't modest and she'd never asked him to be. Until then. "At home, I don't mind around the guys… I don't really mind around anyone… except…" it was sort of cringe-worthy to admit it. "I don't want Ophelia to see you like that."

Without mocking her or laughing, Ryske grabbed the towel she'd discarded on the floor. He wrapped it around his waist and slipped out of the bedroom. Oh, how she loved that man.

Flopping onto her back, she played with the ends of her drying hair and stared at the ceiling. Her position hadn't changed by the time Ryske returned. Dropping the towel, he was quick to leap back onto the bed at her side.

"You stayed put," he said, rubbing her stomach. "You're a good girl."

She tipped her head on the pillow to look at him.

"You flushed it, right? You didn't leave evidence in the trash?"

One corner of his mouth curled. "Should I have checked your ID before I nailed you? Or we role playing that you're back in high school? What part do you want me to play? The jock or the principal?"

"Crash—"

"I flushed it," he said, swaying over to kiss her forehead. "Our secret is safe."

It was insane they had to be secret. They were both consenting adults. But their lives were complicated; the lies were woven into the fabric of their façade. Nevertheless, while her days of freedom were potentially numbered, she had to take precautions.

They lay in silence for a few seconds until she licked her lips and asked, "Did you sleep naked last night?"

On his side, Ryske propped his head on a fist and used his loose hand to stroke her breasts and belly. "Did you?"

"I asked first, and I slept alone."

His brow twitched. "Are you asking if I had sex with Ophelia last night?"

On her back, under his looming body, she felt small and safe.

Taking advantage of the position, she used her fingernail to draw around his abdominal tattoo. "I know you didn't have sex with her. You can be naked without it being about sex for you."

"I wasn't naked," he said, bowing to brush his lips against her hair. "Let's get back to you sleeping naked. Much as I love it, we'll have to talk about whether it's allowed when you're back home full time."

Glossing over that subject, she returned to the previous one. "I know you argued with her," she said and tipped her chin upward, though her focus stayed on his ab tattoo. "We share a wall."

When she'd spied the affianced couple at the breakfast table, their affects suggested neither got much sleep. The tension was conspicuous. Admitting some of that was sexual, from Ophelia's side, was a little creepy.

"She got handsy. I took care of it," he said. "She gets

like that when she's been drinking."

The fake couple had a long history; Ryske knew Ophelia better than Harlow would like to admit. Still, she had to make more of an effort to understand them.

"You've known her for a long time."

"Not that long, few years now."

"How long before Anwen did you meet her?"

"Few months probably," he said. "I told you, me and the guys were running a phony investment scam on Parratt."

"And that's how you met Ophelia," she asked. "At a party?"

He nodded. That's what she'd thought though he hadn't been explicit. During the con on Parratt, Ryske met Ophelia and probably her brother too. The men obviously disliked each other because of their respective relationships with Anwen.

Ophelia's attraction to Ryske would've intensified her sense of a connection between them. It wasn't difficult to imagine Ophelia seeking Ryske out or making herself available to him.

"Yeah. Ophelia and her brother were at a bunch of the functions when we were sliding into Parratt's circle." His hand stopped, resting in a cradle over her breast. "Why are you asking about this now? No lies. Like I said, I'll tell you whatever you want to know. But… why now?"

Her mind was working too fast to process his question. "You never had sex with her?" she asked, shifting her upper body to get a better angle at reading his face.

He breathed out a laugh. "No, I never had sex with her."

"You understand we're talking about Ophelia Hagan?" Harlow asked. He repeated the same kind of breathy laugh as before and nodded. "You never had sex with Ophelia?"

"Where is this coming from, Trink?"

This wasn't about jealousy or insecurity. Lying in bed with Ryske reminded her what life could've been, if it hadn't been for Hagan's murder.

At any moment, she could be dragged back to jail and

once locked up again, freedom would be gone for good, and with it their chance to talk freely. Anything she wanted to know or confirm, had to be asked without hesitation, and maybe without tact.

"I know you have a past, and I don't care about that. I care, but I'm not judging you for it. I just… it's important I'm clear on the details."

Lowering, he traced his lips across hers. "I never had sex with Ophelia Hagan; that clear enough for you, Trinket?"

"Thank you," she said, sliding herself closer to tuck herself beneath him again. Her fingers drifted toward his tattoo, but another thought stopped them. "Why not?"

The confusion on his face spoke to how her questions perplexed him. It was admirable that he answered them anyway, even without understanding why she was asking.

"She wasn't part of the op," he said.

For Harlow, that wasn't enough. Ophelia was beautiful, and would've made her attraction to him obvious. Yet, he'd chosen one woman over another.

"Neither was Anwen," she said.

"I explained that to you."

That conversation had been difficult for him. It wouldn't be fair to interrogate him about such a sensitive subject.

"You did," she said and lifted her head to kiss his chest before it dropped back to the pillows. "Sorry, baby."

Being naked in bed with the man she loved was the safest and happiest place imaginable. Her eyes grew heavy. Her hand left his tattoo and descended to the bed. Part of her wished he'd lie down and hold her. Though, if he did, they'd both end up asleep and that would be disastrous.

Having spent enough time basking in peace and being together, Ryske took a turn to fill in his own blanks. It wasn't like she was oblivious to them. This moment had been coming since the second her house arrest was authorized.

"Ophelia was there the night Hagan died," Ryske stated, rolling her nipple between his thumb and forefinger.

"Mm."

"She was the one who pulled the trigger."

Harlow's eyes opened, but she didn't dare look at him. "Yes," she whispered.

Tense silence reigned until he puffed out a breath. "Shit, baby, three months of asking and just like that, you let it out. Why the hell would you—"

"I didn't want you in the middle," she said, sitting up. "If I told you while I was locked up, you'd have gone to her for answers. I didn't want to be terrified of what she'd say to you first."

"First?" he asked, sitting up too. "What the hell is first?"

"Before I got a chance to explain."

"Explain what? Why she's letting you take the fall for her crime?" he said, rage building to an inferno in a flash. "That's a fucking answer I'd like to hear."

Harlow had to grab for him and use all her strength to hold him back. The only way she could keep him down was to clamber on top of him and pin him with all four limbs. His strength outmatched hers. If he wanted to throw her aside, he could. Straddling his stomach and holding both his wrists on the bed got his attention.

"This is about more than Hagan," Harlow asserted. "I tried to tell you before. A scorned woman is a dangerous thing. Ophelia wants something. That's why she's here. It's all I can come up with. She wants something and that's why she's playing nice. According to what Hagan told me, and what I've seen, she can turn on a dime. We do not want to start a war with Ophelia Hagan."

"Do you think I give a shit about war? I couldn't care less if she burns in hell. How can you expect me to play nice with the woman? To share a bed with her?" he spat. "No, baby. No. There's a line no one crosses. Anyone who even thinks about setting up another player is a traitor. People will see what she is. No way I'm going to lose you for her."

Harlow was already shaking her head. "For three months, I haven't heard a word from her. She's been terrified to come near me… Did she try to contact you while I was in jail?"

He sputtered for an answer like it was irrelevant. "She left messages on the answering service. I didn't return them… Why should I?"

"Pothos," she said and let his arms go. Sitting up on his stomach, she stayed on top of him. "Where's the op at?"

"Who cares?"

"I think she does," Harlow said. "Ophelia orchestrated the whole thing to get to you… She shot him *for* you. At least, in part for you." He didn't react. "She shot him twice and was giddy about it. I've seen men murdered. You were shot down right in front of me. But Ophelia, that night… I've never seen anything like it… Animal took no pleasure in shooting you; it was a job. But Ophelia? She relished killing her brother and said you'd be thrilled. You were the first thing on her mind."

Shit. Laying it out just… Now thinking about it, stealing Ryske right out from under Ophelia at the breakfast table hadn't been a wise move. The murderess would be seething.

Leaving Ryske on the bed, she went to the vanity to brush her hair.

"That's all you've got to say to me?" he asked. "I was the first thing on her mind? I don't even know what to do with that."

Sitting on the vanity stool, she angled the mirror to catch his reflection so they could look at each other. "That's because you still don't understand how much she loves you… Ryske, there are truths I am terrified to tell you."

Shifting to the bottom corner of the bed behind her, his feet found the floor. "I wanna hear them, Trinket. Don't you know by now, there's nothing you can say that will change what's between us."

Twisting a quarter turn, she met his eye. "It's easy to say that now… before I shatter everything you thought you knew."

Sliding off the bed into a crouch, he dropped to his knees in front of her and reached up to drive his fingers into her hair around her ear. "Trust me, Trinket. You are everything to me… Even messed up, you're perfect. Trust me to love you no matter what… Trust me, baby."

A knock on the bedroom door interrupted. When it began to open, Harlow leaped up and grabbed her robe from the hook by the closet door. It stopped after a few inches, leaving just enough space for a voice to seep through.

"Uh… it's me," Clyde whispered through the crack. "I'm not trying to see anything."

Harlow went over, tying her robe, and opened the door enough to see her sheepish friend. "What's wrong?"

"Rupert's here," he murmured, tossing a nervous glance over his shoulder toward the stairs. "Ophelia tried to come upstairs; I told her to keep him busy instead."

Smiling at her friend for saving them, she showed her gratitude. Ophelia would've had no shame about walking in on her and Ryske. Both to break the mood and to get a look at what they were doing. She'd have taken great pleasure in interrupting.

"Rupert will be here to help set up for tonight," Harlow said, guessing the party planner would arrive with the decorators soon. "Thank you. We'll come down… separately."

Clyde disappeared back down the stairs. She closed the door and dipped down to retrieve Ryske's discarded clothes, one item at a time, to toss them his way.

"If you smell like me, Rupert will notice," she said. "Try to keep your distance."

"Because it's a smell he'll recognize." Sorting through the clothes she'd thrown at him, he held up the shirt. "This is the one you slept in."

Spinning this way and that, she located the other shirt half under the bed and snatched it up to throw it to him. "They're both your shirts."

He buried his nose in the first one. "And I don't have a problem wearing either," he said, standing up to dress while she went about finding clean clothes for the day ahead. "But if you're talking about something that smells like you…"

The shirt she'd slept in would carry more of her scent than the one Ryske wore to breakfast. Ryske, in pants and a shirt, folded up the sleeves. While, hmm, she only wore panties. No time to worry about that.

She rushed over. "You can't do that."

"I can't do what?" he asked, letting her fold the material down to his wrists and button the cuffs. "If I'm gonna be hauling shit—"

"Baby, you're not going to haul anything," she said, subduing her smile. "They hire people to do the heavy lifting. You are supposed to be rich. You should know that the rich don't do manual labor…" Once his sleeve was down and his cuff fastened, she held up her forearm to show him her stars. "You don't think people will notice we wear the same mark?"

Grabbing her elbow, he hauled her arm up to run the tip of his tongue over her stars. "I love that you did this for me."

Combing her fingers into his hair, her body drifted closer to his. "Invite Dover over and we can work on getting your name tattooed…" Guiding his hand to the cotton of her panties, she grazed his fingertips across the soft fabric. "Right here."

The material didn't tempt him. The caress of his fingers was way more interested in what was beneath.

"You think I want Dover down there? He can bring his kit; I'll do it myself."

That made her laugh and coil her arms around him. "Do you think I want you down there with a needle? You do remember what's down there, right? And how quickly it distracts you?"

He insinuated his fingers beneath the elastic of her panties, skimming them down to her clit. "I'm sorry, what were we talking about?"

Swatting his chest, she pushed away to go retrieve her bra. "You'll have to take Ophelia out, buy her something for the party."

He scowled. "That's her problem."

His attitude frustrated her. Ryske was supposed to be a professional, above petty animus… Okay, so maybe it wasn't exactly petty. But if she had to take the injustice on the chin, he'd have to get over it too.

"What are you going to wear?"

"I'll have my driver bring me something," he said, smirking.

The amusement demonstrated how he enjoyed, and probably missed, being on the con.

Funny as he found the idea of Noon running to his aid, for her own reasons, she gasped with excitement. The opportunity Ryske's idea presented filled her with eager anticipation.

"You would do that?"

"You're not excited about your parents' party. Why do you sound…?" Ryske paused mid-button to make eye contact. "You're excited I'd ask Noon over?" She grinned. "You miss them that much?"

Raising her shoulders, her shrug wasn't apologetic. "Maybe he could stop by Bale's and get my prescription," she said, tiptoeing over to help him with his shirt buttons.

"Maybe he could."

"And maybe he could bring me a bottle of whiskey from the bar… The one I have isn't going to last much longer."

"Okay," he said and tilted to pick up his tie from the vanity.

Harlow took it from him to thread it through his collar. "And we'll need more condoms. Twelve won't be enough for a week."

"Eleven," he said and bowed to kiss her. "And I agree."

Finishing the knot, she admired her work and, yep, as she'd thought, it wasn't as tidy as Ophelia's. "And another of your shirts."

The game had become a chore, a feigned one anyway. "Want to write me a list?"

She laughed and pulled him down for a quick tongue kiss. "I will. Now go make nice while I make myself pretty."

"Seems to me you're done," he said, kissing her head and heading for the door.

The bra and panties ensemble might work for her lover. For the rest of the family? Not so much. Her mother would faint if Harlow showed her face without blow-drying her hair much less turning up in her underwear.

"Charmer," she teased.

Without missing a step, he ducked to sweep up his jacket and tossed it over his shoulder as he opened the door. Half-out the room, he paused.

"Trink?" Her attention landed on him the same time he nodded at her body. "Lose the panties," he said and winked before slipping out.

Rolling her eyes, she couldn't help but laugh at her wonderful, teasing lover. Just because he was funny didn't mean she'd refuse his request. Going back toward the mirror, she was already slipping them off.

TEN

THE SWEETING PARENTS and Lena were back from the mall before Harlow got down the stairs. The party planner arrived a half hour later.

The rest of the day was filled with decorating and party joy. People in ever increasing numbers kept showing up to do a job until the house didn't look much like her childhood home anymore. Her mom was in her element directing what needed to be done, designating chores to one person or another.

This was a full-service event. A party literally transported to the Sweeting house. Food, music, a bar, the works.

Most festivities happened in the garden. Twinkly white lights and temporary lanterns circled the dance floor and stage, defining each area. Tables were set up both inside and outside the gazebo, giving choice and space to spread out.

The atmosphere was incredibly romantic and seductive. At least, Harlow imagined it would be if she was actually down there to enjoy any of it. From the peeks she'd stolen out of her bedroom window, it seemed to be going well.

Guests had been enjoying the party for a couple of hours. At the start of the night, she'd sat in her bedroom window using the curtain as cover to snoop on others celebrating her parents' marriage. That got old quickly.

Peeking at the guests didn't lessen the likelihood she'd feature highly on the list of topics worth gossiping about. After promising to stay out of the way, she didn't want to be spotted spying like a sniper thinking about picking the celebrators off... She was an alleged murderess after all. Ryske would be safe, her sister too. Anyone else? The jury was out.

Putting aside her curiosity, she made her own fun.

She and her laptop relegated themselves to the middle of her bed. With her legs crossed and her headphones on, the dance music took her mind off life... and liberty.

Moving with the heavy bass-line, her mood was high. Her concentration was intent on the laptop screen until a deft hand snaked onto her throat, closing slow and tight around her windpipe.

Looking up, Ryske was the one leaning over her, forcing her head back, she didn't resist when he stole a kiss.

Once he'd made his point, he released her.

"What are you doing here?" she asked, slipping off her headphones and peering past him to check the bedroom door was closed. "You're supposed to be at the party."

Dropping onto the bed in a slouch, he groaned. "Feels wrong. My girl is alone in a bed and I'm not working to get her naked." His fingertips skimmed down her forearm. "Thought maybe we could play white knight and damsel in distress... I'm here to rescue you from your tower... What's my reward?"

In spite of her unimpressed smile, he winked. True to form, the guy never took his eyes from the potential prize. Much as she played it straight, amused rapture rippled through her.

"A white knight? Really? I'm all for role play, Crash. But there's a limit to my imagination... Maybe you could play the evil black knight here to ravish the virgin princess."

Raising his hand with the seeming intention of snapping his fingers, he stopped mid-inhale to frown. "Virgin? Aren't they supposed to be timid and fearful?" She laughed. Her suggestion was no better than his. "Yeah, we need to rethink the role play."

Tilting toward him, she kissed his cheek and whispered in his ear. "How about you play the conniving conman and I'll be the alleged murderess?"

Now that'd be a game.

Returning to her previous position, she checked what was happening on her screen.

"That, we'd be good at… I brought you food and liquor," he said and nodded at the plate and glass on the nightstand. "What are you doing?"

Though he was subtle about peeking around her screen, she didn't hide it and turned the machine his way. "I'm honing a new skill," she said, leaning past him to grab the glass from the nightstand. "The girls in jail taught me. I'm practicing."

His laugh was half-exhale, half-snort. "Online poker?"

"Yeah, it's not real money…" She'd chosen to start in the practice room to figure out how different the digital version was from the real thing. "I'm waiting for Maze to get back to me with your Swiss bank account number then I'll really be in it."

Another smirk. "Trink, if we had one of those, we wouldn't need to do what we do, and I'd have you out the country already." While she drank and considered life on the lam, he scrutinized the screen. A second later, he turned the laptop back to her. "Go all in."

She almost choked on her drink. "What? Why?"

"You have two pair," he said. "You'll river it." Her eyes narrowed, but his confidence stayed true. "Trust me, babydoll."

Shrugging, she clicked the screen and waited for the round to play out only to find herself winning with a full house. "How did you know that would happen?"

"Experience," he said and leaned over to kiss her again. "Do you know what else I have experience in?"

He opened one button of her shirt and then another. "Mm," she objected, taking the glass from her mouth to slap at his hand. "You have to go to the party."

"You look like you know how to party," he purred in seduction mode.

Dance music still pounded through the headphones looped around her neck. Though the sound was subdued, its bass was apparent.

Leaning past him again, she put the drink on the nightstand. "I'm playing poker."

"Play with me instead," he said, sliding across the bed, catching her hand to press it on his fly.

On a laugh, she worked to free her hand. "You can't be that bored."

"That bored?" he asked. "You were in jail for three months. My girl, locked up, not getting laid. It's my duty as your guy to give it up now you're free. It's my moral obligation to take the edge off for you. Think of all the sex we missed out on… two, three, maybe four times a day for three months. That shit racks up."

Oh, he could talk his way into anything. Or so he thought. "You're forgetting that you went without for months even before I was in jail," she said. "You were dead for four months. Dead men don't fuck."

Accepting that she wasn't giving in, he groaned. "This one didn't." Stretching his arms and his back, he forced himself to stand. "I'll come back in a while… with more liquor."

"Don't," she said. The more she drank, the less resolve she'd have to resist him. "Stay downstairs. Have a good time."

Her new hand was dealt, so her focus moved to the laptop. Reading the cards, she sought her glass without taking her attention from the screen.

"I love you, Harlow Sweeting."

"I love you too," she said in a sing-song voice. "Doesn't mean you're getting laid, Huntley."

Muttering, he slunk out of the room, leaving her to poker and dance music again.

The game kept her distracted, but the food Ryske brought up roused her appetite. Ignoring her hunger didn't chase it away. Just after midnight, it reached critical mass.

Poker was beginning to bore her anyway, so she decided to go on the hunt for something to eat.

Guests didn't have to come through the house to join the party. The side gate was opened to let people in and out from the driveway to the back yard. That made the foyer a pretty unlikely place to be caught creeping. Though the French doors in the dining room were left open for people who needed to use the downstairs restroom off the foyer… She'd have to be stealthy.

Harlow had been to a lot of these parties. They'd been happening every year for as long as she'd been alive. The servers had access to the kitchen for cleanup and prep, and they often discarded things on the dining table too. They weren't really supposed to and often claimed guests were the perpetrators of leaving plates and trays lying around. Harlow didn't care who was responsible, she was hungry, and there would be platters in the dining room.

Figuring everyone who was coming would have arrived already, and that the guests were probably too drunk to notice her, she tiptoed down the stairs to see what she could pilfer. Keeping her wits, she made sure to hide from the guests and servers who may tell her mom that she'd been sneaking around.

Feeling like a child again, she remembered doing the same thing in her pre-teens. Back then, she was supposed to be in her bedroom too, asleep. But being banned from festivities only made them more alluring to her nine-year-old self.

As an adult, she was triumphant that her mission had been a success; that she hadn't been caught. It wasn't until she left the dining room, licking shrimp from her fingertips, that someone stepped out of the entryway from the front door.

Caught.

Each stood startled by the other. It took a few seconds to decide that although she wasn't supposed to be at the party, this was her house, so she should be hospitable.

"Uh, the party's out back," she said, assuming the woman was lost. That was all she planned to say and started across the foyer toward the stairs to get out of the stranger's way. When the woman didn't move, Harlow pointed at the dining room. "You can go through there. You'll find everyone outside."

With blonde-streaked brown hair, the woman didn't look old enough to be one of Jean's cronies. She didn't look preened enough to be one of Lena's either. Most of Lena's posse fancied themselves as trophy wives or Instagram models.

While Lena's friends were triers who hadn't quite made it, this woman was all the way there. Stunning, with clear skin and high cheekbones that underlined exotic, long-lashed green eyes, it didn't take much to imagine this beauty commanding a room.

Her figure matched her face. Long and svelte, she had an ample chest and narrow hips. Something about her was familiar. It was as though Harlow should know her. Yet, she couldn't put her finger on why. There was no way she'd ever have laid eyes on a woman this striking and forgotten about it.

The more they stood, saying nothing, the more awkward it got. The stranger made no attempt to follow the path Harlow tried to set her on.

Figuring they couldn't stand there all night, she edged toward the stairs. The longer she was out of her room, the more likely it was that she'd be caught out of hiding.

"Thank you," the stranger said, side-stepping like she wanted to block Harlow's way.

Confused, and wondering if this interloper had been invited or not, she tried to be polite all the same. "Uh, you're welcome."

The beauty dropped the bag she'd been clutching in front of her to step closer. "No," she said, eyes set wide. "Thank you, Harlow."

Astonished, Harlow's silent mouth was moving when the woman leaped forward and pulled her into a tight hug.

Her lips settled in an O, but she didn't relax. They were strangers. Harlow didn't know this person. This wasn't a standard first greeting. Maybe the stranger was drunk already.

"I really didn't do anything," Harlow said.

The woman eased back and tried to be discreet about wiping the corner of her eye.

Was she crying? Why would anyone cry about being late to a party or coming through the wrong door?

"I'm a mess," the stranger said, trying to compose herself. Unsure if she should stay or go, they stood there at the bottom of the stairs, just… there. The woman startled Harlow by picking up her hand to touch her bracelet. A smile spread on the stranger's lips. "I haven't seen this in forever… Maybe it just feels like forever."

She laughed. The polite sound might have been an attempt at bonding, but it tensed her up. Glancing toward the back of the house, she wanted to send Ryske a psychic message. Maybe he could make sense of this.

"I, uh…" Harlow tried to withdraw her hand.

The woman didn't take the hint. "It's the only thing he doesn't take off in bed, right?" she said, her shoulders rising. "I didn't think it came off at all until he told me he'd given it to you."

Like being tossed off a cliff into the deepest end of a freezing lake, panic and adrenaline vied to take over. She couldn't let them or she'd never make it to the surface.

"You… you know Ryske."

Not only did the stranger know Ryske, but she *knew* Ryske. No one in this house, other than Harlow, Ophelia, and Ryske, knew that this bracelet was his. Clyde had gone home earlier that evening because he had work the following day.

Whoever this woman was, she could blow the lid off everything. If her parents learned the truth of Ryske's identity, and that he wasn't engaged to Ophelia at all, they'd never go on their vacation. On top of that, they'd probably banish him from the house.

Rupert would, by extension, learn that Ryske was the one who'd introduced her to the deal that required the half million dollars. Ryske had been dead at the time and hadn't encouraged her to invest, but that may be glossed over in deference to the fact she'd fallen in love with a conman.

After that, it wouldn't take long for her folks to connect the dots to her being arrested for murder and jump to all the wrong conclusions. Causing scandal at the Sweetings' anniversary event wouldn't be the best way for Ryske to ingratiate himself with the people who may one day be his in-laws.

The corners of the stranger's eyes tapered with a probing curiosity. "He never told you… did he?"

Oh God, all kinds of nightmare scenarios raced through her head. Maybe Ryske was married. Maybe he'd faked his death with another woman. Maybe he had a secret family or was the leader of an off-continent cult.

All the possibilities ended with the same conclusion: she wanted to knee him in the nuts.

"Told me, what?" Harlow asked, endeavoring to paste on a genuine smile. One that looked genuine anyway. "We talk a lot." Though clearly not as much as they should. "He tells me a lot of things, and I—"

"I'm Anwen Windsor."

ELEVEN

HARLOW'S MOUTH CLOSED. Every iota of emotion sank down through her. Like ice it trickled from her blank mind, through her chest, past her hardening heart, her rebellious guts, and out through her desperate-to-flee feet.

Unfortunately, fleeing wasn't an option, neither was giving in to the crushing weight of numbness.

"Come with me," Harlow said, like a stoic member of the household staff.

About facing, she went upstairs, listening to Anwen grab her bag before she followed. Harlow went into her bedroom and held the door open, waiting next to it until Anwen came in. Every second she could use to absorb this new truth was a blessing.

Calm. Measured. Breathe. Don't jump to conclusions. Wasn't that easy to deduce anything when she didn't have a clue what the hell was going on.

Anwen put her bag on the floor at the foot of the bed. With tension and suspicion and a whole host of other things zipping through the air, this could go either way.

Harlow closed the bedroom door, then turned to confront this truth.

The women stayed like that, a few feet apart, just

staring at each other for a score of seconds. Like downstairs they were just… there.

"I…" Anwen started, "don't know where to begin."

"That makes two of us," Harlow said, finding some solace in solidarity.

Neither of them had much of an advantage over the other. Harlow didn't know why Anwen was there, why she'd chosen to show up, or what she wanted. In spite of that, and being fair, she acknowledged it wasn't this woman's fault Ryske hadn't been honest.

So much began to make sense. Ryske never once told her anyone was responsible for Anwen's death and didn't ever talk about his own feelings on it. Harlow assumed it was a difficult subject for him to discuss. Losing a woman he'd been in an intimate relationship with should be a sensitive subject. Except he hadn't lost her at all.

"That's what Hagan will tell you."

Those were the words Ryske used to confirm Anwen's suicide. He didn't say Hagan was responsible. No, she'd made that assumption all by herself. What an idiot!

Though rage tugged at her, this woman didn't deserve to be blasted with it. This woman she knew so much, and nothing, about.

"Jarvis was… he was so controlling. He needed to know where I was every second, needed me to account for every dime," Anwen said, resting a hand on the metal frame of Harlow's bed. "We fought… We argued all the time, and he was—"

"Violent?" Harlow asked. Déjà vu. The JD was in the nightstand drawer. Had there ever been a better time for hard liquor? Marching over to retrieve it, she poured some into the glass Ryske brought earlier. "That's what you told Ryske… But Jarvis wasn't the one to give you the bruises, was he?"

This wasn't the first time she'd had this conversation. It was like a game of Telephone; everyone's account was just slightly different from the last. Gritting her teeth, she fought to maintain her patience.

"His men would—"

"And his sister," Harlow said, sipping from the glass.

Spinning around, she offered it to Anwen who hesitated. "We've shared a man, what's a little liquor between friends?"

Tentative, Anwen came around the bed to take the glass in her fingertips. "I'm not here for him, if that's what you think… I didn't come to steal him from you."

Picking up the bottle, Harlow raised it toward Anwen, and found reason to smile. "Honey, if you can steal him, you can keep him," she said, and swigged from the bottle.

Pointing the bottle at the bed, Harlow sat, indicating Anwen should join her.

After a second, Anwen propped herself on the end. "I… I thought you loved him…" she said. "He led me to believe that you were a fighter… And when I heard about Jarvis…"

"Is that why you came?" Harlow asked. "Because you heard I'd killed him?"

"I haven't been able to get Ryske to talk to me," Anwen said, swirling the liquid in the glass. "I knew something was going on. He's never not returned my calls, and then suddenly, he was nowhere… I thought something had happened with you… He left in such a hurry, we had no time for a proper goodbye."

The coquettish smile Anwen failed to hide was enough to provoke a sneer. "He was with you," she said, figuring things out. "When he was dead… all of them were." Inhaling, she put the bottle to her lips. "Guess that makes sense. Ghosts should hang together."

"I'd been in hiding," she said. "With the money I'd stashed and what Ryske gave me, we had enough for a place in the mountains. A beautiful home with everything I needed and plenty of space for all of them. Ryske needed somewhere to recuperate… I didn't know they were coming. They just showed up and I… I would never turn him away."

Few women would, even if he was in a weakened state. "Of course not," Harlow said. How many nights had she sat in this bed pining for him? That memory deserved another drink. "And if the price of lodgings is sex, Ryske isn't going to say no, is he?"

Anwen's blink became a frown. "I don't think you

understand how badly he was injured."

Of all the things she could be accused of that was the most laughable. Harlow's lips twitched and lowered. They quirked higher and then jumped to a smile that rushed into a laugh. Anwen was taken aback, but even in the face of that Harlow couldn't control her hilarity. After almost a minute, it dwindled to a resigned, whining sigh.

"Oh, honey, I was the one holding his hand when he flat-lined," she said. "I didn't realize how alive he was, not how close to death he was. Far as I was concerned, he was worm food."

Which apparently was a state he coveted. His actions sure suggested that. Already, murder was looking like not a bad deal. Her gaze drifted to the window. The bastard was out there, probably dancing with Ophelia, bonding with the Sweetings, maybe planning his next con.

"Ryske isn't…" Anwen said and moved closer. On edge, her glare snapped to her guest. "You can't take it personally when he lies to you or hides things. You just have to accept he doesn't trust women, especially any he's sleeping with."

"Thanks for the advice."

"I know you're pissed. I probably would be as well," Anwen said. "He'll be angry when he finds out I've come here."

Ryske didn't know Anwen was going to show up. If he had, either he'd have stopped her, or somehow prevented the women from overlapping.

"So why did you?"

"To thank you," Anwen said. "You killed Jarvis." She smiled. "You freed me."

Life was a comedy. She had to laugh. If she didn't, her homicidal tendencies may collide with the dozens of innocent people in the back yard. Good thing she'd stashed Ryske's gun under the floorboards in Floyd's. If it was to hand, she might be tempted to use it… on him.

"Do you know he's here?" Harlow asked, unable to muster anything except negative emotion. "That he's with Ophelia. Engaged to Ophelia."

Not for real, but was anything these days?

Anwen lost her ease, her gaze darted around like the couple might jump out of the paintwork. She stood up to put the glass on the nightstand and went to crouch by her bag at the end of the bed.

"I didn't know if he would be here or not. I didn't think Ophelia would be anywhere near you."

"Turns out she had the same thought you did," Harlow said. "About keeping tabs on her man."

"Ophelia and I were the best of friends," Anwen said, doing something with her bag that Harlow couldn't see and didn't really care to. She was happy lying with Jack there on the pillows. "Until I was with Ryske… I didn't know Fi cared for him as much as she did. Ryske was… impulse. I needed comfort, and he was there."

"It started that way," Harlow said. "But you kept going back for more. Even after you knew Ophelia wanted him."

"We had a complicated relationship," Anwen said, standing up to walk closer. "All of us. Me and Ophelia, me and Jarvis… me and Ryske… But when I needed him, he was there for me. I don't care what he told you about me, I am important to him." Holding out her hand, she offered something. "You are too."

Curious, Harlow raised her palm to accept the mysterious object. Putting down the alcohol, she inspected the short glass tube Anwen handed over, turning it to examine the warped lump of metal inside.

"What is this?"

"A memento," Anwen said, going to retrieve her bag. "Something to remind you of why you did what you did."

"It looks like…"

"It's the bullet they took from his chest."

Shocked, Harlow's gaze flew to Anwen, who was hooking her bag over her arm. "How the hell did you get this?" Harlow asked, leaping to her feet. "This is evidence from my case!"

This couldn't be meant to help her. If Harlow was found with evidence of any nature it would be bad. Worse than that, being found in possession of potentially stolen evidence would lead to a whole barrage of extra charges.

"No," Anwen said, going toward the door. "Not Jarvis… Ryske." What? What did…? Oh, God. This was… this gnarled object was the culprit. The offender. The weapon. Such a small, misshapen thing had been responsible for stealing Ryske from her. "I'm staying at the hotel in town. I'll come back if I think it's safe, but please… don't tell anyone I was here… don't tell anyone—"

"That you're alive?" Harlow asked, less hostile and more curious about the woman bearing gifts… though it may not have been the one she intended to give. "I won't. They'll be gone by tomorrow… I promise."

Anwen nodded and offered another smile before slipping out. The woman could find her own way to the street. She didn't want to be seen by anyone; something she was practiced at.

Sinking back down on the bed, Harlow turned the tube, the deformed bullet rolled inside. This was it. This tiny metal shard set all the wheels in motion and almost took Ryske from her. No, it *had* taken Ryske from her, and delivered him to Anwen. He'd been at his lowest, in his greatest time of need, and he hadn't relied on her. He'd gone to his ex. An ex he claimed manipulated him into bed. Who the hell knew the truth anymore?

Jarvis Hagan had given her a stark lesson in accepting things at face value. Skepticism was her friend. Somewhere in between all the stories, the truth existed. Everyone had their own interpretation based on their perceptions and motivations.

One truth, unfortunately, couldn't be avoided. Ryske promised not to lie to her and he'd been doing it all along. Anwen was alive. His ex in hiding. Was that it? No. He'd facilitated and supported the escape.

Why hadn't it occurred to her? No half-dead person brought back to life would think about faking their own death… Unless they had experience, unless they had done it for someone in the past.

They did it with Anwen. She was the trailblazer. The

pioneer. The success of secreting Anwen away, and convincing the Hagan siblings of her death, informed Ryske's impulsive decision. They'd done it before, why not do it again? Running and hiding wasn't anything new. Faking a death? Sure, no problem. Did they have a code for invoking the practice? Maybe it was a service the crew offered for a fee. Who knew? Anything was possible.

Surging from her bed, she grabbed a chair and wedged it under the bedroom door handle. Tonight, she was too emotional to talk to him. Last time he'd snuck in when she was emotional, they'd ended up having sex and she'd forgiven the lie.

That wasn't going to happen this time. It wasn't going to happen ever again.

TWELVE

SOMEONE DID TRY to open Harlow's door later that night. Lying in the dark, she ignored the tapping that followed the rattle of the handle. She didn't care who it was, or what they wanted. Unless the damn house was ablaze, nothing would rouse her from bed.

After drifting off, her quality of sleep was good, which was something of a surprise. Waking up refreshed, she was renewed, a woman freed, though not from hiding. A lot of her questions seemed irrelevant in the light of the new day.

As she was awake before anyone else, she took the time to pamper herself in the shower. Still no one had surfaced by the time she was finished getting dressed. She didn't rush, but got a lot done without seeing another soul.

Harlow cleaned up the kitchen and made breakfast. Even the table was set and the laundry on when her mother and sister appeared in the dining room. After the partying and drinking of the previous night, they weren't too pleased to see her chipper demeanor.

"Why do you seem so happy this morning?" Lena asked, showing the classic signs of a hangover.

Getting up to pour coffee for the women sagging in their seats, Harlow couldn't erase the smile from her face. "I have an opportunity."

"What kind of opportunity?" Mom asked.

Unless there was a reason, such as a social event, Jean preferred to be in bed by nine thirty. Even when they went out to parties, she'd still always be home by midnight… maybe one a.m. in extreme circumstances.

In a break from the norm, last night, her mom had still been going strong beyond that hour. Harlow heard her in the backyard laughing with the last of the guests around two thirty. God only knew what time she'd actually got to bed.

"You have a plane to catch," Harlow said, finishing with the pouring and going around to take her regular seat, which would be opposite her father, if he were there. "Are you and Daddy packed?"

"Oh," Jean said, like traveling was the worst proposition in the world. "Why do these things seem like such a good idea in the planning stage?"

Lena gave her mother a comforting pat. "You and Daddy should be used to it. You've been doing it for thirty years. You always like going on vacation."

When the sisters were kids, they'd gone on the anniversary vacation with their parents. Thinking back, she and Lena must've put a damper on the couple's plans. Even as an adult, she didn't like to think of her parents having "plans" that kids might ruin, so she pushed that thought out of her mind.

"Lena and I will help you with whatever you need," Harlow said. "I've already cleaned the kitchen and the laundry is on. I'll deal with everything in the house. You just make sure you and Daddy have everything you need."

Jean's tired smile was appreciative. "You always were better at chores than your sister."

Lena made a sound of objection, but Harlow laughed. "And, I thought while you're gone, that Lena and I could go through some of those boxes in the attic. You know, all that stuff that's up there from when we were kids… You keep saying you want more storage space."

As Jean drank her coffee, Brysen came in, looking even more frazzled than his wife. "Good morning," he grumbled.

"Morning," Harlow said, leaping from her chair to serve her father.

"Harlow was talking about cleaning out the attic while we're gone," Jean said. "What do you think?"

"It will save us doing it," Brysen said. "Rupert will help with the heavier items. I've asked him to come and keep an eye on the girls."

"Check in here and at the company?" Harlow asked. "Are you worried I'll get myself arrested again? There will be no one around here to kill." No one appreciated her sense of humor. "I think Rupert has enough on his plate. He doesn't need to be babysitting us too."

"I'll be over at Emma's most of the time anyway," Lena said.

"You mean job hunting," Harlow said. "You need a job. I can help you with that."

Lena tsked and grumbled in protest. "If you don't have to work, why do I?"

Oh and hey, wait. "Do you mean Edgar Charnock's granddaughter Emma? I thought you guys stopped hanging out in high school."

The two had been in the same grade and close as two girls could be growing up. Something happened at some time, some drama Harlow missed while concentrating on learning how to adult. After whatever it was, Emma didn't come to dinner anymore.

"We reconnected," Lena said, reaching over the table for a piece of toast. "And she is dating the hottest guy I've ever seen in my life."

"The hottest guy…" Harlow said, recalling the last time she'd thought about Edgar Charnock and his granddaughter. Putting the pieces together, surprise struck her. "Vane? She's still seeing Vane?"

"Yes," Lena said, spreading jelly on her toast. "He's delicious… He was here last night. You didn't see him?"

"Oh, God," she said. "Check the silverware… count the forks."

"What does that mean?"

"Nothing," Harlow muttered.

"I think they seemed to be in love," Jean said, focusing only on her coffee without entertaining the notion of eating.

Brysen went straight for the bacon. "He's too smooth. I'm wary of men like that," he said. "Never know quite what they're really interested in."

"Oh, Brysen," Jean said. "Don't be ridiculous. I'm sure he's a perfectly nice boy."

Boy? Vane was older than Harlow, definitely in his thirties. At least a decade older than Emma she'd guess.

"You never know. You have to be careful when you have impressionable young daughters. That's why I was thrilled when Harlow and Rupert connected," Brysen said, tossing her a look that betrayed his disappointment at the relationship's demise.

Harlow shrugged. "I turned out okay anyway… except the whole, you know, murder charge and everything."

"Harlow is our burden," Jean said, though she might have been half-kidding, which was better than being scolding. "Edgar wouldn't let his granddaughter be taken advantage of."

Brysen seemed less certain. "There are confidence tricksters everywhere."

As if that was a cue, Ryske came into the dining room with his fiancée behind him.

"Good morning," Ophelia declared.

Given that Harlow sat in her regular seat, Ophelia faltered, probably unsure of where she should sit. With no two vacant seats together either, she wouldn't like the prospect of being separated from Ryske, who was wandering around to the position next to hers where he'd always sat.

Just for kicks, Harlow sipped her coffee and pretended not to notice that the woman was confused. But when Jean noticed it too, Harlow had no choice except to give up her seat. She didn't mind so much because Ryske had just sank down at her side.

"Please, Ophelia, sit here," Harlow said, keeping her cup, but stepping out of the way. "I haven't eaten, so the setting is clean." She raised her mug. "I brought this from the kitchen. I drink coffee by the bucket. None of that dainty teacup nonsense for me."

"Thank you, Harlow," Ophelia said, rounding the table, giving Ryske's shoulder a squeeze as she sat down.

Harlow chose to go the other way, avoiding him completely. "Of course, you're welcome," she said, playing the gracious hostess while strolling to the end of the table. "Please eat our food, drink our coffee, and fuck in our sheets."

Delivering the line through such a sweet smile opposed the words so thoroughly that it took everyone a second to realize what she'd said.

"Harlow," Jean said, outright offended. "You didn't really—"

"They're not going to stay anyway," Harlow said. "They've done what they came to do."

"We—we—"

"Yes, you, Ophelia," Harlow said, putting her mug on the table and folding her arms on the back of the dining chair to peer at her parents and sister. "Don't you think it's odd that the sister of the man I supposedly killed wants to hang out with us? Maybe it would be less odd if she'd rushed to my defense after I was arrested or contacted me in jail. But she did neither. I get out on house arrest and pouf, here she is like magic."

"Harlow, I—"

"But it's okay," Harlow continued, pushing up to grip the back of the chair in both hands. "Because her dashing, charming fiancé came rushing in to protect her virtue from evil, villainous me." Leaning closer to her family, she stage-whispered. "Secret is, the fiancé isn't all that virtuous himself."

"Harlow," Ryske said.

She raised a hand without bothering to look at him. "Don't worry, that's all I'll say… I'll just let that percolate. So…" Standing up straight, she clapped her hands. "Here's the plan for today. I'm going to check the laundry, then help Mom and Dad get ready for their flight. Lena, call for two cars, one for Mom and Dad, and another for Mr. Ryske and the beautiful Ophelia Hagan." Dropping her smile, she glared at them both. "Because they are going to pack their shit and get the hell out of our house."

Spinning around, a spring in her step, she left to go through the kitchen into the laundry room. It didn't surprise her that Ryske came in just seconds after. He stepped down into the room and closed the door at his back.

"What happened?"

"Nothing," she said, pulling everything from the dryer to dump the clothes in a basket. "I don't want to be with a liar anymore."

Grabbing her arm, he hauled her away from the appliances. "Look at me," he snapped. "What happened?"

"Haven't you been hearing me for months?" she asked, yanking her arm back. "I don't need this hanging over me. I don't need you hanging around."

Considering her, he rubbed his lips together before holding up his hands in surrender and backing off. "Okay… Okay, fine. You want me to take Fi out of here? I'll get rid of her for you."

That hit a nerve. "You think I couldn't get rid of that psychopath on my own?" Shoving him aside, she went to grab the chef knife used by the caterers to cut the cake and raised it up. "Bring the bitch to me."

"Okay," he said, coming over to curl his fingers around hers on the handle of the knife. While he tried to push it down, she held it firm. "Do you think it's a good idea to threaten someone with murder while you've got that bracelet on your ankle?"

"I think if I'm going to prison for murder, maybe I should take out as many people as I can before I go," she said, jolting her hand out of his to touch the point of her blade to the underside of his jaw.

"Bullet's quicker."

He didn't look worried or indicate any intention to retreat. Pushing onto her tiptoes, she tilted her mouth close to his. When his jaw descended, she let the knife move with it.

"Don't tempt me," she whispered, her pout almost touching his. Assuming a kiss was inevitable, Ryske tried to follow through. Not a chance. She pushed the knife upwards to keep their mouths apart. His hiss confirmed she'd cut him. Good. The wound wouldn't be deep, but it was enough. "Take your fiancée and get the fuck out of my life."

Backing off, his fingertips ascended to the bead of blood to give himself a look at it. His lips curled to an ironic smirk that joined a laugh. The sound grated, but it didn't last long. Drawing in a breath between his teeth, his laugh died and the smile was replaced by ferocity in a wild glare.

"If you're gonna do it, Trink, do it properly," he said, lunging at her to seize the knife.

Leaping back against the counter, she clutched at the corner, fearing his savage growl. Without any acknowledgement of pain, he dragged the blade across his palm, cutting himself open.

"Ryske," she screeched, bounding forward to grab for his arm. He yanked it out of her reach and squeezed his fist until the blood dripped from his palm onto the floor. "What the hell are you doing?"

Blood reminded her of the night they'd met. Seeing it on her hands, fear pulsed through her. She didn't remember much about the blood from the night he'd been shot, but the scent of it sparked all kinds of devastating flashbacks.

In the past, whenever he'd bled, she jumped to action. Before she could think, Ryske grabbed her wrist and jerked her arm out straight to drag the blade across her palm, slicing it open. In a silent scream, frozen in shock, pain seared through the sensitive nerve-endings.

Ryske dropped the blade and rushed her backwards, slamming her hand against the wall with his own torn palm clamped against hers. Their blood merged and mixed, flowing into each other's veins. Now it was his turn to get in close. She was too stunned to think about fighting when he grabbed her chin to haul it up.

"That's how far I am from you," he hissed against her mouth, untamed in his determination. "I'm in your blood, Harlow Sweeting. I flow through your heart and give you life. Send me away. Cast me out. But don't kid yourself. Every breath you are is me. You are my soul." Forcing her to take his kiss, he kept it brief and then backed away, opening his arms. "You always come back to me, baby. Every single fucking time…"

Blood stained the cuff of his shirt. The warmth of it ran down her arm too. His blood? Hers? Though he hadn't cut them deep, their wounds were extreme enough to ensure they'd both have a permanent scar.

His arrogance scared away the shock.

Pushing off the wall, she stood tall. "Not this time, Ryske. That's it. You'll never have me."

With his uninjured hand on the door handle, he grinned at her. "Again," he said. "You mean, I'll never have you again. I remember you telling me I'd never have your mouth on my body and, baby, those sweet lips have been every damn place on me."

"Glad you remember because memories are all you have of me now," she said and raised her forefinger to taste their blended blood. "With the smell of blood in the air, I'm surprised your bitch hasn't come running already. Better get to her while it's still fresh… she'll want to suck you dry."

"Only bitch allowed to suck on me is you," he said with a wink and opened the kitchen door. "I'm on call whenever you need me, Trinket."

Bounding into the kitchen without any hint of being dispirited or crestfallen, the bastard had the nerve to whistle a happy tune. Jerk.

Looking down at the gash on her hand, she touched the edge. Which of the blood was hers? Which was his?

It didn't matter.

Going to the sink, the water washed away the evidence of their blood union.

Ryske might love her, and she wasn't naïve enough to think her feelings for him were gone, but he was a liar. She couldn't trust a liar. Without trust, there could be no relationship.

THIRTEEN

CONVINCING HER PARENTS she wasn't insane wasn't easy.

Harlow had just finished cleaning the blood from the laundry room floor when her mother appeared in the doorway to ask what happened. Ryske and Ophelia were gone. All for the best. Ryske would have found a way to conceal his hand. Hate or love, trustworthy or deceitful, the man knew how to be discreet.

Her mother assumed something transpired between her and Ophelia. At least, that's what Harlow overheard Jean telling Lena a while later. Her explanation was a spat between the two girlfriends and Ryske had gone to defend his fiancée. As any good fiancé should.

Restraining herself wasn't easy. What she really wanted to do was leap around the doorframe and tell Lena no woman needed a man to do a damn thing for her. If someone wronged her, she should stand up for herself.

But given the way Jean ignored the blood, her mom deserved a break. Any more drama and she'd be permanently traumatized.

Her parents' flight ended up being a reprieve. Harlow reminded her mother they had a plane to catch, made them snacks, checked their carry-on, their chargers, their passports, everything. When she wanted to be, Harlow could be a good organizer. Keeping busy was a distraction from the Ryske mess.

Once they were gone, Lena went for a soak in the tub while Harlow made dinner. The sisters rebelled and watched a movie in the living room while they ate; something their mother would never allow them to do.

After dinner, Lena left Harlow to do the cleaning up and vanished back upstairs, making her feel like the surrogate parent to her younger sibling. When Lena re-appeared in a cocktail dress, surrounded by a strong aura of perfume, her instruction was not to wait up. Lena gave no hints on where she was going, which was completely her prerogative. The Sweeting family might like to be in the know, but they were smart enough not to pry.

In spite of that, it was on the tip of Harlow's tongue to say that, if she had one, Lena's boyfriend was welcome there. They were grown women; their mother never needed to know.

Just before opening her mouth, Lena scurried into the entryway, and it hit her that she was about to be… the door slammed and that was it.

Harlow was alone.

For a minute, silence was alien. In jail, it didn't exist. Even before that, silence only lived when Ryske died. Except, he hadn't been dead, had he? He'd been shacked up with his ex and his buddies.

The piercing sound of the phone made her jump. It cracked through the air like the snap of a sniper's bullet.

Leaping around, she snatched for the handset under the clock that was her father's pride and joy.

Pressing answer, she raised it to her ear. "Hello?"

The expectation of Ryske's voice brought the greeting out as snide.

"Harlow?"

The female voice wasn't a member of her crew, her sister, or even Ophelia. That left only one possibility.

"Anwen? Where did you get this number?"

"It's listed."

Right. Listed. The basic answer to the stupid question reminded her how complicated life had become. Before city living, questioning someone on where they got the phone number wouldn't have occurred to her. Now she just felt ridiculous for being suspicious.

"Right," Harlow said, shaking off her paranoia.

"Is he still there?"

"Ryske? No, he's gone. Ophelia too. I'm here alone."

In another situation, Harlow might be more hesitant to reveal that. Her ankle monitor gave her a safety net; a direct link to law enforcement. If anyone tried to hurt her, all she had to do was run out onto the street or damage the device and the blues would come directly to her pad without passing go. There would be no two hundred dollars for her. She'd be straight back to jail, but she'd be alive… and might take the assailant along for the ride.

"I was hoping you'd say that," Anwen said. "I think it's time we talked."

"I agree."

"I can be there in ten," Anwen said.

"I'll be waiting."

The line went dead. Anwen was coming. Before the night was over, Harlow was going to know another ghost in the flesh.

***

ANWEN LOOKED MORE perfect than she had the previous night, the Meadowbank's caliber of hospitality never failed. If a good night's sleep at the local hotel could put a glow in people like Anwen's, Harlow wanted to be signed up… if, you know, jail didn't happen.

"Would you like a drink?" Harlow asked before she'd even closed the front door.

"Yes," Anwen said and followed her to the kitchen where they selected drinks from the illuminated glass cabinet.

The party last night would at least give them cover for whatever they drank. Marking the bottles wasn't her parents' style. Didn't matter much. The alcohol would probably be gone by the time the vacation was over.

She and her guest didn't say anything on the way into the living room. Sitting down, both sipped, and Harlow got another chance to absorb some silence again.

"I'm going back to the city tomorrow," Anwen said. "I haven't been there since I died."

That could've been a joke meant to lighten the mood, but Harlow didn't crack a smile. "I'm not on the inside of that joke," she said with misdirected irritation. "You and the crew are part of that little game. I'm happy for you all… Are you going back to him?"

"To Ryske?" Anwen asked, elegant in the way she perched herself on the edge of the couch. It almost appeared that she was hovering rather than actually sitting.

Ryske said Anwen came from nothing. Except by all appearances there was nothing common or lowly about her. Other than an apparent tendency to commit fake suicide, Anwen looked to be the perfect lady.

"Yes, to Ryske."

Even Anwen's sigh was dreamy and sophisticated. "I don't know. I… I don't know what will happen between us now that Jarvis is out of the picture."

Toying with an earring, Anwen's gaze sank into the middle distance.

Harlow gulped her alcohol, keen to avoid obsessing about the beauty's imaginings. "He doesn't have marble floors," she said. "But you'll never want for anything. Anything's possible where Ryske's concerned. If it's important to you, he'll find a way to get it."

"That's true."

"And life's never boring," she said, looking at the bandage on her hand.

Anwen put her glass on the coaster stack on the coffee table. "Sounds like you're trying to talk me into it… To be honest, he didn't factor into my decision to come back. He didn't even tell me that Jarvis was gone, can you believe it?"

How awful. What a joke. She'd be laughing if her anger wasn't still simmering. "Oh, I can."

Anwen must have sensed the tension weighing on Harlow's shoulders. After a pause, she became softer, contrite. "I really thought he would've told you about me," she said. "I didn't come here to stir anything up. I wanted to say thank you. You have no idea how grateful I am to you for taking Jarvis out of the picture… I wasn't brave enough to do it myself… I tried to convince Ryske it was a good idea. I begged him to do it… To be honest, that was a part of the reason I cultivated my relationship with him in the way I did. I knew he was capable of anything; I thought he might take care of Jarvis for me." Harlow's frown made Anwen smile. "I'm not revealing any secrets, Ryske knows everything. I stopped lying to him a long time ago. I don't know how he sizes people up so fast, but he could read me from the first minute… Have you noticed that about him?"

Ryske liked to think he could read her. In truth, feeling the way she did right then, she wasn't ready or willing to admit how many times he'd been right about her. Not when she'd been so wrong about him.

"You've known him longer than I have," Harlow said, wishing she could be an observer to this conversation rather than a participant. "Personally, I think he's an arrogant asshole."

Anwen laughed. "He's arrogant, that's for sure… Unfortunately, that's my type… The cockier the better."

If that was what Anwen wanted in a man then Ryske was the one for her. No doubt about that.

"You've got yourself the right guy then."

"I really thought he was off the market," Anwen said. "I thought you would be an obstacle to me even considering it. I'd assumed that when you learned he was alive…"

"That I would jump on and never let go?" she asked. "I don't like being lied to. Sometimes I withheld from him, but I never lied to him. It wasn't easy for me to get over what he did… but I did…" her voice trailed off. "I thought I did."

"You didn't?"

"I've always been independent. Ryske was the first guy who didn't resent that about me. I learned a lot about myself when I was with him," she said and nodded at her guest. "But this, you… I can't get over this lie that easily. Finding out he stayed with you for those four months I thought he was dead… Guess I'm not as forgiving as I thought."

"We were never exclusive," Anwen said. "Ryske and I… If that's what you're thinking. He didn't cheat on me with you. He was a free agent. I had relationships too. Not that I could tell my dates anything about myself or where I came from. But I had to do something. After riding a guy like Ryske on demand, a girl can't live in a drought."

There was nothing genuine about the smile Harlow forced. That statement was the first peek at Anwen's heritage.

"When you go to jail, you don't have much choice," Harlow said, recognizing her flat, taut tone.

Anwen sat taller. "Gosh, you're right, listen to me." She touched her chest. "I understand now; you're asking me to look after him. I will. Of course I will. I owe you so much. I knew I couldn't live with Jarvis any more, but he made it clear that he wasn't going to let me go. I worked on Ryske for months and he just wouldn't do it… He said vendettas ruin people. Passion doesn't motivate smart decision-making."

Ryske changed the rules as they suited him but expected everyone else to abide by what he said; yet another example of his arrogance.

It had only been earlier that day she'd kicked him out. Given that, she wasn't in the right frame of mind to talk about him with anything close to objectivity.

With Anwen going back to the city tomorrow, this could be the last chance Harlow ever had to talk to her. There was no way to put this off, especially since she could be dragged back to jail at any minute.

Putting her own glass aside, she shifted to the front of her seat. "Talk to me about Ophelia," Harlow said.

She needed to understand Miss Hagan more than she needed to deconstruct Ryske.

"What do you want to know?" Anwen asked. "She's a passionate woman who was always close to her family."

Less than a minute ago, Anwen commented passion didn't equal smart decision-making. Maybe her choice of words to describe Ophelia was no accident and a nod to that statement.

"Was she home schooled?"

"Yes," Anwen said. "I didn't know her back then. We didn't meet until college."

"Did she graduate?"

"Neither of us did. Ophelia didn't like authority figures and I preferred to party. My grades dropped, I lost my scholarship and I went to stay with Ophelia. I knew Jarvis for years before we got together. I don't think he noticed me at first, not when I was just Ophelia's friend.

"It wasn't until she started to work for him and brought me in as her assistant that he noticed me… It was flattering to be pursued by the CEO and he wasn't exactly bad to look at."

"No, he wasn't."

Referring to him in the past tense still felt surreal and Harlow hadn't been close to the guy. She hadn't even liked him.

"After we started dating, both of them changed in their attitudes towards me. The change was almost overnight. I couldn't believe it…" Anwen paused. "I hadn't understood their underlying competitive natures. This was sibling rivalry on a whole new level. Both of them wanted all of my attention all of the time. If I ever had to pick one over the other, even just who to have lunch with, all hell would break loose… behind closed doors of course."

"So much happens behind closed doors," Harlow said, thinking maybe honesty was too much to expect. Every time she'd been honest, her life combusted in some way. "Honesty's a rare trait."

Anwen exhaled a laugh. "If honesty is your priority, you're with the wrong man," she said. "Ryske's job requires him to be deceptive… I didn't know that when I met him… I learned so much more about him after I died. Before then, he was suspicious of me. After, I was completely dependent on him. He was the only one who knew who I was, where I was, he was my only link to me. At any time, he could've pulled the rug out from under me… He never did. He could've told Jarvis where to find me and got me off his plate... He never did... He might be an asshole and a criminal... But he's an honorable one. I owe him my life... and I owe it to you too."

Anwen's gratitude was maybe a little too zealous. "It sounds like you're trying to convince me."

Still, her guest's sympathy seemed genuine. "I'm just sorry my freedom costs yours. Are you on house arrest until the trial?"

All she'd said was that Ryske hadn't told her about Jarvis. So...

"How did you find out about me?"

"Ryske told me all about you," Anwen said, assuming Harlow meant in the first place, rather than the current situation. "It's funny, I faked my death to escape a man who wanted to stifle me. Ryske faked his to save his girl from being stifled."

That was one way to put it. Harlow wasn't in the mood to cut him any slack. Ryske was the last thing she wanted to talk about, yet Anwen kept bringing the conversation back to him.

"How did you know I was here?" Harlow asked. "That Jarvis had died?"

"The media," she said. "I read about it online. I knew I'd find nothing on Ryske." Even if there was something out there on him, Maze would make short work of eliminating it. "He'd talked about you so much, I thought you could lead me to him... I was worried maybe Jarvis finished the job."

While in hiding, Ryske was the only one who knew her location. According to Anwen. If something happened to Ryske, Anwen would've been cut off. In that scenario, fear made sense.

Except the whole crew had stayed with her when Ryske was dead. Anwen had to know there were contingencies in place for looking after her if something happened to the point man.

Speculating about the specifics of their relationship made Harlow queasy. She moved onto something more productive.

"Was Ophelia violent with you?"

"She could be," Anwen said. "They both could... Though Jarvis preferred to have his goons do the dirty work... That was one thing I always loved about Ryske, he never asked anyone else to do it for him."

FOURTEEN

THE DOORBELL STOPPED Harlow from asking Anwen exactly what that meant.

A breather wasn't unwelcome. "Excuse me," she said, trying to figure out who could be at the door.

Rupert wouldn't ring the doorbell, neither would Lena… even Ryske would just storm in.

Apprehension tensed Anwen. "Will that be him?"

Twirling in an open armed shrug, Harlow wasn't in the mood to be tactful. "If you're going back to the city tomorrow, you'll have to see him sometime."

It was likely to be a neighbor or one of Lena's friends, not anyone scary. When she opened the front door, a surprise awaited.

Doctor Bale. And he didn't look impressed. Not that she blamed him. The doctor was pushed and pulled with the crew's tide with no control or notice on when it would turn.

Opening his hand toward her, he had an expectation. "Let me see it."

Dropping the back of her bandaged hand into his open palm, the med bag over his shoulder was no fashion accessory. It made more sense to turn her hand over and take his to bring him inside.

"Didn't I tell you the night we met that he's an asshole?" Bale asked when she dragged him into her parents' foyer. "If I didn't, I should have."

"Do you want a drink?" she asked. "You can stay the night if you promise to tell him we had sex… and that I said you were better than him. *Way* better than him."

The doctor might not have been the instigator, but he'd been complicit in the lie. Teasing distracted him on the trip to the living room. The moment they entered, Bale stopped. Time for someone else to be shocked. She let go of his hand to return to her seat and her drink.

"Oh my God," Anwen said.

"Anwen," Bale said. "When the hell did—"

"She came to visit me last night," Harlow said and held her Scotch toward him. "Drink?"

In a kind of stupor, Bale got the glass to gulp down the liquid while dropping into the seat at her side. Once the liquor was gone, he handed back the glass and met her eye.

"I told him he was crazy," the doc said. "He came to me with the idea. He knew an undertaker, had paid off a coroner. It was a full-scale operation, not like when he—"

"Faked his death?" she asked. "Everybody's dead. Nobody's dead. Who even knows anymore?"

Except that wasn't fair. She'd already concluded Anwen's fake death inspired Ryske's. The crew knew they could pull it off; that they had a safe haven to hide in. His wouldn't have happened if it wasn't for his ex's.

"It was protection; that was how he convinced me."

Funny, Ryske said that was his reason for fake dying too. Only she was supposed to buy that it was for her protection, not his.

"Do you think that's why I'm pissed?" she asked.

The doctor took her injured hand to his lap to unwind the bandage and inspect her wound. "No," Bale said. "I'm going to guess he didn't tell you she was alive."

"Yahtzee," she said without intonation. "He said she killed herself when Hagan found out about the affair. He gave me some line about, 'at least that's what Hagan would say.' I thought he meant Hagan was responsible, not that Hagan believed Ryske's lie."

"Jarvis was responsible," Anwen said, defending Ryske. "He made my life miserable and wanted to control every little detail. Yet, he'd go out there, making a fool of me, screwing anything he wanted to. I told Ryske he had to help me or I would kill myself… I basically put a gun to my head and asked him to pull the trigger. Faking it was the only alternative."

Bale took a couple of things from his med bag and stood up, drawing Harlow to her feet too. "I need to wash this out, is there a restroom?"

"By the front door," Harlow said and with their hands linked, she led him through the house to show him.

At the sink, he held her hand under the stream of water. "My brother's an idiot."

"Duh," she said, leaning on the vanity.

"What the hell was he thinking of cutting you like this and letting you bleed into each other?"

Bale's job was to make people better. He wouldn't be able to understand anyone deliberately injuring another person.

"I can wash my own hand," she said.

He was too intent on his work to pay attention to her words. "God knows what kind of diseases you could've picked up in prison. Did you get any tattoos?" He twisted her arm to look at her stars. "Anyone touch Dover's work?"

"The stars are pure Dover," she said. "Did you just call me diseased? I thought you were being sweet and concerned. You're supposed to be the caring sibling."

Snagging the towel from its metal loop, he sat her down on the closed toilet and crouched to pat her hand dry. "I came all the way over here after my shift to treat you. I'm your crew's personal physician; I don't enjoy running around after you all. I was looking forward to a couple of days off."

"If it wasn't for the idiot, I wouldn't be cut."

"Sends him crazy when you do this, when you tell him you're through," Bale said, holding her hand inside the towel, looking into her. "You don't understand how much he loves you… how much power you have over him."

Harlow wasn't swayed. "He lied to me," she murmured. "He told me he'd never do that."

The doctor's grip tightened. "He trusts you more than anyone else in the world. His crew are the only ones who know about my connection to him… You're on that crew."

Shaking her head, she got closer. "No. How can I be when I didn't know she was on it too? Anwen knows all about me while *I* didn't even know she was breathing."

Turning her arm again, he showed her the stars. "She's not on the crew. She doesn't know about Ryske and I, and you're the only woman in the world with these."

"That means nothing," she said, snatching her arm back. "How will I ever be able to trust him when we live surrounded by these half-truths?"

"The way I hear it from both of you, you've been omitting a few details yourself. Hasn't he been asking you what happened the night Hagan died? Word is you won't tell him."

In her mind, the two things weren't even close to similar. "Not telling is not the same as lying. I've been honest about my withholding… *I* had to learn that he was shacked up with his ex for four months from her," she hissed, keeping the volume down when what she really wanted to do was scream. "Anwen came back from the dead to tell me… How many other truths has he kept from me? Is he married? How many kids does he have?"

"You want to talk about this all night? We'll do that," Bale said, pulling her onto her feet. "Before that, I have to get you patched up and we have to tell Ryske Anwen is here, out in the open. That wasn't part of their deal."

Like she gave a shit about any deal Ryske had with his ex… oh, that was another assumption. Maybe Anwen wasn't an ex at all. Harlow couldn't be sure of anything anymore.

"Bet he'll be so disappointed. He was just desperate to tell me himself," she said, letting herself be dragooned out of the restroom and back to the living room couch.

"I don't remember you being so sarcastic when we met."

"Ryske does that to women. He makes us bitter and

vindictive," Harlow said, glancing over at Anwen. "I suppose you two got close when Bale was with you in the mountains."

"No, actually," Anwen said. Harlow only half watched what Bale was doing to her hand. "The doctor stayed in the basement with the rest of Ryske's friends. Ryske was the only one who slept upstairs."

As if sensing what she was about to say, Bale interjected. "Because it was warmer and cleaner and he was recuperating."

Long days with just him and Anwen alone, bonding. Great, an unsolicited mental picture that wouldn't go away in a hurry.

"I didn't say a word," Harlow said. "Anwen and I have already established that Ryske didn't promise either of us fidelity. We weren't ever each other's other woman."

Anwen smiled. "Ryske said you were reasonable."

Bale snorted a laugh. "There's no way he said that about Harlow."

Something he did with his little sticky things stung and she flinched. "Ow!"

"Sorry," he mumbled.

"Maybe I should go," Anwen said.

"You're free to stay if you would like… We'll tell Ryske Bale had both of us," Harlow said, but her joke fell flat. "My parents are out of town, and I have a feeling my sister won't be home tonight."

"Thanks," Anwen said, leaving her seat. "But my things are at the hotel and I've said all I came to say. You saved me, Harlow. Anything you need, just let me know."

Harlow slapped at Bale's hands to stop him working so she could go with Anwen to the front door.

"Thank you for coming," Harlow said and was surprised when Anwen hugged her again.

"I'll look after him," Anwen whispered in her ear and made eye contact as she retreated to the driveway.

Harlow closed the front door and turned to find Bale behind her. "You know the rules about doctor's orders for your crew," he said. "Let me finish with your hand. After that, if you want to spend the night ripping Ryske apart, you know

I'm game."

Bale was like his brother in so few ways. Yet, there were times they were so alike she didn't know why their similarities always astonished her.

"I need something else first," she said and went over to slide her arms around him.

Embracing her in return, he gave her a squeeze. "You've got the world on your shoulders, babe… None of us have helped much, have we?"

"You help," she said. "I feel like you get sucked into these messes. Ryske isn't an easy man to say no to… Believe me, I know."

"You seem to say no to him a lot. I haven't known anyone to stand up to him as much as you do… You know how to put him in his place. He might say out loud that he's confident, but when you guys are in limbo, he's a fucking mess."

Bale didn't swear much, so it meant something that he chose that moment to use such a strong word. "Aren't brothers supposed to cover for each other in front of girls?"

"He has enough people covering his ass," Bale said. "You and I need to give him some perspective."

"You do," she said. "You share blood with him; you have to stick at his side."

Stepping back, he turned her injured hand to show where Ryske had sliced her. "I'm not the only one who shares blood with him… Did you use condoms while he was here?"

Groaning, she shoved his arm. "You're just a doctor every minute, aren't you? Yes, we used condoms."

"It's too early for a pregnancy test, but if there's a chance—"

"God, Bale," she said, grabbing his hand to drag him into the kitchen. "You're not going to be an uncle. Let's get you a drink and loosen you up… We have a lot of bitching to do."

She didn't really care about bitching, but she would look forward to hanging out with Bale. He was the smartest man she knew. Despite his connection to Ryske, he was the only one who didn't actually want anything from her.

Harlow trusted Clyde and knew his loyalty was with her before Ryske, which she couldn't really say about Bale. Problem was that kiss Clyde laid on her, it stuck there in the background, hanging over them… not that it would ever happen again.

Bale didn't want her like that. Their relationship was what it was. They had no expectation of each other and that was exactly what she needed.

FIFTEEN

LENA HADN'T DISAPPOINTED expectation. She'd called to say she wouldn't be coming home. If it hadn't been for Bale, Harlow would've been by herself. Much as she was independent, she hadn't been alone for a long time. The silence unsettled her more than she'd care to admit out loud. Given how much was on her mind, it was nice to have someone around to distract her.

Bale shared stories from his job at the hospital. The role was basically the same as his old one. Upon his return from disappearing with the Floyd's crew, he'd accepted a demotion. He said it was temporary and she hoped that was true. It wouldn't be right for his career to suffer because he'd chosen to care for his wayward brother.

Another popular topic? Apartment hunting. Apparently, choosing a home closer to Floyd's was a deliberate decision. Switching location meant he was nearer the hospital and, in the less desirable neighborhood, could afford two bedrooms. The undercurrent being he could be on call for Ryske and his crew in case of any more stabbings or shootings.

They agreed that with Hagan gone, the threat to Ryske had decreased. But neither were naïve. The crew lived in a dangerous neighborhood and did dangerous work. Anything could go wrong any minute.

More than once Harlow got the sense that the doctor wanted to question her about Hagan's death. He asked about jail and learned everything there was to know about her family but didn't inquire about the night of the murder.

Lena didn't come back the next night either. Bale stayed over again on the understanding he had to leave early for work the following day.

His staying might have gone unnoticed, except Rupert walked in to find her friend the doctor on the stairs… in a towel. There hadn't been any screaming or hollering when the men came face to face. Nope, she'd been oblivious to the meeting and only heard their voices in the foyer when she came in from the backyard.

Bale had come down with a question about the shower at the same time Rupert walked in to check on her. Apparently. The two men did their own introductions and got on to talking about Bale's stock portfolio. For how long? She had no idea. Surreal. Neither man got awkward. They'd said their goodbyes, shaken hands, and Rupert kissed her cheek, telling her to call if she needed anything.

He didn't ask if she and Bale were sleeping together, not outright, though she assumed that was his deduction. In a way, her ex-fiancé seemed relieved. Given what she'd told Rupert about her boyfriend, it probably *was* a relief to find out he was a doctor, not a ruffian. Harlow was in no hurry to correct his supposition.

Once Rupert was gone, Bale had his shower and headed off to work. Saying goodbye to her friend wasn't easy. Still, not everything was about her. Respecting his commitments was more important than her anxiety about being alone with her thoughts.

Leaving his numbers and his address, Bale told her to visit any time. The invite was bittersweet. As long as the murder case was hanging over her, she wasn't going to be dropping in on anyone.

Harlow wasn't good at staying put and doing nothing. There were only so many times she could wax her legs or pluck her eyebrows. So it was a relief when Lena eventually came home for dinner. Having someone to look after kept her busy.

By the end of the week, the house was spotless and she was preened to within an inch of her life. It had been fun to clean out the attic with her sister. They'd had a laugh over the family photo albums and old yearbooks.

On Friday, Lena seemed less like herself, which made Harlow wonder if she was apprehensive about their parents returning. Lena had never lived away from home and must have enjoyed the freedom that came with having the place to themselves.

Sure that Lena was seeing someone, Harlow's other theory involved issues in the relationship. If the boyfriend was playing with her sister's heart, being a suspected murderess could work in her favor. Given her own relationship history, she wasn't qualified to give out advice. But if the guy stepped out of line, she was the perfect person to scare him.

While Lena chattered on the phone with Emma, making plans for the evening, Harlow cooked dinner.

The doorbell rang.

Grabbing a towel, she wiped her hands and started through the foyer. Who could be dropping in on them? Since the night Bale arrived, she hadn't heard a peep from Anwen. Ryske hadn't been in touch either. None of the crew had.

After all her talk and cajoling, her wish was coming true. They were moving on, letting her go to prison in peace.

Except, she couldn't think of anyone else who might be coming by.

Bale wouldn't finish at the hospital for another hour and Clyde was on call tonight, so—

On opening the entryway door, the distorted glass panel in the front door gave her a clue. Three people stood on the doorstep. Although she couldn't see precise details, it looked suspiciously like two of them were wearing uniforms.

This was it.

Somehow, she just knew.

They'd come for her.

Her freedom was over.

For a second, Harlow thought about spinning around and running into the dining room to impart some last minute wisdom on her sister or grabbing the phone to call Floyd's. But there was nothing to say.

Resigned to her fate, she untied her apron and draped it over the table next to the shoe closet door.

With a hand on the front door handle, she was about to open it when Lena spoke behind her. "Harlow?" she asked. "Who is it?"

Whoever was on the other side must have seen her outline. That didn't stop her from letting go of the door. The doorbell rang again; she ignored it. These were her last seconds with her sibling.

Going to her sister, unfastening the bracelet from her wrist, Harlow stayed calm.

"Take care of Mom and Dad, okay?" she said, putting the bracelet on her sister's wrist and taking the long leather necklace from her neck to put it over her sister's head. "They love you so much. Tell them not to visit. I don't want any of you to visit."

Witnessing her mother's discomfort and her sister's fear at a prison facility would tear her apart. It wouldn't do any of them any good.

"Harlow," Lena said, touching the bullet tied to the strand of leather around her neck.

The littlest Sweeting couldn't possibly understand what the damaged metal meant. There was no time to explain. There was no time for anything anymore.

Pulling her into a hug, she kissed her sister's cheek and raised her lips to her ear. "Get what you like, and like what you get, little one," she said and touched her hair as she drifted away, smiling at the tear on Lena's lashes.

"Harlow, I don't want them to take you," Lena said, rushing after her. She opened the front door to two cops and her lawyer. Lena grabbed her shoulders and tried to pull her back into the house. "No! You can't take her!"

"It's okay," Harlow said, prying her sister's hands away and easing her back into the foyer.

Crying, Lena tried to grab for her again, but she

pushed her hands down. "Harlow!"

"They're dropping the charges."

Greta's words froze both sisters.

Harlow couldn't process… It was… It didn't make sense. Even her lawyer spoke the words with disbelief.

Whipping around, Harlow made eye contact, seeking clarification. "They're… what?"

Lifting her arms, Greta was incredulous. "I got the call and… they're dropping the charges."

"No more court?" Harlow asked. Greta shook her head. "No more jail? It's… over?"

The tentative smile on Greta's lips dropped. "I can't say that. If new evidence emerges, they can charge you again. We never went to trial. This could still come back. But with the evidence going missing, there's nothing else that they can do right now. The State's Attorney isn't confident they'll get a conviction."

"Oh my God," Harlow whispered.

Since this started, since her arrest, she hadn't let herself think about the future beyond the next lights out. Even throughout her week at home, Harlow hadn't let herself think about what life could be. As far as she was concerned, the rest of her life would be spent incarcerated.

Suddenly, every thought she hadn't let herself have crashed into her. Without even realizing it, she was making plans.

One person was top of her list in those plans.

"Why are they here?" Lena asked. "Those uniform guys. If Harlow's free, why—"

"For their monitor," Greta said. "They have to get it back. There's some paperwork to sign and then you're… free."

"Am I going to get a formal apology?" Harlow asked, letting the trio into the house and leading them into the living room. "Lena, go turn the stove off, will you?" Nodding, Lena darted toward the kitchen. Harlow sat on the couch to present her bracelet. "Quick as possible, if you wouldn't mind."

One of the two uniforms went about removing the monitor while the other shuffled papers around.

Greta scurried over to sit at her side. "Don't forget," the lawyer murmured. "A man died… and they still think you did it."

"So they're looking for any excuse," Harlow said, understanding the subtext. "I hear you. I won't push my luck."

"We should keep in touch…" Greta said, "just in case."

Harlow would need some time to wrap her mind around the prospect of being free from the bounds of the state. The lawyer's suggestion that they stay in touch implied Harlow would need her again. This was progress, but not necessarily permanent.

Once the bracelet was gone and the paperwork signed, and after clarifying several times that she was a free woman in every way, she ushered everyone out of the house.

Harlow was free.

SIXTEEN

AFTER CLOSING THE front door, Harlow spun around and took a breath. Looking down at her bare ankle, she tried to recognize what she was… herself again. There were no bounds, no rules. No more obligations to anyone.

From being idle, and living on pause, she got moving fast. Running up the stairs, her mind was racing with plans of what to pack. Being thorough, she tossed everything into one large suitcase and grabbed the phone to call a cab.

She'd just put the phone on the nightstand and was thinking about money when Lena came into her bedroom. Ryske had access to all her bank accounts, so they were probably empty.

"Do Mom and Dad still keep money stashed under that figurine in the dining room?"

Lena nodded. "There's around a hundred bucks."

"Okay," she said, nodding. "I need it… I'll replace it."

"I'll take care of it," Lena said, removing the leather necklace to lay it across the center of the bed. "I thought you'd want this back."

"Thanks," Harlow said, grabbing it to loop it around her neck.

She tucked the bullet into her cleavage where it had nestled since she'd attached it to the leather string.

"Is that it… the… Is that what killed him?"

"This?" she asked, touching the leather tied around the bullet. "No. This is something different."

"It means something to you?" Lena asked, sitting on the corner of the bed.

Tugging the bullet from her cleavage, she rolled it in her fingertips. "Yeah. It means love is fleeting."

Not because her love had been taken from her, but because her love had never been hers in the first place. The bullet meant so much. It served as a reminder to be aware, not naïve, and never let herself be fooled by her eyes again.

She was so caught up in her contemplation that she didn't notice her sister's state until the sound of Lena's sob startled her. Red-faced, with tear-stained cheeks, Lena had gone from tentative to a mess in the space of ten seconds.

"You're leaving," Lena bawled.

"Oh, God, honey," Harlow said, running around the bed to sit down and pull her into a hug. "It will be okay, little one."

"No," Lena said, returning the hug with startling force. "No, it won't! It won't be okay."

"I'll come home to visit."

"You said that before, when you moved away."

Sitting back to get a better look, Harlow tucked her sister's hair away from her face and tried to smile. "And I came back, didn't I? I would've been away for a lot longer if they'd sent me to prison."

Lena threw herself forward, launching into another embrace. "I don't want you to go! I want you to stay here! Please stay, Harlow."

No one had ever begged her to do anything. The closest anyone had come was when Rupert asked her to stay with him. Looking back, Harlow was sure that even then, even while saying the words, he'd known that she wouldn't.

Holding her sister, Harlow soothed and murmured her platitudes, but Lena kept crying.

After about five minutes, she grew concerned.

"Lena," she said, holding her sister back to look at her again. "This isn't about me, is it?" Lena blubbed. "Lena, what happened?"

Her sister was a full of life, bubbly person. She always had been. Until that week. That week she'd been more subdued. Harlow had noticed. Except she'd guessed her sibling was distracted by love or annoyed about sharing the house with her felonious sister. No doubt Lena would've preferred to be with the friends and the possible boyfriend.

"I did something stupid," Lena said.

When her sister's chin fell, Harlow widened her smile and scooped her hands onto Lena's face, holding her head like Ryske usually held hers. "You're talking to the queen of doing something stupid... What happened?" Lena hesitated. "You can tell me anything."

"Mom and Dad are going to be so mad when they find out... I don't know what to do."

"No, they won't be mad," she said. "I meant what I said downstairs, they love you so much... You didn't kill anyone, did you?" Lena shook her head but didn't look her in the eye. It broke her heart to see her beautiful sister so downtrodden. "They didn't cast me out when they thought I did... Whatever you did, they'll accept it. They're not going to—"

"I'm pregnant."

Harlow's open mouth froze. After a moment, she let it close while she exhaled an, "Oh."

"I just found out today," Lena whispered and peeked up. "I don't know what to do... I don't know if I want to keep it. I don't know if it's a good idea."

"What does the father say?" Harlow asked. Lena's head descended again and she fidgeted with the comforter beneath them. "Lena?"

"I haven't told him," she said on a shrug. "I thought maybe if I wasn't going to go through with it that I shouldn't..."

"Tell him? You have to tell him, Lena... Who is the father? How long have you been together?"

Lena was so young, though plenty of younger women

had children. But Lena had such a clear dream of what she wanted her life to be. The dream didn't include career or success in the workplace. The youngest Sweeting wanted the perfect man, the perfect wedding, the perfect marriage. From what she was witnessing, Harlow guessed that whoever the father was, he wasn't the dream man Lena pictured herself with.

"We're not exactly… we're not together."

Though there was only seven years age difference between them, it wasn't always easy to picture her innocent baby sister even knowing what a one-night stand was, much less engaging in one.

Remaining calm and non-judgmental, Harlow liked to think she'd react with this kind of understanding even if she didn't have her social work training to fall back on.

"You're not together?"

Lena shook her head. "He… he's sort of hung up on someone else."

Her sister's meek tone offered Harlow clarity. Something Lena had said at the breakfast table last week came back to her. Something about Emma's boyfriend: Vane.

"Oh, God," she groaned, casting her eyes to the ceiling. "Sweeting women have a type."

The last person she wanted her little sister to be involved with was a devious conman like Sam Vane. There was no way they could be talking about anyone else. Lena said he was the hottest man she'd seen in real life. It was no wonder her little sister felt guilty enough to consider not revealing the truth. She didn't want to hurt her friend.

Lena didn't know the truth about Vane. Harlow didn't know the details, but there had to be a reason Ryske called the man 'Penzance' and she doubted it was because he was funny.

"I didn't mean for it to happen," Lena said, grabbing for her hand. "Neither of us did, it just… did."

"Sex doesn't just happen," Harlow said, taking the bracelet from Lena's wrist to put it back on her own. "Trust me, I've slept naked with the horniest man on the planet. If there was a way, he'd have found it. I managed to keep his cock out of my body just fine."

Maybe not easily, but she'd managed it. Where Ryske was concerned that was an achievement worthy of the podium.

"Harlow," Lena said, grabbing her hand when she tried to stand up. "What should I do?"

Exhaling, her sister's desperation softened her. It wasn't like Lena could go to her friend, Emma, for help. Damn Vane and his wandering eyes… though it wasn't his eyes that had caused this problem.

"Look," Harlow said, pulling both of Lena's hands onto her lap. "You have to tell him. There's no way you can't tell him."

If this had happened in her life pre-Ryske, Harlow might not have advocated for telling a criminal he was going to father a child. The felonious connection could be dangerous for both mother and child.

"And… if he tells me to get rid of it?"

Startled by the question, she frowned. "Are you kidding me? If you want to have an abortion, I will support you every step of the way. Mom and Dad never have to know. I'll go with you myself. But if you want this child," she said, putting a hand on her sister's stomach. "Then this guy can go fuck himself if he thinks he's going to make you bend to his will… You don't need a man, Lena. No matter what, you'll always have my support, even if Mom and Dad don't want to accept it." Lena tensed. "I think they will, but even if they don't, you can move into the city. I'll support you… both of you."

"You… You're moving back to the city?"

Sitting up straighter, the decision was only made the moment the words came out of her mouth. "I think I am," she said, leaning over to kiss her sister's cheek. "Here." Leaving the bed, she went to grab a piece of paper and a pen. "If you're ever in trouble, or you need to get hold of me, call this number." Scribbling down Bale's number, she tore off the paper and took it to her sister. At the last second, she pulled it back. "Don't share this with anyone, not ever."

Nodding, Lena took the number from her and read

it. "I didn't know you had a phone."

"I don't," she said, going to finish her packing. "That number connects you to a man I'd trust with your life."

She'd trusted him with Ryske's life and he had saved it; not that he'd been honest about it. At first, she'd considered sharing Clyde's number, but her former colleague might be more inclined to panic than jump to action in a desperate situation.

Bale would know who to call no matter how serious the situation, and the people he'd call wouldn't hesitate to go to any lengths. Clyde would hesitate. But her crew, they had weighed their limits and knew their boundaries. They would act and if her sister needed help, that's what Harlow wanted: action.

With freedom came possibilities. While zipping up her suitcase, she admitted, only to herself, that Anwen was right about Ryske. Though Harlow could never be in an intimate relationship with a man who lied to her, Ryske was who he was. She couldn't take his lying personally. In his own way, he had honor… when he wanted to. Trusting the Floyd's crew to be capable professionals wasn't the same as trusting Ryske with her heart.

If he wanted to be a liar, he could be a liar. Just like if she didn't want to be intimate with a liar, she didn't have to be.

Nothing surprised her. In many ways, that was a gift. After living in jail for three months and watching two men die, nothing scared her either. Ophelia once told her that Ryske dubbed her fearless. She used to have fear, used to be afraid. Not anymore.

Pulling the case off the bed, the blare of a car horn outside got Harlow moving. "I'm sorry to leave you like this," she said, going to stroke Lena's hair. "Spend the night spoiling yourself and think about how you'll tell him. I'll call you tomorrow."

She gave her sister another kiss, then went downstairs. Just as she opened the front door, the phone rang. In two minds about answering it, hesitation held her still. She didn't want it to be Greta with news her freedom was all a mistake. Except, if it was Bale or Clyde, Lena was too emotional to explain what was going on.

Putting her suitcase on the external stair, she waved to the cab driver who got out to scurry across the drive. Dashing back inside, she grabbed the phone and spun around to watch the cab driver carry her suitcase to the trunk of his car. Cleavage worked wonders, even from a distance.

"Yeah?" she said into the phone, impatient about being delayed.

It was dark and might be raining, but out there was freedom and it smelled sweet.

"Harlow?"

The female voice surprised her. "Anwen?"

"I… I didn't know who else to call. I don't know what to do."

Forgetting impatience, concern overtook her again. "What is it?" Harlow asked, sensing Anwen's apprehension. "What's going on?"

"Ophelia's on her way over," Anwen said. "I'm staying at a motel. I… I don't know if I should stay and talk to her. I don't know what she wants… or how she found me."

"Call Ryske."

"No, I… I can't get hold of him," Anwen said and inhaled a shaky breath. "You asked if she'd been violent… You know something… Something more than he does."

Yeah, she knew a lot. Hagan had told her what his sister was capable of and Harlow had seen it with her own eyes. As much as she resented herself for it, Harlow didn't want Ryske or the other guys anywhere near that kind of danger.

"Tell me where you are," she said, going to get her parents' cash from the figurine after almost forgetting about it. Anwen recited the motel address and her room number. "Stay where you are. I'm on my way."

"What? How can—"

"If you see so much as a glimpse of a weapon, get out of there. Don't wait. I'll be as quick as I can."

Hanging up the phone, she ran to the cab and leaped into the back, instructing the driver that she needed to get where they were going. Fast.

SEVENTEEN

THE CAB DRIVER did his best to get her to Anwen's motel as quickly as possible. Despite his appreciated effort, there was no way she'd get there before Ophelia. Staying in the had frustrated her as a teenager when she wanted to be in the thick of things in the city. Until that night, the journey had never been one of life or death.

Every single one of those minutes in the cab crushed her. Exuding tension, the driver quickly got the message she wasn't in the mood for small talk. The guy's best was nothing to what Noon's would've been, where was her friend when she needed him?

By the time they pulled up outside the motel, rain poured. Tossing money at the driver, she grabbed her suitcase and sprinted into the motel, ignoring the front desk to bolt up the stairs.

Anwen's room was right there at the top. The number on the door bore ominous omen to what lay inside. Like a horror movie, the ajar door beckoned. This would be the moment she'd scream "run" at the screen. Going inside probably couldn't lead to anything good, but what choice did she have?

Leaving her suitcase, she tiptoed closer, listening for

sounds of… anyone. Nothing, not a peep.

Without a weapon, how could she defend herself? Her ring was in her suitcase. Looking for it would take time she didn't have. With her back to the hallway wall, she used just the tips of her fingers to open the door farther. Anticipating movement or activity, she waited a second in silence. When nothing happened, she peeked inside.

There was no one there. No signs of… A prone foot on the floor at the other side of the bed got her rushing inside. Glancing left and right, she saw no one else. Restroom was open. She didn't notice anyone in there, but kept one eye on it just in case someone was hiding. Her wariness relaxed though. The abrupt confrontation she'd expected hadn't come.

Relief didn't last.

She moved around the end of the bed, the foot, oh… Anwen lay on the floor, her perfect body loose and motionless.

Her panic spiked. "Oh shit."

Dropping to a crouch, she rolled Anwen onto her back to feel for a pulse.

This was some luck. On the same day she got out of one murder charge, she could be taken in for another. Pressing her fingers to Anwen's neck, the slow pulse was better than nothing, but not great.

"Oh, shit, shit," she whispered, seeking out a phone… and coming up short.

Harlow didn't have one in her suitcase either. Her mind was racing. 9-1-1 wouldn't be the best idea for a dead woman. Anwen was dead. Officially. Hagan had believed it; people were paid off to make it real. If Harlow took Anwen to a hospital or called the authorities, all those promises she'd made to Bale about keeping his secret would be broken.

Still, it wasn't like Harlow could just watch the woman die for real.

Shaking her did nothing. Anwen was out. She brushed her hair from her face. Bruises, blood she'd been beaten. It turned Harlow's stomach. Searching for gunshots or stab wounds, none were apparent.

There was bruising around her wrists and on her stomach too. Linking those injuries with the blood on her skirt, she deduced Ophelia hadn't come alone, or she'd violated her once-upon-a-time friend in a more intimate, and perhaps permanent, way.

Anwen groaned.

A spark of hope.

"Anwen," she said, stroking her cheek. "Anwen, honey, I need you to wake up. It's Harlow. You're safe now."

"Harlow," she muttered without opening her eyes.

Though that could be attributed to the swelling on her face.

"Okay. Okay," Harlow said.

Anwen was awake. Good sign, a step in the right direction.

Leaving her side, Harlow ran to haul her suitcase into the room. Opening it up, she got the closest thing she had to a jacket and took it back to Anwen. Laying it over the woman, she tried to cover her as she scooped her arms under her to pick her up.

It wasn't easy. Anwen was taller than her, the lift was awkward and painful on her muscles. Her pain didn't matter. The slight woman needed her and wasn't capable of walking on her own. Adrenaline had a lot to answer for. Somehow, Harlow managed to find her feet.

Carrying her out of the motel room, Harlow took her time about balancing Anwen on the way down the stairs. She said nothing to anyone who may or may not be behind the Plexiglas at the check-in desk and took Anwen to the street.

Anwen groaned again and her head fell back. Harlow had to stop to steady her again. The new position made things harder, but she got moving. Every step took her closer to where she needed to be.

"You're okay," she said, trying not to strain in the slippery rain. Only two more blocks. "You're lighter than Ryske."

Her joke fell on deaf ears. Didn't matter. No one else would understand the parallel between her walking the streets of this less than savory neighborhood with an injured person relying on her to get them where they needed to be.

Grateful for small mercies, Harlow was glad Bale's new apartment was on this side of town. In the crappy neighborhood, she could walk in without a doorman or security holding her up.

One flight of stairs, narrower than those at the motel, forced her to go up sideways. Her arms screamed in pain. Her body was tense and sweating, but she was capable of anything. Anything. This was about strength of mind, not of body. Repeating that in her head encouraged every step.

By the time she got to Bale's door, her lungs were tight. While trying to knock on his door with her aching hand, she almost fell against it.

"Please be home," she whispered, gritting her teeth and letting her head go back in response to the pain. "Oh, please be home."

A clunk on the other side of the door heralded it opening.

Bale stood there for half a beat, processing the view. "Oh, fucking hell," he said.

Putting his beer bottle on something by the door, he quickly leaped forward to scoop Anwen out of Harlow's arms.

Instant relief was short-lived. The moment Anwen was taken, Harlow's body relaxed, but her muscles went into spasm. Adrenaline nosedived, hitting her with exhaustion. She dropped onto her hands and knees without the power to stop the collapse.

Bale appeared in a crouch at her side. "Harlow, look at me," he demanded in his doctor voice. "Are you injured? Having trouble breathing? Where's the pain?"

Shaking her hand, she kept her head dipped. "I'm fine," she wheezed and tossed her head back to attempt eye contact. "Anwen… help Anwen."

"Let's get you inside too," he said, putting an arm around her to help her onto her feet.

Once she was up, she went into the apartment. It was open plan with three doors leading from a central living and kitchen space.

"Is she okay?" Harlow asked, rubbing her arms,

fighting to ignore the throbbing in her head.

"Through here," he said, going to the internal door that was open. Anwen was on the bed, her eyes closed. She was whimpering, which was at least a sign of life. Bale went to a closet to retrieve a bunch of supplies. "How are you here, Nightingale? Your ankle monitor—"

"They dropped the charges," she said, sitting by Anwen.

Bale dumped some medical stuff on the bed, then donned gloves. Taking her shoulders, he moved her away from his patient, giving himself space to do his thing checking vitals and wounds.

"Anwen," he said, his voice firm. "Can you hear me?"

"Mm," Anwen whimpered.

"Why did they drop the charges?" Bale asked. "The missing evidence?"

Harlow nodded, wringing her hands. "I need to do something. What can I do?"

"Go into the kitchen and boil some water. We need to clean her up."

Doing as she was told, she brought him water and kneeled on the mattress by Anwen. Taking the doctor's direction, she bathed Anwen's wounds. Bale was seated in a chair angled at the side of the bed.

"This isn't right," Harlow said, holding Anwen's hand on hers and wiping the back of it. "She fought back."

"Wouldn't you?"

Harlow had fought back when she'd been attacked, but her wounds weren't like these. "Do you think she was raped?"

Her attention left the blood on Anwen's skirt to meet Bale's, he shrugged, his expression solemn.

"I don't know," he said. "She was certainly beaten, and if she wants to go to the hospital—"

"No hospital," Anwen muttered, attracting their focus. Her eyes were still closed, but her head moved. "It was Ophelia."

"She did this to you?" Harlow asked.

"Animal."

Just like her brother. Hagan claimed that he'd never laid his hands on Anwen. Ryske's account spoke to the physical abuse she'd endured. There was little Animal wouldn't do for Jarvis Hagan. Now that he was gone, had Animal's allegiance switched to the woman in charge: Ophelia?

"Were you raped?" Harlow asked. "If we can get evidence—"

"No," she said. "No evidence."

That wasn't an answer either way. Bale must have had the same thought because he looked to her and they shared a moment.

"None of the cuts are too deep," Bale said. "I think he split his knuckles from the way some of the blood is swiped… They can collect DNA—"

"No," Anwen said. "Where's Ryske?"

Anwen was out of it, dazed and disoriented. Given what she'd been through, that was no surprise. Except, if she was so confused, could they rely on her assertion that she didn't want to be taken to a hospital?

"I don't know where he'll be," Bale muttered, picking up a med bag.

"It's Friday night," Harlow said, waiting for him to remember that Floyd's basement would be open.

Ryske would be at the bar keeping things in order with his crew.

Their eyes met again. "There's a phone in the kitchen," Bale said, opening a new syringe. When her lips parted in objection, she squeaked. Why should she be the one to call and summon him? "He's not going to come running because *I* call, Sweeting."

According to Anwen, Ryske had been avoiding her. So if he didn't understand how serious this was, he might be tempted to ignore his brother's request.

Groaning, Harlow clambered off the bed to make her way to the kitchen.

This wasn't the best night to phone Floyd's. They would be at their busiest; everyone would be occupied with their job. On other week nights, she'd get either Dover or

Lowan because they were usually the only two likely to be behind the bar. Friday through Sunday, anyone could pick up.

Dialing the number she knew better than any other, Harlow took a calming breath. No matter who picked up, she wouldn't cause tension or start an argument. This wasn't about her. This was about Anwen and what she needed.

Noon was the one to answer the phone. "Hello?"

"Noon," she said. "I need Ryske to come over to Bale's."

"Nightingale?" he said with obvious shock. Like Bale, he'd expect her to still be under house arrest. "You're at—"

"If he's there and he wants to come, I'm here. If he's not, I don't give a shit."

Hanging up the phone, she didn't let herself stop to think about whether or not he'd show up. Pouring three glasses of water, she took them through to the bedroom.

"Is he coming?" Bale asked, putting butterfly stitches on a cut on Anwen's jaw.

"Who knows with him?" she said and went to sit on the end of the bed.

On her first night back in the city, she hadn't expected to see the man she'd vowed never to call again.

"Want to tell me what happened?"

"I don't know what happened," she said, resting a hand on Anwen's ankle to offer a comforting stroke. "She called my parents' house and said Ophelia was coming over… I haven't heard from anyone this week. I don't know how everyone reacted to her being back."

"I haven't been over there this week," Bale said, concentrating on what he was doing. "Ryske's a mess when you're fucking with his head. Why do you think I choose not to live with him?"

"I'm not fucking with his head," she said and stood up. With tensions running high, she didn't want to talk about the man who seemed to delight in fucking with her. "I left my things in Anwen's motel. I'm going over to pack for her. She can't go back, she won't feel safe."

"And you're going to be safe over there on your own?" Bale asked, leaping up to follow her through to the living room. "You're running away because you don't want to see him."

"I don't give a damn about him," she said, opening the front door. "I'll be back soon."

She did want a breather. The motel was three blocks over, and it was still raining, giving her a chance to cool down. Although she told herself that she wasn't trying to avoid Ryske, she did cut across an alley that would ensure there was no chance of their routes overlapping.

Her suitcase was where she'd left it. She took a minute to retrieve her pointed finger ring from inside to put it on, just in case there were any unexpected visitors. Anwen didn't have much. Most of her things seemed to be in the bag that she'd carried during her visit to Harlow at her parents.

Gathering up the things in the bathroom didn't take long. Harlow emptied the nightstand before checking under the pillows of Anwen's bed. In the nightstand was some underwear, all expensive and lacy. Anwen might have come from poverty, but she'd learned to enjoy the finer things in life.

Much as she didn't want to go back to Bale's and deal with whatever drama was waiting there, Harlow couldn't put it off forever. Hanging around at the motel was a bad idea anyway. Ophelia, or her men, could come back any time.

EIGHTEEN

ON THE WALK back to Bale's, Harlow tried to figure out how Ophelia had gained Animal's loyalty so fast. Maybe it wasn't so fast; she was out of the loop. It only seemed fast because she'd been in jail for three months. Ophelia had all that time to recruit Hagan's men as her allies. Sometimes it was difficult to remember that life went on outside.

Maybe they'd been in it since before Hagan's death. Maybe Brash was loyal to her too. Sex was Ophelia's weapon. It had been the woman's suggestion to use it with Parratt and Yarker to gain their support. Maybe she'd adopted the same tactic with her brother's goons.

With Anwen's bag on top of her case, Harlow's free fingers toyed with the bullet hanging around her neck. Animal shot Ryske. She couldn't imagine even standing near Animal by choice, much less working with him or paying him. The man may not have been the one to wish Ryske dead, but he'd been the one to take him closest to it. Ophelia was apparently fine with that.

Harlow didn't see anyone on her walk back to Bale's, but she recognized the car parked on the street opposite the entrance. Going into the building and up the stairs, she noticed Bale's apartment door was open a crack, much as Anwen's had been. Except this time, she didn't have to loiter, the raised voices were obvious from afar.

"She was fucking here," Ryske said.

"Calm down a minute and listen, would you?" Bale said.

Pushing the door, Harlow's entrance caused the three men present to turn in her direction.

A grunt of satisfaction came from Ryske. "Good, your shit is packed," he said, marching toward her and grabbing her hand. "Noon's gonna take us over the border."

She tugged her hand away before he could pull her into the hall. "Uh, what are you doing?"

His frown seemed cemented on his face. "You want to run, we'll run. I don't need to have a fucking discussion about it..." Some of his tension ebbed. "That's why you called."

"No, it isn't," she said, shaking her head while switching her focus to Bale. "You didn't tell him?"

"I didn't get a chance. He came storming in here calling for you."

"The cops could be here any minute, Nightingale," Noon muttered.

"Why? What did you do?" she asked, dragging her suitcase into the apartment and removing Anwen's bag from on top. Thrusting the bag at Ryske, she pointed to the bedroom door. "That's where you're needed."

Confused, Ryske took the bag and stepped out of the doorway, letting her close it. "I don't understand."

Picking up her leg, she gestured at it with two hands. "They dropped the charges," she said.

It took him a second, but he did smile. "You're free? Trink, that's—"

"No," she said, pushing his arm away when his hand came toward her face. Again, she pointed at the bedroom. "I don't need you. She does."

"She?" he asked, his brows rising.

Bale took a backwards step. "She's waiting for you."

Noon was as confused as Ryske, but no one was directing him to do anything. After Harlow gestured at the bedroom again, Bale did too. Frowning at them both, Ryske probably thought they'd lost their minds. Still, bag in hand, he headed toward the bedroom.

The moment he opened the door, his arm dropped to his side, the bag hanging in his hand. "Fuck me," he murmured and went inside, closing the door at his back.

The three of them in the living room breathed for a moment. There wasn't much to say.

Harlow spoke first. "Any good Chinese food places around here?"

Noon smiled at her. "You never change, Nightingale."

"God, I hope that's not true," she said, sharing a smile with him before focusing on Bale. "What's the prognosis, doc?" Noon frowned again. "Anwen got beat up."

Given she was the only one the crew liked to keep secrets from, she didn't feel the need to be discreet. The crew, the real crew, knew everything there was to know about each other. Noon lived with Anwen while Ryske was dead, so he knew she was alive. He'd also been privy to whatever transpired since Anwen reappeared in the city that week.

"She'll need rest. I'll have to keep an eye on some of the wounds. They'll have to be cleaned and redressed every day… She'll need someone with her for a few days. Like I said, I'd like a CT to rule out hemorrhage."

"Ryske will convince her," she said, folding her arms. "But how will you scan a dead woman? I don't think you can bring her back to life."

"She'll need a new identity," Noon said. "Dover's working on it."

So everything worked out. Anwen's return must've been accepted by the crew; they were working for the woman already.

"Great," Harlow said. "Ryske will convince her to have the scan… She might let you do a rape exam too."

"She was raped?" Noon asked.

"We don't know," Bale said. The doctor had taken Anwen's response in the same ambiguous way she had. "I guess she'll tell Ryske."

Leaning back on her suitcase, Harlow shook her

head. "Don't count on it."

"You think she wouldn't tell him?" Bale asked.

"I think that…" The bedroom door opened. Ryske came back in while she was talking. "Rape victims often feel shame," she said, drawing her eyes away from Ryske to look at Bale. "You know that."

Bale nodded. "You think she won't want Ryske to see her as unclean or damaged in any way? She wouldn't tell him about being violated by another man in case it repulsed him?"

She raised her shoulders. "I don't know. I wouldn't tell him."

Ryske stopped walking. "You wouldn't tell me if a guy forced himself on you? Why the hell not?"

"For one thing, because I don't answer to you," she said, and went into the kitchen to put on the coffee machine.

There may be liquor somewhere, but she didn't want to dull anyone's senses… at least not yet.

"That's not fucking good enough," Ryske barked. "Any fucker touches you, Trinket, and I'm your first damn call."

Her experience with Hagan taught her that if the need arose, she could take care of herself. Though, every situation was different and that might not always be the case. Her first thought actually hadn't been about not answering to him; she'd worried about his liberty. Old habits died hard. For a second, the visceral sensation of terror Ryske might go to prison for avenging the crime had been intense.

She shook it off. "I'm not the victim here…" Harlow said, taking the things she needed for coffee out of the kitchen cabinet. "Anwen is."

"Is she okay?" Noon asked.

"She's out of it," Ryske said, exhaling his frustration, though he seemed to accept the progression of the conversation. Harlow hadn't been violated; getting into an argument about a hypothetical was insane. Reality needed their attention. "She started to get upset, so I told her to rest. I don't want to upset her… I do want to know what the fuck happened."

"Animal beat her," Harlow called from the kitchen

without slowing in her coffee prep. "At Ophelia's behest… Your fiancée's a real bitch."

"What the fuck?" Ryske said. "How the hell did Annie get here?"

"Harlow brought her," Bale said. "Damn near passed out on my doorstep."

"I'm a magnet for bleeding people," she said, gathering mugs from the cabinet. "At least that's how it feels." A thought occurred to her; she turned to address the trio. "Wait a second, with you two here, who's backing up Dover?" Leaving the coffee, she went to take Noon's hand. "We should get over there."

"Whoa, wait a second," Bale said. "Anwen can't stay here… I mean, she can stay tonight, but I have to go to work in the morning. You can't leave her here alone."

"She's not my girlfriend," Harlow said. "If I can carry her here, Ryske won't strain himself lifting her. I have to get across town."

"You're going to take her to Floyd's?" Bale said.

"What's across town?" Ryske asked her like Bale hadn't spoken.

"The doc just spoke to you, Crash."

Ryske didn't acknowledge that and came striding across the room. "Flaxman… You're in town, you're free, and you're gonna spend the night with him?"

She balled a hand on her hip. "Who should I spend the night with, Crash? You?"

"Your crew," he said, getting up close. "You get your butt back to Floyd's."

If he thought crowding into her personal space was going to intimidate her, he hadn't learned much from his time with her. "I know math isn't your strong suit, Grifter, but there are more bodies than beds, and you're going to have an extra one in yours. Are you offering up Noon's bed or Maze's?" He was about to retort, but she interrupted, inhaling feigned clarity while bowing back. "Oh, I get it! I'm on the list now."

"What the fuck are you—"

"Ryske's little black book," she said. More than once,

she'd heard him discussing hooking Noon up with women he'd already passed on or finished with. "I get to work my way around your friends now…" She pretended to ponder. "I think I'm going to start with Maze…" Bowing to the side, she sought Noon. "No offense, honey, it's nothing against you. I just know who you sleep next to. I wouldn't want to be enjoying you and glance his way. I think it would kill my buzz."

Ryske's hand leaped to her throat and he thrust her back against the fridge. "Don't fuck with me, Trink."

"I'm not interested in doing anything with you," she said. "You can let me go and I will leave."

Her chin rose when he squeezed tighter. He was trying to break through to her, but she couldn't let him. Passion had always been easy for them. She'd been drawn into her attraction to him before and it had made her forget about his deception.

"You're not going anywhere," he said. "Whether we're fucking or not, this is your crew."

"Yeah?" she asked. "How many lies am I supposed to ignore, Crash? I can trust them with my life but not to treat me with respect?"

"If you'd just told me she showed—"

"That's not how it works," she said, shaking her head as best she could while his strong fingers restricted her. "You said no more lies."

"I wanted to tell you. I tried to."

"When?

"In the apartment, when I came back. Same day I told you I would never lie," he said, coming in even closer. They weren't alone, so this conversation wasn't going to be private no matter how close he got or quiet he spoke. "I asked if you had questions. I said I would tell you anything you wanted to know… I'd have told you everything, baby… In your room, when we…"

She dug the point of her full-finger ring into his hip around where his actual stab scar would be. Ophelia's comment about business and bedfellows came back to her in sync with the memory of Anwen telling her Ryske didn't trust the women he was sleeping with.

Harlow had thought she was different; he'd made her believe that.

"Do not tell me we were too busy having sex for you to tell me something like this," she said. "You knew it was important, and you knew I was oblivious."

"Would you trust me with your life?" he asked. "You said you trusted the crew. Do you know I would do anything to protect you?"

"Including fake dying…?"

"Hate me, Trink," he said, keeping her throat while driving his other hand into her hair to hold the side of her head. "If you have to, hate me. Never abandon your crew. If we're assholes, we're your assholes. It's your job to make us better."

Damn him, but that got through to her. The guys had accepted her and stood by her even when she was in jail for murder. They'd told her she could bring all her baggage and be herself and they'd still accept her. Yes, they messed up. But it wasn't like Harlow could claim to be a saint.

Ryske was right. They were assholes for lying about something this huge. No one was denying that.

The thing was, even when she'd fucked up, they'd never judged her or made her grovel. Whether she and Ryske were fucking or not, the guys were her crew. Ryske had told her that even if they fucked their relationship up and hated each other, she'd still be on the crew.

Yeah, they were a bunch of misfits who'd rustled up a family, but they'd opened their arms to her. Running from them wasn't an option anymore. No matter what. They were her assholes.

"We need her new ID from Dover," she said. "And you have to convince Anwen to get a scan at the hospital."

"Does she need a scan?"

"Have you seen her face? He beat her good," she said. "We don't know if she was raped… You have to talk to her."

"I don't want—"

"You were the one she asked for," Harlow said. "You have the power over her."

Bale moved behind Ryske. There was distance between them and the doc, yet, he was intent on her. He looked so serious and wise. Just like that, it hit her. She got it. Her words clashed with his in her mind.

The doctor had said she didn't understand the power she had over Ryske, and there she was telling Ryske he didn't understand the power he had over Anwen.

"Noon and I will go back to the bar and help Dover. Spend the night, help Bale take her in for the scan. If she gets the okay, bring her back here... I'll come back in the morning."

"You'll stay at the bar," he said. "Stay with the guys? I don't know what Ophelia's game is. She could come for you next."

Being wary made sense. They didn't understand Ophelia's motivation yet, and Anwen couldn't give them a full account. It was only a matter of time before someone told Ophelia the murder charges had been dropped. Her brother's case was back in limbo.

"I don't see why she would," Harlow said. "I can take care of myself. But, yes, I'll stay at the bar."

"We're gonna figure this out," Ryske said.

It was possible he'd been following her train of thought. In that moment of weakness, in bed, she'd answered his question about who pulled the trigger. He knew Ophelia was responsible for Hagan's death, and that the fall guy was free.

Would Ophelia come for her? Who knew? She still hadn't figured out exactly why the murderess had shown up at the Sweeting house. Not that it mattered. If Ophelia didn't come to her, Harlow would go hunting for her.

NINETEEN

THERE WAS MORE deja vu the next morning when Harlow asked Noon to swing by the coffee shop to grab pastries and coffee before they went to Bale's. Different apartment, different patient, but they'd held this kind of vigil before.

"I'm just saying the apartment was spotless before my arrest," she said, leading the way up the stairs. "You guys can't keep anything clean."

"And I'm saying it pisses Maze off when we don't pick up."

"So you do it on purpose? You do it to piss off Maze? Is that the excuse you're trying to sell?"

Opening Bale's front door, they went inside to find Ryske lying on the couch under the window on the opposite side of the room. He had a foot on the floor and an arm outstretched, hanging in midair like he'd just flopped down.

The closer they got, she noticed his eyes were closed and his lips slightly parted.

"What will we do with his coffee?" Noon asked.

It was a stupid impulse, but Harlow bent over to check the pulse in his neck. "Still alive."

Noon slid the tray of coffees onto the end table. "You thought he wouldn't be?" he asked, dropping into the armchair.

Almost every day when she woke up, there was a split second when she had to remind herself that Ryske was alive.

Harlow didn't share that embarrassing truth. "Thought maybe Christmas had come early," she said, putting the pastry bag on the table.

Leaving the men in the living room, she went into Bale's bedroom. Anwen was asleep. Now developed, the bruising told a stark tale of what the woman endured. There were pain pills on the nightstand. For a moment, Harlow second-guessed leaving pills with a woman who'd overdosed, but quickly reminded herself that had been a con.

The swelling in Anwen's face was bad, though probably not as bad as it would've been if they hadn't got the ice packs on it. Bale was good. No. He was an excellent doctor. Still, Anwen would need considerable recovery time.

Bale's work day started early; Harlow felt bad that they'd disrupted his night. The guy had no chance at a normal life when this kind of drama kept landing on his doorstep.

To her surprise, Harlow slept well. That may have had something to do with the party atmosphere that accompanied the celebrations of her freedom. In Floyd's, patrons and employees alike were happy to see her. The place had been crowded. Even though it was impossible, it almost felt like they'd planned a party for her. Afterwards, Harlow had crashed and woken up to Dover making coffee. Nothing beat waking up to that scent.

Recalling what Bale had said about infection, Harlow checked Anwen's temperature. Everything looked good. Rest was important, so she left the sleeping patient alone to return to the living room.

Noon was searching around for something. "What did you lose?"

"Remote control."

The small TV was on a stand next to the bedroom door. "Don't put it on loud. Anwen needs to sleep."

Noon kept on hunting. Harlow went over to the now snoring Ryske. No need to worry about his breathing anymore. His crashing out was a strong indicator he'd been up most of the night.

Crouching down, she squeezed her hand into Ryske's back pocket to retrieve his money clip. He didn't wake, which was just fine with her. It wasn't like she wanted to explain robbing him.

While she stood over him, counting the bills, he breathed out hard. She froze. His eyes didn't open, so she was still in the clear and tucked the bills in the pocket of her dress.

Looking down at him, so loose and relaxed, regret cramped her gut. Last night, he'd come when she'd called. They were in a fight, broken up. Their relationship was in tatters after their last heated exchange. Yet, he'd come. Ryske hadn't asked questions or made her work for it. He'd just been there when she needed him.

Bale had known he would come. She hadn't considered having power over another person; she wasn't sure how to feel about it.

What she didn't want to do was abuse that power.

Crouching down, she unlaced Ryske's boots and pulled them off. He needed rest and deserved to be comfortable after doing the right thing by Anwen. Pushing up the hem of his tee-shirt, she popped the buttons of his fly.

Muttering, he opened his eyes. The moment his gaze kissed hers, his eyelids descended again.

"Shh," she whispered, opening her fingers to comb them through his hair, pushing it from his forehead.

Turning her hand, she let it float lower. By the time she brushed her thumb across his lips, his eyes were closed and his breathing even.

Catching sight of the remote behind a couch cushion, she fished it out and tossed it at Noon who just managed to snag it.

She started toward the front door. "If I were you, I'd get him a blanket from the closet in Bale's room. He'll wake up with a boner. You probably don't want that distracting you from the TV."

"Wait, where are you going?" Noon asked. "I thought we were going to hang out."

As she opened the front door, she glanced over her

shoulder. "I've been inside for months, Noon… I've got a list of places to be."

***

CLYDE HAD BEEN on call the previous night. Harlow didn't want to phone or go over in case he'd worked an emergency that may have kept him out late.

Her reunion with Felipe was emotional. Meeting his baby cousin, Tiffy, brightened the mood. The infant was beautiful. Although Camila looked frazzled, she beamed over her daughter.

After offering to babysit any time, she'd handed the baby back. Felipe was due at Floyd's anyway. Harlow walked him over there and put him to work cleaning up in the bar before slipping out again.

She went to see Charlie to reserve some time with him later in the week, and ended up buying jewelry from the new stock he had. After spending some of Ryske's money, she'd gone next door to see Costello and they went to lunch. Isla, his girlfriend, had dumped him. He needed a pick me up; she convinced him to meet her in Floyd's for a drink later. Before then, she'd have to find time to talk to Bale too. The doctor wouldn't finish work until later, crossing paths with him wasn't guaranteed.

Being back in the neighborhood felt like home. For the first time in weeks, in months, her shoulders were loose, tension eased.

Another reason to avoid heading across town to Clyde's? She'd be tempted toward Ophelia's. Before visiting her old friend, she needed to talk to Anwen.

Anwen might not feel like eating anything, but to get her strength back, she'd need sustenance. Ignorant to what their patient would like, she grabbed a selection of food from the lunch place. The guys would eat anything; someone would polish off the leftovers.

She didn't really think about what she'd find on returning to Bale's. Noon lounging in the living room watching TV, exactly where she'd left him, seemed about right.

"Where have you been?" he asked when she walked in.

"I brought food," she said, carrying the box to the kitchen counter.

Even though there was something of a grump on his face, Noon came over and investigated what she'd bought.

Bale didn't have a lot of furniture; he probably hadn't had time to decorate since moving in. The lack of possessions made the space feel really big. But it was nice. An excellent find on the doctor's part… in this neighborhood anyway.

Going into the kitchen to make coffee, she was surprised by how much she enjoyed doing normal things. Things that weren't a part of her life in jail.

"We should go tell Ryske there's food," Noon said, opening one of the boxes.

"If there's one thing you should've learned from my relationship with Ryske," she said, getting mugs from by the sink to rinse them out. "It's that he doesn't appreciate being interrupted when he's alone with a woman."

"Yeah, but…" Noon came around the counter to retrieve a fork. "He'd be doing stuff with you. He won't be doing stuff with her." Tossing him a quick glance over her shoulder, she bobbed her brows and then went back to washing the cups. "Wait, you don't think that they're… do you?"

"I think that even after he'd been stabbed, he loved to express how capable he was in bed," she said, drying her hands to put a filter in the coffee machine. They had a better machine at Floyd's and given all the doc did for them, they should really consider gifting him something similar. "If Anwen is interested, her injuries won't stop him."

"If Anwen is interested," he said, leaning back against the counter. "And if Ryske's interested… which he won't be."

"I'm not accusing him of anything," she sang out like a parent appeasing a teenager. "I don't make his decisions for him. He's a big boy."

Noon snorted. "Don't have to tell me. I've seen his dick swinging around the apartment probably more than you have."

She laughed. "He's not shy with it," she said, thinking of what she'd said to him about being naked in front of Ophelia.

In that moment, he could be in the bedroom with Anwen in any state of undress. Despite her roiling stomach, she had to do her best to ignore the aversion. Finding a way to co-exist without reacting to seeing him with other women was going to take a while. In the meantime, faking it would help hone her skills of deception.

No matter what, she couldn't show any crack or he would exploit it. Ryske had told her as much. Before jail, he'd promised to take advantage of any moment of weakness she had in her relationship with Rupert.

"Ever bother you?" Noon asked, sliding up to sit on the counter.

The coffee was percolating and the mugs were ready, so she went to join him, stealing a mushroom from his pasta as she did.

"That he waved his cock around all over the place? Not at home," she said, licking her fingers clean. "Was that another reason you didn't invite Frida back to the apartment?"

"Ryske's dick? Yeah," Noon said. "Figured if she saw him wandering around like that she'd think we were some sort of tag team. You know he'd never have left her alone in the shower."

Harlow laughed. "Yeah, well, I guess that's karma. None of you leave me alone in there."

The Floyd's shower screen was distorted glass. Partially distorted anyway; the distortion faded out as it ascended from the floor. The top quarter was clear, but with the steam of the spray, she never worried about anyone spying on her. Other women, who weren't so used to the system, might be uncomfortable with men wandering in and out of the bathroom like it was a common room even when it was in use.

"Yeah, but you'd hand any of the three of us our asses if we tried to hop in."

"Uh, three of you?" she asked. "All four of you are in

the same bracket now."

Noon's food box lowered, he didn't really believe her. "You think if Ryske got in the shower with you that you'd tell him to get lost?"

Showing him her pointed ring, she lowered it to his knee and dragged it up his thigh. "I think I'd love for him to try."

Noon dropped a hand onto hers, stopping its motion before the point got to anything too sensitive. "Uh huh, yeah, I get the point," he said. Laughing, she tapped the point on the end of her chin. "Jail made you a little nuts." When her smile dropped, he smirked. "Scratch that, you hooked up with Ryske... you've always been nuts."

He laughed. She feigned offense before joining in, prodding the point of her ring into his arm.

"What the hell's going on out here?"

Leaning to the side, she saw Ryske coming from the bedroom. "Oh," she called out, leaping sideways before he could close the bedroom door. "Tell Anwen there's food... If she's up to coming out, we can set her up on the couch."

Eventually, Harlow would want to talk to Anwen, preferably in private. But that would have to wait. For now, she wanted the woman to eat something and to try to get a feel for her state of mind.

Reversing back into the bedroom, Ryske didn't close the door, though the angle meant they couldn't see into the room anyway.

Taking the large food box over to the end table by the couch, she returned to the kitchen to pour coffee. Movement made her glance back to see Ryske carrying Anwen from the bedroom to sit her on the living room couch.

"Noon, go grab a pillow, man," Ryske said, helping Anwen get comfortable.

Jumping to action, Noon discarded his own food and dashed into the bedroom to get a pillow from the bed.

"Anwen, how do you take your coffee, honey?" Harlow called.

"Uh, just cream."

Once she'd prepared the coffees, Harlow carried

Anwen's to her. Propped on a couple of pillows with her back against the arm of the couch, her legs were stretched out over the middle. Ryske sat at the end next to her feet.

Giving Ryske his coffee, and Noon his too, Harlow went to retrieve her own. "Do you want this food?" she called to Noon while grabbing a couple of forks from the drawer.

"Nah," he said. "Finish it if you want."

"I've eaten," she said, sipping her coffee as she went to join them in the living room. "I had lunch with Costello."

Noon was in the armchair; the only chair in the room. He started to stand, but she caught his shoulder and pushed him down before he could get all the way up, then sank onto his lap. For a minute, he stayed rigid. To relax him, she kissed his cheek and ruffled his hair.

"We need to get the doc some new furniture," Ryske mumbled.

He probably didn't like her sitting on his friend, but Noon was her friend too. Being tactile with Ryske's friends was normal. He'd never had a problem with it before. The state of their relationship meant finding a new status quo.

For all Harlow knew, Anwen was going to be sticking around too. This was a new normal for all of them and it would take time to find their way.

TWENTY

TURNING HER SMILE to Anwen, Harlow made sure to bypass Ryske. "How are you feeling?"

"Sore," Anwen said, wincing as she shifted position.

"Do you need more pain pills?"

Anwen shook her head. "We just took some," she said, rubbing Ryske's thigh with her toe. "They'll kick in soon."

"That's good," Harlow said and nodded at the end table next to Ryske. "There's food there. I got a bunch. I didn't know what you'd like."

Ryske began opening food boxes to check what was in each one. He kept putting them aside until he had a couple on his lap; seemed he'd picked for himself and for Anwen without consulting her. Judgment about his presumption flitted through her mind, but she bit her tongue. It wasn't her place to criticize their relationship, so she just handed over the forks.

"Remember when I was laid up?" Ryske asked. "You made soup and cookies."

That was so long ago, it felt like a different lifetime. Back then, she'd been eager to do anything to help him recuperate... almost anything.

"Maybe I'll do that later in the week if you're still here," Harlow said. "I haven't been to the store and I don't have time to shop and cook today."

"Those were good cookies," Noon said.

"I've never had a culinary bone in my body," Anwen said. "I burn toast."

"What do you mean you don't have time?" Ryske asked, narrowing his focus to what she'd said. "Where are you going?"

"I have plans tonight," Harlow said and slurped her coffee before bowing to put it on the floor. Leaping off Noon's lap, she retrieved her suitcase from the corner. "Anwen, you can help me."

Distracting the woman from her pain would help. Whenever she distracted Ryske at Bale's it seemed to improve his mood. No reason it wouldn't work just as well with Anwen.

"Okay," Anwen said, shifting again.

Harlow put the suitcase down flat and unzipped it to root around inside. She pulled out three different dresses and stood up to show each to Anwen. "Which do you like best?"

"Middle," Anwen said and raised her arm, reaching for the garment, even though there was ten feet between them. "Let me feel the fabric." Going closer, she let Anwen touch the skirt. "You'll have VPL in this."

"That won't be a problem," Harlow said, returning to the case to toss the other two inside.

"Who's the lucky guy?" Anwen asked.

Draping the dress on her lap as she kneeled beside her suitcase, Harlow sought heels that might match. "It's not like that," she said, flashing her a smile. "It's complicated."

"Meaning it might be like that," Anwen said, obvious teasing in her voice.

"You're going on a date?" Ryske said. "Where?"

"What's VPL?" Noon asked.

"Means she's going smokeless," Ryske said, making no attempt to disguise his disapproval.

The heels that she wanted weren't in her suitcase. Harlow got up and went to the phone in the kitchen to dial.

"It's not a date," she said, raising the phone to her ear to listen to it ring. "I'm having a drink with a friend."

As it rang, she slipped her hand in her pocket. Ryske's money clip was in there. Still listening to the phone, she returned to the living room to toss it at him.

He held it up. "This was full this morning, Trink."

"It was not full."

The phone stopped ringing. "Yo?" Dover asked.

"Where are you right now?"

"Upstairs," he said. "Maze said Ophelia left a message for you on the answering service. Said you should get in touch."

Her eyes ascended and she shook her head. "Sure, I'll get right on that." In her own sweet time. "Listen, will you go into the closet for me and look under Ryske's clothes rack?"

She heard movement. "What am I looking for?"

Being at the mercy of Dover's interest wasn't promising. "A pair of nude stilettos."

"Oh, he's tall," Anwen said.

Harlow smiled.

"There are like twenty pairs of shoes in a mess down here."

Which betrayed Ryske hadn't kept them neat and ordered like she'd left them. She glared across the living room at him, but he was already glaring back.

"If they're not there, I have to go to the store," she said to Dover. Ryske held up the empty money clip as if to show they had no funds. She grinned and lowered the mouthpiece to talk to him. "Maze has plastic."

"How many pairs of shoes does one woman need?" Dover muttered.

She tried not to wince at the sound of shoes being tossed around and clattering to the floor. "Some of them are really expensive, Dover. Could you just… treat them nicely… please."

In sympathy, Anwen's expression matched hers.

"I don't know what the fuck I'm looking for, Nightingale," Dover said. "There are four that might be nude…"

"Skin tone, honey," she said. "Look for shoes that match my skin tone."

"Are you shitting me?" he grumbled and she laughed. "How the fuck do I know that?"

"I don't have long legs," she said. "Nude lengthens." Anwen nodded in agreement. Having another female around was nice. For once, someone else was able to feel Harlow's pain. "It's okay. Just take the ones that you think match down to the den… They're all heels, right?" Another grumble. "Ask Martina. She's coming to get Felipe in about an hour. If none of them are right, call Bale's." She twisted to look at the clock. "I can get Bale to stop somewhere for me on his way back from work. Do you think he knows my skin tone?"

"I have no fucking idea," Dover mumbled.

"Okay, thank you for that, honey," she said and blew him a kiss before hanging up. The phone stayed in her hand when she went over to give Ryske a kick. She sank back onto Noon's lap. "Will you be nicer to my shoes, please?"

"They're shoes," Ryske said. "They don't have feelings."

"I have feelings," she said, pointing the phone at her chest. "It hurts me when you hurt my shoes."

Anwen laughed. "I feel the same way about my purses."

"They just don't get it," Harlow said.

"They don't… So tell us about the guy, you're going to a lot of effort for him."

"It's nothing to do with him," Harlow said, reaching down to get her coffee from the floor. "I've been in jail for three months… I just want to live again, you know? I want to be me. Stilettos weren't exactly standard issue in jail."

"I can't imagine what it was like," Anwen said and shivered. "You must have been so scared."

"It's not that scary," she said, shaking her head. "Not after the first couple of nights. The first place I went to was worse than the second."

Anwen shivered again.

Harlow put her coffee aside and went into the bedroom to get a blanket. Opening it out, she laid it over

Anwen and Ryske's lap.

"You must be determined to never go back," Anwen said, smoothing the blanket.

"I don't know," Harlow said, sitting on the floor, facing the couch. Crossing her legs, she kept the phone on one side and her coffee on the other. "There's less mystery now. I wouldn't be as scared if I had to go in again. If they came for me, I'd know what to expect... When my lawyer showed up at my parents, before she told me the charges were being dropped, I thought that was it. That they were coming to take me back. I wasn't afraid... I was prepared for it... My sister was more upset than me."

"It's scarier for those around us, I guess," Anwen said, glancing at the guys. "This is crazy, isn't it?" The blanket moved like she prodded Ryske with her toe. "Did you ever think you'd be sitting in a room with both me and Harlow?"

Harlow laughed. "I think it's safe to say he didn't."

"What's the plan?" Noon asked, shifting to put his elbows to his knees. "I've got that thing on tonight... Will the doc be enough as backup, or do you want me to call Maze?"

Even though it was likely he was talking to Ryske, Harlow answered. "I think you should call Maze," she said. "Or I can ask Martina to work tonight and Dover can come over... I don't think anyone saw me coming here, but I don't want to take the risk Anwen could still be in danger... Especially since the man who hurt her is the same one who came for Ryske twice."

Noon was nodding. "That's a good point."

"I was going to shower and change here. But I can go home early and do it there. Whenever Maze gets back, I'll send him over."

"You're..." Anwen's voice wasn't as confident as it had been. "You're living with them?"

Harlow relaxed her weight onto her hands behind her. "I guess I'm without a fixed abode," she said. "I haven't really thought about where I'll be full-time... I told my sister I wouldn't go too far, so that means staying in the city... Which reminds me." Climbing off the floor with her coffee and the phone, she dialed as she rose. With the phone at her ear, she headed for the kitchen, but glanced back at Ryske. "You should pay the doc's phone bill this month."

"Why?" he asked. "I'm not using the phone… And someone bled me dry today."

"I had to pay Charlie," she said just as the line connected in her ear.

"Sweeting residence!" Lena chirped, her usual happy self.

A good sign, right?

"Hey, honey, you okay?" she asked, tipping the rest of her coffee into the sink.

"Oh my God, Harlow," she said. "Oh, thank God. You left here so fast. What happened?"

"It's a long, complicated story," Harlow said, hooking the phone against her shoulder so she could wash her cup. "How are you doing? Have you thought about what we talked about?"

Lena huffed out a long, tired exhale. "I haven't seen him. I haven't told him. I… I don't know, maybe I should get things checked out first… What if it's nothing? What if I'm wrong?"

"Have you seen a professional?"

Someone came up behind her, curving an arm around her to put another mug in the sink. Someone? Ryske. Standing way too close to her back. Harlow snatched the mug to wash it, hoping he'd take the hint to leave. He didn't.

With a finger, he hooked her hair away from her chest, taking it back over her free shoulder.

"No," Lena said. "I should… shouldn't I? What if there's a problem and I can't have it anyway… There would be no point in telling him then, would there?"

Trying not to sigh, Harlow licked her lips. "I guess not."

Ryske's fingertips worked on the back of her skirt, gathering it just slightly. With both hands occupied by the washing, she couldn't stop him.

When his lips moved to the back of her ear, she tensed. "I could fuck you right here," he whispered, kissing the shell of her ear. "And you couldn't do a damn thing about it."

Tilting her chin to her shoulder, she couldn't see him, but glared anyway. "Try it. You'll find out fast exactly what I'll do about it."

"Are you with someone?" Lena asked with a thread of panic.

"No, honey," Harlow said, using her butt to shove Ryske back. "A dog just walked in. A dirty, mangy animal. I'm ignoring it now."

Sliding out from between him and the sink, she grabbed a towel to dry her hands, taking extra time over drying her pointed ring, which only made him smirk.

"An… animal?"

Harlow had almost forgotten about her sister. "Be ready tomorrow morning," she said into the phone. "I'll come pick you up."

"But… if we go to the clinic, someone might—"

"Don't worry about that," Harlow said. "I know someone who can help. No one will know."

"No one? What if your friend tells someone?"

"He won't," Harlow said. "My friends are professionals at keeping secrets."

They hung up and Harlow put the phone back on its base.

Whether Ryske cornered her for a reason or not, she didn't hang around in the kitchen to find out.

Swerving around him, she went back to the living room. "Noon, I need a ride tomorrow," Harlow said. "Can you help me out?"

"Sure can," he said. "Where are we going?"

Taking Ryske's place, Harlow sat on the arm of the couch rather than on the couch itself, but she didn't leave any space for him to sit. "No, I mean… I need a car."

"I can do that too… Any make or model in particular?"

The question was genuine, he would steal to order. Still, it was funny. Really she'd meant borrowing his car.

Ryske came storming over, breaking up the light, happy mood. "If you need to go somewhere, Noon drives you."

"It's a personal errand," she said. "Not professional."

"Doesn't matter," Ryske said. "You need someone with you."

"I really don't," she said, peeking in the food box to see what was left.

The remaining boxes would be well received at Floyd's. Their patrons would make short work of hoovering up the leftovers. That would make more sense than leaving it to go to waste. Bale wouldn't be back for a while. He probably wouldn't want food that had been sitting for hours going soggy.

"You might," Anwen said. "I don't think Ophelia's feeling reasonable."

"I'm not afraid of Ophelia Hagan," Harlow said. "Or her minions… She and I will be having a pointed conversation soon… I'm happy to leave her to her anxiety until it suits me."

"You think she'll be anxious because you've been freed?" Noon asked.

"Might make her mad," Anwen said. "She could come for you if she thinks justice hasn't been done."

Running the edge of her ring down her jaw, she inhaled. "Oh, justice will be done," she purred.

"Trink."

She blinked up at his tone of warning. "What?" she asked. "What's between Ophelia and I is between us… You don't have to worry about it spilling over."

Ryske nodded at Anwen. "It's spilled over… All of it is part of the same thing."

"No, it isn't," she said. "None of this has anything to do with you…" Pushing up, she took a couple of steps toward him, blocking out the others. "I can't talk about this with you."

She tried to walk past him, but he grabbed her arm, forcing her to stop. "Why not?"

Looking to the side, she met his eye. "Because you don't want to hear what I have to say."

His expression tensed, trying to figure her out. "We've talked about this before," he said. "Nothing you could say will change what I feel for you."

"This is not about feelings, Ryske," she said, facing him. "You know that since I was arrested, I've been hiding things from you."

"Yeah," he said, his head moving in a nod. "Yeah, and I know you're busting my balls for doing the same."

"Hiding things is not the same as lying." Just as he was about to say something else, she raised a hand. "We don't want to do this in front of other people."

"Don't mind us," Noon said. "Some of us have heard worse coming from your corner of the apartment."

Noon's bed was right next to Ryske's, where they often enjoyed their oral sessions behind their curtain. Except Noon wasn't the one who concerned her. Anwen seemed like a reasonable person. Yet Ryske had attributed some horrible traits to her.

Curious, Harlow was almost tempted to drag Ryske into the bedroom to find out what she'd have to do to blackmail him into bed. Though given what he'd just said to her in the kitchen, she guessed it wouldn't be much.

With Anwen back in the picture—an unattached, free and single Anwen—it was likely they'd start up their relationship again. Even if Ryske was hesitant, Anwen had proved she'd find a way to get what she wanted.

Looking from Ryske to Anwen and back again, she tried to picture them together. Would they be affectionate and tender or would they be fractious and passionate?

"Do you guys argue a lot?" Harlow heard herself asking.

While Ryske folded his arms, Anwen laughed. "Not out loud," she said. "He just goes all quiet and grumpy when he's pissed off at me."

That wasn't the Ryske she knew. He had a habit of following her around and talking even when she was long done with a conversation. Ryske didn't pout. At least, *her* Ryske didn't. Tilting her head, Harlow looked at him with new eyes. This man was a chameleon who could be anything to anyone, at least for a while. Which one was the act? Were any of them real... did he even know?

"Quit looking at me like that."

Did he know what she was thinking? From personality and temperament, it wasn't a leap for sex to sneak into her thoughts. Ryske was an incredible lover, strong, passionate, intuitive; everything a woman wanted her man to be.

"Got any sex tapes?" Harlow asked.

Anwen laughed. "I was just thinking the same thing."

"Wow, man, they're talking about comparing technique," Noon said. "Hope you didn't have an off night."

Ryske wasn't embarrassed; the knucklehead didn't know how to be. With his eyes becoming heavier in their fixation on her, his lips widened to betray his swagger. "I'm about three questions away from a threesome, Noon. Let the women work."

"Ha," Harlow said, prodding his hip with her ring. "You wish." Turning to face Anwen, Harlow let her shoulder rest on his arm. "If I got that beauty in bed, what would I need you for?"

Noon's laugh was loud and sudden. Anwen's smile was more demure. Harlow didn't check Ryske for a reaction.

"I didn't think he'd be attracted to a sense of humor," Anwen said. "But you're funny."

"Thank you," Harlow said. "Do you need me to draw you a bath? The doctor told me last night you should be able to bathe today. A shower might be a little much."

Gratitude swept over Anwen. In her predicament, she probably wanted to wash, but might fear asking too much.

"I should wash," Anwen said. "I'd appreciate that… Ryske will you help me?"

Her cockiness may have backfired. No. Remember. No cracks. Impervious, that's what she had to be.

"I'll get towels for you both. The tub at home is bigger," she said. "But this one should fit two people."

Harlow only got one step before Ryske snatched her wrist. When he spoke, it wasn't to her. "I'll help you in the tub, Annie," Ryske said. "But I'm not getting in with you."

Anwen sighed. "Ryske has a bathtub phobia," she said, moving on the couch to change position so her feet were on the floor. "He'd never get in a tub, with a woman or on his own."

"That's true," Noon said. "Maze said it's 'cause your momma never bathed you as a baby."

"I'd be surprised if he even had a bathtub growing up," Anwen said, pushing back to change her angle.

It was all a joke and the mood didn't feel heavy, yet her arm moved until her fingers grazed his. What did Anwen know of his upbringing? Everything Ryske had revealed about his relationship with Anwen related to before her death. She had no idea how close they'd gotten, or what they'd shared, after it.

Ryske was Anwen's only link to who she'd been; that's what the beauty had said. Their trust had grown when they were in hiding together. Maybe his feelings had grown too. If he felt for her and trusted her, maybe he confided in her. Regardless, Harlow's instinct was to comfort him when he was reminded of his childhood.

"I don't have a bathtub phobia," Ryske grumbled and tried to lace his fingers through hers, but she withdrew her hand.

Harlow wanted to comfort him, not give him a way in.

Hmm, maybe it was kind of like shower sex.

Smirking, she peeked over her shoulder. "Maybe you just haven't done it with the right gal."

"Lead the way, Trink."

Choosing to take his comment as a joke, she laughed and slunk around him to head for the bathroom. "I'll put the water on, Anwen. I'll call the doctor to find out if there are any special instructions."

Going into the bathroom, she got the water going in the tub and found some candles under the sink. They were just basic white stick candles, maybe even left from before Bale moved in. Still, they were fit for purpose, so she took a few from the box.

The door creaked. Ryske was coming in.

"Do you have a lighter?" she asked.

Slipping his hand into his jeans pocket, he offered one to her. She smiled. "What?"

"It's so like a con man to be carrying a lighter," she said, carrying it and her candles to the tub.

Kneeling down, she lit one and let the wax drip onto the enamel in the corner. Once there was a circle of wax, she pressed the base of a candle on it, gluing it to the spot.

"It's a good way to start a conversation," he said. "Or it was in the old days."

Fewer people smoked now than probably did when he'd started his career.

"No more ladies perched at bars looking for debonair heroes to spark their flame?" she said, gluing another candle down.

"You're enjoying this."

Glancing up, she tried to figure out what he was talking about. "Enjoying what? Drawing a bath or playing with candle wax? Have you heard of wax play? That's a thing, right?"

"Where we get naked and pour hot wax on each other? Sure," he said. "You into that?"

Concentrating on her job, she watched more wax drip from the lit candle. "I don't know. I've never done it… You get actual candles designed for it… I saw some in a store once."

"Want me to pick some up?" he asked, sauntering closer.

"I don't know," she said, letting go of the last candle and standing up to toss his lighter back to him. "Ask Anwen if she's into it before you spend your money."

He stepped into her path, blocking the way to the door. "I haven't had sex with her."

She touched him with the point of her ring. Using the accessory to make contact meant she didn't have to actually connect with his body.

"We both know that's a lie."

"This week," he said, reaching for her face. She stepped backwards. "Since she came back… Fuck, Trink, I don't know why you didn't tell me she was—"

"We're not doing this," she said and tried to side step. "We're in the same crew, nothing else."

Holding up his hands, he seemed to acknowledge that, which was good given he'd been the one fighting that case the previous night.

"And that's why you have to tell me where you're going tonight." Oh, she wasn't buying that, not for a second. Crooking a brow, she leaned back, drumming her fingers on her hip. "Crew protect each other." Grabbing her hand, he pulled it up to display her stars. "Highs and lows, baby. You want to go out and get yourself laid? Do it. But if there's a chance the fucker will touch you without consent or hurt you... You need me and the guys around to keep you safe."

"I don't need anyone to keep me safe," she said, but had to pick her battles. Harlow couldn't tell him they were only friends and then react to his concerns with suspicion. "But you don't have to worry about me. I'm only going to the bar." That truth relaxed him, which made her think maybe he was just concerned for her safety rather than annoyed about the potential of her going on a date. Dipping closer, she grinned. "You know, the rule is no women in the apartment... What's the rule about me bringing guys back?"

"Don't push your luck, Trink," he said, hooking his arm around her neck and pulling her out of the bathroom.

Being Ryske's friend might not feel natural, but for now they were both playing the game. If he didn't let her make her own choices about their relationship and kept trying to force the issue, he'd only push her away.

Harlow didn't want this chapter of her life to close, not in this way, so she'd be patient with him. But if there came a time when she had to put her foot down, she wouldn't hesitate to tell it like it was.

TWENTY-ONE

AFTER A COUPLE of drinks, Harlow figured out that Costello wasn't going to talk to her at the bar. There were too many people around there. It was easy to get drawn into conversation with others. Everyone wanted to talk about her time in jail or to Costello about their workout.

Getting him away from the busy spot, Harlow took him to a table in the corner.

"What are we doing over here?" he asked when she pushed him into the corner and sat down beside him.

"We need privacy."

"Do we?"

Costello had made his gym his life. Not only was he good at what he did, he was a great advertisement for it too. His father was some martial arts guru, and had trained Costello from a young age. The tough guy wasn't all muscle without substance; he had a solid, decent personality.

In the last year, she'd learned a lot about making assumptions about people based on their appearance. Even the roughest, most sturdiest of guys could have a softer side.

"Yes," she said, getting close and slapping both hands to his thigh under the table. "You haven't mentioned Isla once." His demeanor shifted. "We arranged to meet so you could talk… what happened?"

"It's not a big deal," Costello said, using his drink as a prop to cover his discomfort. "She wanted something, you know?"

For all the difference between levels of affluence in the world, some things were the same in every walk of life. Especially when it came to relationships. In her experience, the female in a couple wasn't always the one who wanted to leap into commitment. When either person wanted to take that step and the other didn't, there was little that could be done in the way of compromise.

"A ring?"

He shrugged. "I don't know… She wanted us to live together but didn't want to live at the gym. I tried to fucking tell her that's where I live, you know? I don't want to move."

Nodding in understanding, she held his hand. "Why doesn't she want to stay at the gym?"

"I don't know," he said. "She never liked it there."

How could Isla love Costello yet not support what he loved? She could understand the woman being intimidated or wanting more space. The apartment above the gym where he lived was small. But to dislike the gym when it was Costello's life made her question the woman's commitment to the man.

"I don't know her well," Harlow said. "Where did you meet?"

"A nightclub," he said. "Downtown."

A nice club and a hot guy… Isla had hit the jackpot.

"How long were you together?"

"Six months maybe."

That was a reasonable amount of time for a relationship to move up a level. Living together was a good next step. Harlow had moved in with Rupert only after she agreed to his proposal. Sometimes she wished they'd lived together first.

They'd never made that leap. Rupert was always at her parents anyway, and he worked with her dad, so he was always around. They saw so much of each other that it often felt like they lived together anyway.

"What do *you* want, Cost?" she asked. "Do you want

to get her back?"

Smiling, maybe to put her off the scent, he leaned back and slid an arm around her. "I want a girl like you, Har," he said. "You're all grit, no fuss."

That was a laugh in itself. "I'm easy to love from afar," she said. "You think it's no fuss but I'd drift in and out of your life, making impossible demands, imposing my high expectations… then I'd go and get myself arrested for murder."

"Good point," he said on a laugh. "Though I'm not sure I agree about the impossible demands and high expectations. From what I've seen, it's obvious you push yourself harder than you push anyone else."

Looking at him could mean looking into the face of the truth. "I'm my own harshest critic," she said, and picked up her drink, wondering if she was using it as a prop like Costello.

"I'm serious, Har," he said, squeezing the back of her neck. "I've seen you at the gym with the other guys. You're always telling them to give themselves a break and then demanding five more minutes from yourself. It's always five more minutes. You don't give yourself a break."

"Flatter me, why don't you?" she said, but he wasn't kidding around.

He pulled her back and forth maybe in an attempt to loosen some of her growing tension. "There's a lot to flatter. I've never known anyone so willing to trust their own instincts and adapt. You don't have any problem learning something new or finding out something and letting it change your opinion or your path. You don't get stuck in your ways like so many of us. You make a decision one day and change it the next without blinking."

"So I'm fickle?" she asked. "How did this conversation become about me?"

"Not fickle," he said. "You're… accepting and tolerant. You can think a guy's a dick, but still give him a chance to change your mind."

Not in Ryske's case, though he'd changed her mind on so many things that she'd lost count. Costello was describing the way she'd always been. Hence why social work had been such a good fit. Judging people or situations and sticking to that judgment was the undoing of so many. In her opinion, people had to be willing to learn and change or they would never grow.

"If you're not worried about losing Isla, then I'm not worried about you losing her," she said, happy to lean on him when he pulled her to his side for a half hug. "But don't ever forget I'm here for you. I'm just around the corner."

"Yeah, this week," he said, pressing his mouth into her hair. "What you gonna get arrested for next week?"

Digging her elbow into his ribs, she followed it with a slap on the thigh, which only made him laugh harder. They sparred together all the time. It was a running joke that while she gave it her all to battle him, his heartrate barely moved above resting.

A shadow cast over them. Harlow looked up to find Ryske standing at the other side of the table.

"Up," Ryske said, but he wasn't talking to her.

Shit. Harlow knew that growl in his voice and it wasn't his one of passion. "Ryske—"

"You're Costello, right?" Ryske asked. "The gym guy?"

Costello had been to Floyd's before he'd met her, though it wasn't his regular haunt. He spent too much time on his business to be out drinking in bars on a regular basis.

"Yeah, man, I—"

"Get up. Let's go outside and see what you've got."

Ryske stepped aside like the proposition was reasonable. No way would she let him make something out of nothing.

Shoving out of her seat, Harlow leaped around the table. "Oh my God, you're not serious," she hissed, glancing around in hope that no one had noticed what was going on.

Everyone had. Even though they were being discreet, she could see other patrons peeking and turning to catch a glimpse of the potential scene. Most people would have assumed she was having a drink with a friend, because that was what she was doing. The introduction of Ryske, displaying this rigid, puffed up, proud stance, would alter those opinions.

It wasn't a secret that she wasn't with Ryske anymore; it hadn't been advertised either. They'd done this dance with each other since they'd first met. People probably didn't try to keep up with whether they were on or off. Not when one thing had been made clear by the Floyd's crew: she was Ryske's property.

If she wanted to change that opinion, she could. She never had because she was in no hurry to get herself entangled with another man, especially not when the last one kept proving so difficult.

"You think he's some master, Trink? It shouldn't take him two minutes to knock me flat," Ryske said, taking his attention from her to turn a threatening eye on Costello.

Grabbing his chin, she forced Ryske's head back around. "I'll knock you flat myself if you don't get your shit together," she said. "Costello is my friend. We're having a drink and enjoying a conversation. That's it. And you have no right—"

"A man doesn't come into another man's house and finger his property."

"No one is fingering me," she said, almost groaning at the choice of words. "I'm not your property. This is enough, Ryske. You can't be this way every time I'm talking to another guy."

Seizing her arm, the strength of Ryske's fingers bit into her. When he hauled her close, Costello leaped to his feet.

Sensing that Costello thought she was in danger, Harlow threw up a hand to halt him. "Don't," she said, glancing at her friend. "No one's going to fight in here tonight."

Angled away from the bar, she couldn't see Dover or the other guys. Even if they were around, if Ryske had told them to stay away, they would.

"You don't make the rules," Ryske growled, bowing closer to her ear. "I should take that fucker apart just for the way he looks at you."

Pulling hard, she yanked her arm away from him to retreat. "I'm done, Ryske. Done with this. You want to fight, knock yourself out, 'cause I'm through."

Turning on her heels, she marched across the width of the bar and out the corner door to the street. Harlow hadn't got half a block before he caught up and tried to pull her back, but she resisted and kept on walking.

"Where the fuck are you going?" Ryske demanded.

"Away from you!"

"Baby, that guy—"

"Is my friend," she screamed and stopped to spin on him. "I was consoling him. He had his heart broken and I was doing what friends do, trying to make him feel better."

He rocked back on his heels. "I know how the fuck he wanted you to do that."

She sneered. "Yeah, that's it. I said, 'You know what will make you feel better, Costello? A hand job under the table. Blow job in the restroom… Better yet, my ex-boyfriend's bed is right upstairs, let's do it!' Do you really think I would do that to you? To any of you?"

"I know what I saw!"

"No, you don't," she said. "This is Clyde all over again. You did the same thing with him. You assumed you saw something and made a huge deal about it! In every other area of your life, you can switch off and distance yourself, but with this… With me and other guys—"

"You want to hang with other guys? Hang with your crew. You know the rules, I won't let another man have you. I told you that from the start."

Frustrated, she growled and balled her fists, letting her head fall back. "I can't do this, Ryske! I tried to tell you today… I can't talk to you!"

"Why?" he asked. "Why do you think I act so crazy, huh? You don't think I know it's crazy? I do it because I love you!"

That was just the cherry on her sundae; she socked his chest. "But you don't give a shit about me," she said. "You don't give a shit! I have been trying to tell you to give me time, trying to tell you to give me space… You said that I was on this crew even if we weren't fucking. I want to be a part of your team. But that can't happen if you can't let it go and give me space to live my life! You're supposed to be at Bale's. You're supposed to be with Anwen. Instead of doing what you're supposed to be doing, what the crew need you to do, you're skulking around, spying on me, and challenging innocent men to duels!"

"I didn't—"

"If Costello and I wanted to fuck, don't you think we'd have done it during one of our sessions?" she asked, putting the last word in air quotes. "I could go over there any morning, and sandwich a workout between fuck sessions. We've never had sex. We've never kissed. He's my friend and he helped me out when you weren't around to do it; when none of you were around!"

"Trink—"

"Do you know what the worst part about this is?" she asked, trembling with the tension and adrenaline that threatened to turn into tears. "I fucking love you too." Letting him absorb that, she took a breath while he stepped away. "I'm acting like this, putting this space between us, because you hurt me! You fucking bastard! You hurt me… again!" A tear slipped from her eye. With an angry hand, she swiped it away. "I didn't tell you I didn't want to be with you because I didn't love you. I didn't do this to us because we weren't working or I wasn't happy. I do love you! We were working! And fuck you, Ryske, I was happy!"

After a beat, he came closer, raising his hand and softening his voice. "Then, baby, why—"

She swatted his hand away from her face and grabbed hold of her anger. "Because I will not be made a fool of, Huntley Ryske, I swear to God," she growled. "You think you can fuck around with me? That you can lie to me or tell me half a story and I'll let you walk all over me? No fucking way."

"That wasn't what happened," he said. "You're a fucking rock, baby. No one can take advantage of you. I learned that damn quick."

"If you want me…" she said. "If you want there to be any chance for us to ever be together again, you have to let me find my own way back to you. It'll be hard. Yeah, I know that. I've struggled with not having ownership of you too. I admit it… But you said that I was on this crew. You need to treat me the same way you treat Dover, and Maze, and Noon. Tease, play, flirt, fine. Show up when I need you; that works too." Setting her stance, she pointed to the concrete between them. "But do not cross that line, Ryske. I don't care how much you hate what you have to see, or what you have to hear. Whatever you're living through, I'm living through it too. Yes, we love each other, but I told you when we started this that you'd break my heart and you have, Ryske… more than once… You told me that reliability seduced me, that I wanted a man who'd be there for me every minute—"

"I also told you that you shouldn't want to tie yourself to me," he said. "That I was a crook."

Stepping back, she couldn't believe how naïve she'd been back then. "I told you that was one thing about you, and that it wasn't the most important thing."

"You said I cared about you."

Her smile was nostalgic. "And I was wrong."

Surprised, he became offended. "Wrong? I love you. I do fucking care—"

"Not about that," she said, folding her arms, and moving in closer, grazing a finger on his chest around where his tattoo would be. "I said you didn't lie to me. Back then, you told me that you could feed me lines to get into my panties. You said you wouldn't because you wouldn't mean what you said. Even when it was guaranteed that you'd get me on my back, you wouldn't make me promises that you couldn't keep. Something about it left a bad taste in your mouth. I believed you… But that was a line in itself… wasn't it?"

"Trinket, what happened with Anwen wasn't… I didn't want to set it up. She told me if I didn't kill him that she'd kill herself… Getting her out of the city, putting her in hiding, it was the best way to—"

"I know. She told me."

"The deal was, she went there, stayed there, and she'd only contact us in emergencies… When I made my stupid decision to leave you, she was already setup. It was just a bolt hole, a quick stop. I needed somewhere safe—"

"Crash," she murmured, touching his lips. "I don't want you to grovel. I know why you went there. I know that what you did for her gave you the idea to fake your own demise. I know you needed somewhere private and safe to recuperate. I get all that. I even understand how you could have sex with her while you were there. It's a comfort and you have a history."

"Baby, we didn't have sex," he said, his lips moving on her fingertips. "It's only been you since we met."

Taking a deep breath, she let her hand drop to her side. "We've been through a lot. Our lives have been intense since the start of us. You wouldn't make me promises you couldn't keep back then, and I'm not going to make you promises now."

"I promised I would never leave you again."

She remembered. The memory made her smile. "The only way you can keep that promise is to appreciate that we are not a we right now. We can have each other's backs because I trust you; I would go to war for you. You know the players. We're ensnared in a bunch of messes together. You have my loyalty."

"But not your heart."

Picking up his hand, she pressed it to her chest beneath her breast, almost smirking when her eyes rose to his. "This will never belong to anyone else," she murmured.

One side of his mouth lifted. Those were the words he'd said to her. Though she meant them, there was an edge of mocking in her tone too.

Bowing down, his smile grew wider. "I still plan to do everything in my power to protect you."

"Good," she said. "So long as that doesn't involve beating up men who buy me drinks. Shit, Ryske, the guy had his heart stomped and then you come along and try to kick his ass… He'd have owned you by the way."

"Yeah, right," he said. "I've got to check out this guy in action."

She patted his chest. "You can do that when you go and apologize to him in person, which you're going to do tomorrow." He groaned. "Now, can you go back to Bale's and do what you were supposed to be doing? I want to go home and take a bath."

Harlow took notions for soaking in the tub every once in a while. During her period of house arrest, when the ankle monitor was a part of her life, she hadn't been allowed to submerge herself. Knowing it was against the rules just made her want to do it more. Life hadn't slowed down long enough for her to do it yet.

His brow arched. "Need company?" Hitting his chest, she raised her finger in warning too. "What?" Opening his arms, he was all innocence. "You said I could flirt with you."

Backing up the way they'd come, she shoved him in the other direction. "Yeah, and flirting is the limit. Go do what you're supposed to be doing."

Walking backwards, he put more space between them, tapping his temple. "Thinking of you in the tub," he said and winked. "Got it."

Flirting could be dangerous, but it was part of Ryske's nature. As long as they kept a lid on it, she was sure they'd be fine. Raising her hands, she swept them toward him to show she was done with him and turned around to head back toward Floyd's.

Costello would be gone, if not by his own choice, then one of the guys would probably have suggested he split. She would apologize when she next saw him.

A soak in the tub and an early night sounded like a dream. The next day would start first thing; she'd have to get Lena. Harlow had spoken to Bale about bringing her sister to the hospital to get checked out and he'd been happy to help. Of all the things he'd been asked to do, a pregnancy test and an ultrasound were sort of low on the scale of hindrances.

After she'd dealt with her sister, she'd have to figure out how to go about dealing with Ophelia. Not that confronting the murderess worried her.

The possibilities before her were endless. Harlow had learned what a blessing it was to have that kind of freedom. Things couldn't stay as they were. Something had to give. Whatever it was, Harlow felt strong enough to deal with it.

She had confidence that whichever way things went, she'd be the one steering the car.

TWENTY-TWO

LYING ON THE COUCH in the Floyd's apartment the next evening, Harlow was turning the copy of her sister's ultrasound picture around trying to work out which end was which. She didn't hear anyone coming until someone's stubbly chin bumped her forehead.

"He looks just like me," Ryske said.

He kissed her hairline and then walked toward the back of the room.

Crunching up, she hung over the back of the couch to watch him approach the gym in the corner. "Really? When did you fuck my sister?"

He sat on the end of the weight bench to unlace his boots. "Lena's pregnant? Who's the lucky guy?"

Her groan was one of disgust. "It won't work in your favor for me to talk about that," she said, pushing up off the couch.

Ryske stood to take off his hoodie. He tossed it aside and unbuttoned his jeans, which quickly joined the first garment.

From the unit by the closet door, he grabbed a pair of sweatpants. "Because I'm male?"

"Yes," she said, reaching him at the same time he tied

his pants and put his feet into sneakers.

Harlow flicked his arm, startling him.

"What was that for?" he asked, rubbing the spot she'd assaulted.

"You men really suck, you know?"

Smirking, he leaned down to whisper, "Well, not right now, babydoll, I'm about to work out. But if you want to wait 'til my shower after…"

"I'm never getting in a shower with you again," she said, twirling away to head into the kitchen where she put the scan picture on the fridge.

All she had to hold it in place was a beer magnet, but it would do. Smiling, she touched the corner of the picture. That was her niece or nephew. Planned or not, that kid was going to be a big part of her life.

Grabbing a bottle of fruit juice from the fridge, she was turning it upside down and right way up, shaking it as she wandered back to the gym.

Ryske was done with his warmup and standing on the mat doing an exercise with the dumbbells. She propped a shoulder on the unit containing the gym clothes and opened her juice bottle.

"Can I ask you a question that has nothing to do with us?"

"Ask anything you like," he said, blowing out a breath. "But if I'm not getting oral, I reserve the right not to answer it."

"I said you could flirt with me. I didn't say you had to do it every minute," she said, twisting to let the unit catch her weight on her shoulder blades. "I'll ask one of the guys."

"I'm teasing, babe. Ask me," he said, carrying on his reps.

Finishing her mouthful of juice, she rolled her upper body again so her arm was between her and the drawers.

"Is it possible for a grifter to be a good father?" His frown implied he'd forgotten the question wasn't about them. "I'm not pregnant."

He seemed to relax. "You mean you don't think you are."

She shifted to lean on her shoulder blades again. "No, I really know I'm not. Doing a test was Bale's price for checking Lena out." Harlow twisted the bottle around in her hands. "You know he would've done it anyway, but he put me on the spot."

Ryske sat to do concentration curls. "Your sister didn't think it was weird that the doctor wanted you to do a pregnancy test?"

"They think I'm sleeping with him," she said, enjoying another drink.

"They?" he asked, raising his brows. "Who's they?"

"My family. Rupert met him when he stayed over at my parents."

In a strained effort at restraint, his neck vein popped. "Who stayed over? Bale or Marlowe?"

"Bale," she said.

He stopped pumping. "He stayed over?"

She held up two fingers. "Two nights."

"In your bed?" As soon as the question was out, he immediately started to work again. "Forget it, don't tell me. I don't want to know."

Smiling, she appreciated his attempt at adjusting to their new rhythm. Harlow brushed that tangent aside and returned to the point. "I suppose Rupert must have said something about meeting Bale. Lena guessed we were going to see the hot doctor who'd been traipsing around our house in a towel."

Ryske paused again like maybe he wanted to ask why Bale had been in a towel. But he shook his head and went back to his workout, lying down on the bench to do something else with the dumbbells.

"Rupert said Bale was hot?"

"I think that word got added," she said, without specifying which of the Sweeting sisters was responsible for the addition.

Going over to lie on the mat next to the bench, Harlow started to go through one of her Pilates warm ups.

She'd worked out with Costello that morning, so didn't need to exercise again. But it seemed silly to stand there doing nothing when the mat was calling to her. After apologizing to Costello and learning that Ryske had already done the same, she'd stayed to work up a sweat, and to ensure there were no lingering issues.

For a few minutes, she and Ryske each focused on their own tasks. At least that's what she thought they were doing until she cracked open an eye and saw Ryske on his side on the weight bench, his head propped on his fist.

"I love when you do that pelvic thing," he said, a salacious smile on his face.

God only knew how long the idiot had been lying there perving on her. She grabbed a towel from the floor to toss it at his face.

On a laugh, he dropped it and got up to head over to the treadmill. "Do you think I'd be a good father?" Ryske asked, pressing buttons to begin his jog.

She gave up on her routine and rolled onto her side, scooping a hand under her hair to support her head. "That's different."

"It's not different. It's the answer to your question," he said. "You told your family if you'd been pregnant when you went to jail that you'd leave your kid with the father: me."

She hadn't identified the father to her family, but both she and Ryske knew who she meant. "Yeah."

"You wouldn't do that if you didn't think I'd make a good father. Ipso facto…"

"Grifters can be good fathers," she said, finishing his thought. "But there is one major difference you can't deny."

He pressed a button to increase his speed. "What's that?"

"You would be present. If you had the kid full time or we were pregnant now, we know each other. We have a relationship. We could make exchanges and communicate because we're not strangers."

"Lena got knocked up by a stranger?"

"She got knocked up by Vane."

Slapping his hands to the rails on the treadmill, he jumped to drop his feet onto the static sides of the running conveyor. "No!"

What a scandal!

Sitting up, Harlow crossed her legs. "Lena hasn't confirmed it. She wouldn't tell me who it was. But from what she said, that's what I think… I didn't tell Bale, so don't say anything."

It took about half a minute for him to process the news.

Delight and mischief lit his grin. "Sweeting women have a type."

That she'd said the same thing only made her groan. "Vane's with Edgar Charnock's granddaughter."

"Not that much with her if he got Lena pregnant," he said and winced. "That's careless. Amateur hour, to be honest. A disappointment to the profession." He leaped back onto the treadmill to start running again. "An affair while you're running a con is risky enough, but with your mark's friend… and to get her pregnant…"

On a loose nod, she rolled her eyes. "Yeah, yeah, I get it," she said, sighing. "He's a novice and you're the guru."

"Don't mock. I never got a girl pregnant."

Harlow pointed at him. "That you know of. You can't be sure of that."

"I can be sure I used rubbers with every woman I had sex with."

Her mouth opened with a disbelieving squeak. "Oh my God, you can't help yourself. That is such a flat lie."

He flashed her a frown. "Are you shitting me? How would you know? I used rubbers with Anwen every single time. If she told you different, she's the liar. She's the only woman you know who I've slept with—"

"Another lie."

"Trinket—"

"You had sex with me," she said. "Did you forget that already? We were unprotected the first time we had sex. You didn't know if I was on the pill. You didn't even ask."

"Now *that's* different."

She dropped her weight to her hands behind her. "How, pray tell, is that any different? You said you used condoms with every woman you had sex with. Did you forget to add the caveat that you didn't use them every time you had sex with every woman?" His smirk made her suspicious. "What?"

"You're doing that prim thing again when you use fancy words."

"I'm telling you off for lying to me... and you just used Latin."

With his eyes ahead and his smirk in place, he side nodded. "Little trick I sometimes pull out that makes me sound smart and rich... I get that you're telling me off, mistress, but you're missing the point. I came back from the dead for you. I don't lump you in with every other woman I got naked with. You're the love of my life."

Sitting slowly, she didn't think he understood what a huge thing that was to say because he kept on running, pressing the button to speed up for a sprint again.

A couple of minutes later, he slowed it down as the sound of a rabble in the kitchen drifted their way. The other guys were coming up the spiral stairs into the kitchen, conversing about that night. At least they were until Maze spotted something, which she only knew from the way he cut Noon off mid-sentence.

"Whoa, hold on, shut up," Maze said to Noon. "What the hell is that?"

"Where's Nightingale?" Dover demanded.

The three came around the end of the fridge in a troop.

"What's going on?" Ryske muttered, decreasing his speed until he came to a stop.

"I put the scan picture on the fridge to freak them out," she said from the corner of her mouth and grinned when Maze held it up.

"What the hell is this?"

"Looks like me, don't you think?" Ryske asked, never one to miss a prank.

"You're pregnant?" Dover said and drove a hand through his hair. "Where the hell are we going to setup a crib?"

Maze sighed and shook his head. "We'll clear space

in the closet," he said. "Make room for a bed and a crib. She'll need privacy to nurse." He turned to her. "Are you going to feed yourself?"

"It's best, right?" Noon said. "We want what's best for him… He'll need space to play…" He inhaled an excited gasp. "We should get him a racetrack!"

"You've got to build up to that shit, idiot," Maze said. "All newborns do is cry and crap their pants."

"We'll move the gym stuff to the basement," Dover said. "It's too dangerous to have around kids anyway."

Harlow was so dumbfounded that she didn't hear Ryske approaching. Before she snapped out of her daze, he bent down to haul her onto her feet.

"Backfired on you, didn't it, Trink?"

"I… I…"

"She's not pregnant, guys," Ryske said. "False alarm."

Maze frowned at the scan picture, probably wondering how it could be false when there was a baby right there.

When Ryske rubbed her back, she stepped away from his teasing comfort. "My God, my child would have four fathers, wouldn't he?"

Like it was inevitable, Ryske nodded. "Long as he or she follows the crew hierarchy, they'll be fine… They'll be the most protected and capable kid in the schoolyard."

That was true. Her child would have Ryske teaching him the chat, Maze showing him how to hack, and Noon teaching him to drive while he was still in diapers. Dover would educate him on how to cut an ID, how to appraise the loot and launder the proceeds… and how to make an honest living too.

It wouldn't be a typical upbringing by a long shot, but as she thought more about it, she realized that it wouldn't be so bad.

"What's the youngest you can get a tattoo?" Noon asked, looking at his stars.

"You're not taking a needle anywhere near my child until they're at least sixteen," Ryske said.

"You're the only parent in the world setting a date for

the tattoo before the kid is even born," Maze said. "And who knows? They might want to be like their Uncle Bale."

Bale didn't wear the same tattoo they did; he was more an honorary member of the crew than a fully-fledged one, by choice.

"That's true," she said, and looked at Ryske. "We should let him or her decide what they want to do with their life before we mark them permanently." His brows went up, and he was damming a laugh behind his infuriating lips. Shit, she deserved it, her words implied… "I'm not pregnant."

"No, you're not," Ryske said, sliding an arm around her shoulders. "But any time you want to change that…"

Picking his curling fingers off her arm, she slapped his hand away. "I'm going to get changed," she said, ignoring his amusement. "Dover, I'll help out downstairs tonight."

"Whatever you want, Nightingale."

Dover didn't let much phase him but she felt out of whack. Rushing into the closet, she dampened her agitation. Just like that the guys accepted the prospect of her having a child.

More than that, they'd discussed ways of accommodating her and her offspring. Their shock had only been momentary. While they didn't ask if it was Ryske's, they probably assumed he'd be the father. Even if he wasn't, they hadn't cared or judged. The guys wanted her there, wanted to support her.

They were her crew. All the way. Baggage and all.

TWENTY-THREE

OVER THE NEXT few days, Harlow got a chance to re-learn how to be a free citizen. The adjustment wasn't as easy as she'd thought it would be. That was after spending only three months locked up. How people returned to society unscathed after years in prison mystified her.

A week had gone by since Anwen's desperate call to the Sweeting house.

Bale was doing an excellent job taking care of the patient. Ryske stayed at his brother's place every night. For security sake, there was usually at least one other guy with them. As yet, no one nefarious had shown up at Bale's. Though that didn't mean the threat was over.

The breathing space gave both her and Anwen time to reorient themselves. But the unfinished business was still looming. The time had come to get to work. Hence why Harlow was walking into Bale's apartment.

Bale was in the kitchen, stirring coffee. "Hey," he said, turning to her. "Are you staying here tonight?"

"Not exactly," she said, removing her jacket to hang it by the door.

Going to him, they shared a mutual cheek kiss.

She started for the bedroom. "Anwen in here?"

"Yeah, but—"

Without waiting to hear what Bale had to say, she entered the bedroom. Ryske and Anwen were lying in the bed, facing each other. When she walked in, the couple checked who'd intruded. Ryske's hand dropped from Anwen's temple.

"Sorry to interrupt," she said, slipping off her shoes and kicking them out into the living room. "Can I have a minute, Crash?"

"Sure," he said, rolling off the side of the bed to walk toward her.

The swagger in his step suggested an assumption she wanted to talk to him. Unfortunately for him, he was wrong.

Stepping aside, she let him pass to go into the living room. "Great, thanks," she said, slamming the door and flipping around to look at Anwen.

Seeming a little unnerved, Anwen pushed down to sit up, propping herself on the pillows. "You want to talk about Ryske?"

"No," Harlow said, going around to climb onto the bed. Sitting in the center, she crossed her legs and linked her fingers. "I want you to talk to me about Ophelia."

"O… Ophelia?"

"Yes," Harlow said. "What happened when you got into town? After you left the Meadowbank and came back to the city?"

"I… I went to the motel," Anwen said. "I knew I had to reach out and I… I wanted to go to Ryske, but he didn't pick up on the number I had for him. I left a message, but I couldn't wait. I was edgy, you know? I knew where Ophelia lived, I could take action, so I…"

"You went to see her?"

The nervous shift of Anwen's mouth didn't compensate for the practiced innocence she tried to convey through her eyes. The simpering contrition didn't really work on Harlow; she didn't have the patience for that sort of thing. Anwen nodded.

Harlow inhaled. "What happened?"

"She was… surprised… I don't know… I thought she was happy to see me, but then she started to get kind of paranoid. I don't know."

Having experienced what it was like to have someone come back to life, Harlow understood the shock of it. The maelstrom of emotions would've hit all at once. Ophelia had had two people come back to life on her now, but that was nothing compared to the fact that she'd murdered her own brother.

Ophelia hadn't confirmed her brother's death; Harlow had been the one to check for a pulse. It was possible that Ophelia was concerned her brother could come back and surprise her too. Facing a resurrected person was shocking, but facing your victim would be a different level of surprise.

"She didn't hurt you at that first meeting?" Harlow asked. Anwen shook her head. "When did you next hear from her?"

"When she called to say she was coming over to my motel the night I called you," Anwen said. "I didn't even tell her where I was staying. I don't know how she figured it out. Maybe Ryske told her. While I was in her apartment that first time, she left a message for Ryske. He didn't call back while I was with her, but he could've called her after."

"He was the only one you gave your location to?"

She nodded. "On the message I left for him… And he did visit me."

The less said about that, the better. Ryske wasn't the one on trial and Harlow didn't doubt his integrity. Not on the subject of a woman's safety. He wouldn't have endangered Anwen by revealing her location to Ophelia.

"How did you leave things with Ophelia?" Harlow asked.

"I left her apartment with the promise we'd meet up later in the week… In her apartment, I don't know, it was weird, like she wasn't all there… Like… her mind was somewhere else."

Harlow had thought Ophelia was together until the night she'd watched her put a bullet in her own brother. So many things had changed that night.

"Did she seem to trust you? Did she talk to you as a friend?"

"Yeah, she… she told me about Jarvis, about how he'd been murdered. She inherited the company and his assets… She's planning to sell almost everything; she's taking it apart piece by piece. It almost seemed like she was happy to be dismantling his life."

It was sad that someone could be so happy about destroying the life's work of another. But having been in the unique position of seeing Ophelia literally destroy the man when she took his life, Harlow wasn't surprised.

Picking out something Anwen had said, Harlow leaned in. "Almost everything? What isn't she selling?"

"There's a… club, something downtown. It's a hotel and gentleman's club type place, I think. I don't know why Jarvis had it. It didn't fit with anything else in his portfolio… He didn't have it when we were together… If Ophelia sells everything, she'll have millions. I don't know why she'd want to keep that one building."

Harlow knew. She was thinking about Windsor's and Pothos when the bedroom door opened. Ryske appeared, but she threw up a hand to show him a finger before he could speak.

"I need one more minute," she said.

The way his eyes moved between them betrayed his confusion. But he didn't ask questions. He backed out of the room and closed the door, leaving them alone again.

"I can't get through to him," Anwen said.

Harlow was still thinking about the consortium. It took her a second to readjust.

"To Ryske? What do you mean?"

"I can't stay here forever," Anwen said. "But I don't have family. I need to face Ophelia—"

"I'm going to take care of that," Harlow said, picking up her hand. "You don't have to handle anything… not while you're recovering."

"That could take another month," Anwen said. "And, like I said, I can't stay here. I'm not working, I don't have any money—"

"Ryske will give you money. He'll get some from somewhere."

Or one of the guys would. Noon could find them a car to sell or Maze could do some of his freelance work. There was always a way to pull in a few bucks if they needed it. They managed to cover daily expenses with the income from Floyd's. Part of the reason they crowded into the apartment was to keep costs down. Dover owned the building, so they didn't have to worry about rent.

"I thought maybe I could... stay with you for a while."

"With me?" Harlow asked, recalling what she'd told Anwen. "I'm of no fixed abode."

"You sleep somewhere, right?"

Yeah, in Ryske's bed because he'd been sleeping at Bale's. Harlow had already checked that the couch in the living room pulled out into a bed. The one in the den did too, but that room was far more public, and wouldn't make much of a bedroom. Felipe hung out there most evenings because Tiffy irritated him at home. His aunt and mother tended to bicker a lot too. Sometimes the kid needed a break.

Given that she'd also found Tom, Dick, and Larry in the den more than once, hanging out or watching sports, Harlow wasn't sure she'd like to sleep down there.

"Yeah," she said, "in Ryske's bed because he's not in it."

Stroking Harlow's full-finger ring, Anwen appeared to be admiring it. "How did you talk him into letting you do that?"

She shrugged. "I didn't ask him, I just did it."

Ryske wasn't in his bed, it made sense to use it. She'd have done the same thing with any of the guy's beds if they hadn't been in them and she needed a place to sleep.

"He won't even tell me where he sleeps."

Anwen peeked up. If she thought Harlow was going to give out Ryske's address, she was mistaken. The trouble was, it wouldn't take a lot for Anwen to find it.

Back in the day when they were having their affair, she might have had more difficulty. But in this neighborhood, Anwen could stop just about anyone and ask. Once she recited their names and convinced said person she wasn't going to do damage, she'd be told where to find Floyd's.

Clearing her throat, Harlow tried to get the conversation on course. "How do you—"

"Would you talk to him for me?" Anwen asked. "I think if you tell him it won't upset you, that he'll be okay with it."

The situation was beyond awkward. Harlow wasn't in a place with Ryske that she could tell him to do anything. Beyond that, she wasn't sure how she felt about facilitating the pair's potential relationship.

"You asked him if you could stay at his place?" she asked. Anwen nodded. "If he said no, there's nothing I can do."

"You live there too."

Harlow winced. "Yeah, but that wasn't exactly by choice. The night he took me there, I was in danger... Well, he thought I could be and I was being used against him, so he felt responsible."

"I could be in danger," Anwen said. "The night, in the motel... Ophelia did this because of him."

That was interesting and drew Harlow closer. "She had you beaten because of Ryske?"

"Her whole attitude when she came to the motel... she was crazed. She asked a million questions about Ryske and about our relationship... Mad doesn't even... She said I was the reason she'd never had a chance with him. I... I think she thought that after I was dead, they might get together. Finding out that I'd never really been dead..."

"She never had the chance she thought she did," Harlow said. "You were the obstacle."

Rubbing a hand over her mouth, she tried to imagine Ophelia's state of mind. With her in jail and Anwen apparently dead, Ophelia must have believed her chances with Ryske were as good as they'd ever been. Especially with Pothos on the horizon, linking them together.

Then, both she and Anwen sprang back into the picture, ruining Ophelia's opportunity to seduce the man she loved.

Anwen pointed at the bottom edge of Harlow's zip

up corset top that sat just on her hip. "What's that?" she asked. "Did you hurt yourself?"

"What?" The white of the long dressing on her ribs peeked out. "Oh, no… It's a tattoo I got done this week… I figured it was better to cover it under leather like this."

"You got a new tattoo?" Anwen asked, perking up. "Can I see it?"

"I'm not wearing a bra, but sure," Harlow said, lying down and unzipping her top.

Letting the leather open, she put one arm across her bare chest and peeled back the dressing to reveal the tribal rib tattoo beneath. Wider where it scooped under her breast, the hourglass shape descended on her ribs and stopped in a curve on the angle of her hip.

"Oh my God, it's amazing," Anwen said, leaning over to inspect the delicate curves and points. "They look like thorns."

Anwen's exuberance was funny. The bedroom door opened again. Anwen twisted to look over her shoulder while Harlow slipped one hand behind her head.

Ryske's mouth closed when he took in the view. "Okay," he said after a few seconds. "This is not what I expected to walk in on."

"Come look at this," Anwen said, gesturing him over.

Walking around to Harlow's side of the bed, he didn't seem to be that interested until he spotted what Anwen was stroking.

"You got it fucking done," he said, picking up the pace.

Harlow didn't think anything of him dropping down onto the bed behind her. Not until his fingertips landed low on her hip and began to slide up toward her tattoo. She twisted further in an attempt at eye contact, but he was as intent on her tattoo as Anwen.

With one forearm behind her head and the other covering her breasts, she was more like an art exhibit than a human being.

"It's beautiful, isn't it?" Anwen said to Ryske, but glanced up at her. "I never had the guts to get a tattoo."

"Harlow's impervious to pain," Ryske said. "Didn't blink when she got her stars done."

Anwen faltered. "I noticed that... That hers are like yours."

"Same artist and everything," Ryske said, mesmerized by the lines his fingertip was learning. "I told her not to get this fucking done."

"Yeah, and gave me no reason not to," Harlow said.

"This is why," he said, tracing his finger along the lines that curved under her breast. A ticklish shiver of pleasure shimmered through her. Ryske noticed her flinch but didn't retreat. "Look how close this guy got to my girls."

"Don't belong to you," Harlow said in a sing-song voice, managing to bump her elbow on his head.

He flashed her a smile. "Were you wearing a bra today?"

"Noon keeps moving my bras," she said and Ryske snickered. "Your friend is a little creepy... I mean I love him, but he's a creep... I don't think I own panties anymore."

Interest raised his brows. "Really?" he said. His hand moved from her ribs to her thigh. When it began to ascend, she clamped her thighs tight together to prevent it from disappearing under her skirt. "Just testing your honesty, Trink."

"It's not my honesty that was ever in question," she said. "And don't pretend panties ever slowed you down... You should use some of those skills to educate your friend on how to respect women's underwear... What does he even do with them?"

"I'll talk to him," Ryske said, going back to learning her new ink. "Good misdirect on my question though."

"I wasn't wearing a bra today, no. But I didn't get this done today, so your question is irrelevant."

Ryske hadn't closed the bedroom door all the way. It swung open and Bale came in with Maze and Noon just behind him. Bale stopped first, forcing Maze and Noon to come up short against his back.

All three took a second to absorb what they were looking at, much like Ryske had done when he came in.

"A week," Maze said then turned to Noon. "Who had a week in the pool?"

"You," Noon said.

Maze grinned. "Cool. You owe me a thousand bucks."

"Four hundred," Noon said. "It's in the freezer at home."

"A week for what?" Anwen asked, sitting up against the headboard.

"Until he got both of you in bed," Bale said, letting the other men filter into the room.

"We're in bed," Harlow said. "We're not having sex."

"It's going that way," Maze said. "Or it was."

"Before you bastards interrupted," Ryske said. "Payback's going to be a bitch for you pricks."

Ryske's hand spread on her waist, slithering around to flatten on her abdomen so he could pull her body back against his, which was when she learned just how much he liked her new tattoo.

Harlow's eyes dropped. "I don't know what you think you're going to do with that."

"I have a few ideas," he murmured, his mouth moving in her hair.

"And that's all they're going to be tonight, Crash," she said. Taking her hand from behind her head, she got a handful of his hair to pull him back. "Get up."

Grumbling in disappointment, Ryske flipped out of the bed, which gave her the room to roll into a seated position on the edge. Retrieving her top, Harlow kept her back to the room so no one could see her body when she took her arm off her breasts.

No one except Ryske, who wasn't a gentleman. Standing in front of her, he slid his hands into his pockets and scrutinized her with blatant admiration as she pressed the dressing back into place.

Wrapping her corset around her back, she caught the bottom of the zipper and glanced at him as she pulled it up. "You don't have to watch."

"Oh, I do, babydoll," he said and stepped closer to

stroke her hair. He kept on stroking and turned his attention to his boys. "Aside from ruining my good time, why are you guys here?"

"We came to get you," Maze said. "Noon and I were on our way back from… something."

Were they being discreet because Anwen was present? Was the woman conscious of their caution?

Because she didn't want to have her face so close to the lump in Ryske's jeans, she stood up, turning her back to him as she rose. Except he gave her such little room that she almost fell forward onto the bed. Probably sensing her wobble, he put an arm around her waist to steady her; an arm she chose to ignore because it was doing its best to pull her back against his hard body.

"You guys all have some place to be tonight," she said. The Floyd's casino would be open. Friday nights were all hands on deck. "All except the doc."

"I have to be at work in the morning," Bale said, glancing at Anwen. "I'll be leaving early."

"I can stay here tonight," Harlow said. "I have something to do first, but I'll come back after."

Bale nodded; the others weren't as understanding.

"What do you have to do?" Maze asked.

"Something," she said, squeezing out from between Ryske and the bed. As soon as she was free, she turned to face him. "There's a comforter on the bed at home, Crash. If you don't want it, put it in the closet. Fold it. Don't just dump it on the couch."

He offered a mocking salute. "Were you getting cold without me, baby?"

When he tried to slide his hands onto her waist, she pushed them away and started to back off. "I used it to muffle out the noise of Noon's snoring," she said. The Floyd's guys laughed, all except Noon anyway. "Make the bed in the morning, Ryske, please… Just try it, just once. I put clean sheets on the mattress yesterday."

Maintaining her slow backwards steps, she used the bullshit about the bed as a way to prevent further questions. Just as she was about to make her getaway Anwen spoke.

"Harlow," she said. "Make sure you aren't followed."

The advice was genuine.

Harlow smiled and winked. "This isn't my first rodeo."

Curling a hand around the back of Bale's neck, she pulled him down for a kiss. She gave Noon one too, pressing for just a fraction longer than she had with the doctor.

Grabbing her shoes and running out of the apartment, Harlow put as much space between herself and the guys as she could before anyone probed further. Ryske hated her going anywhere without backup. If he knew where she was going, he'd want to come after her. The guys would too. But, as she'd told Anwen, she was no rookie. Visiting Ophelia on a Friday was a deliberate choice; the guys were needed at the Floyd's basement casino on a Friday.

Anwen may or may not tell the guys about their conversation. Ryske may or may not come after her. Reducing her travel time meant maximizing her time at her destination… That was why she'd been naughty.

Opening her hand to look down at the keys in her palm, she knew Noon would forgive her for picking his pocket while distracting him with a goodbye kiss. The guys weren't reluctant to show off their skills, and she wasn't shy to learn them.

With a car, not only would she get to Ophelia's faster, but she'd have a getaway vehicle too. Ryske could get to her without a car, and Noon could steal one if they decided to get to her fast.

She didn't know what would happen at Ophelia's. All Harlow knew for sure was that they'd need time alone because there were some truths only they shared.

TWENTY-FOUR

OPHELIA WAS EXPECTING her. She didn't say it, but Harlow could tell when the woman opened the door that she'd known this moment would come.

Neither of them spoke. Ophelia stepped back to hold the door open, granting her entry. Going over to the couch, Harlow took a seat without invitation. Her nerves were solid, not a hint of anxiety. They only wavered when she noticed the three urns on the mantelpiece. The central one took the place of the glass display box that had once showcased the engagement ring as a monument to Ryske. The sight served as a reminder of the real human cost of Ophelia's game.

Only one of the urns was the same as before; the other two were new. One of those, she guessed, would contain Jarvis Hagan. The man who had spoken his last words to her; the man who had died right before her eyes.

"That's our father at the end," Ophelia said, probably following Harlow's line of sight. "The one in the middle was meant to be for Jarvis… but they wouldn't authorize a cremation."

So it was just empty? Harlow didn't quite understand the hollow monument. Though even if Jarvis' remains had been in there, the monument would still be hollow. After all,

Ophelia had killed the man. A shrine to him would serve no solemn purpose. It would only remind Ophelia of her deed. If she was okay with that, as apparently she was, it could stand as a mark of triumph.

Ophelia went to the sherry decanter in the corner and poured two glasses. She brought one back to Harlow, and didn't say anything as she sat down.

The last time they'd seen each other, Harlow had been kicking Ophelia out of her parents' house. Tension permeated the air. Yet, she also sensed exhaustion. Ophelia seemed to be under a lot of strain.

Sympathy wasn't on Harlow's agenda. "Why did you come to my parents' house after I was released from jail?" she asked, putting the sherry on the table behind the couch without drinking.

"You don't beat around the bush, do you, Harlow Sweeting?" Ophelia asked, sipping her sherry.

"You thought Ryske would come," Harlow said, hazarding a guess. "He hadn't been returning your calls and you wanted to see him."

Shaking her head, Ophelia licked the liquor from her lips. "I was worried about Ryske and I did want to see him… But I didn't know he would go to your parents, not so quickly…" Her gaze drifted back to the mantel. "I was naïve."

"About what?"

Shifting her position to angle her body in Harlow's direction, Ophelia grew more discerning. "Do you want to know when everything changed for me?"

Whether it was relevant or not, it might provide a clue to something she'd need in the future. "Yes."

"The night he came back from the dead," Ophelia said. "Do you remember?"

"If you're talking about Ryske, yes, I remember."

It would be insane to suggest that she wouldn't. At the meeting about a multimillion dollar drug deal, she'd been attacked, beaten, and almost raped. She'd stabbed Hagan, fought back, been ready to commit murder… Even before Ryske called out to her, the night had been memorable.

"I was ecstatic," Ophelia said, sinking against the

back of the couch. "To see him there, to have him back… It was like a dream." Harlow remembered Ophelia's exuberance. "Except… he didn't see me." Her eyes narrowed. "He didn't see me at all. I was invisible." The exhaustion Harlow sensed morphed into determination in the next glare Ophelia pinned on her. "All he saw was you."

"I was mad at him," Harlow said, reasoning Ryske's dismissal away. "He wanted to get through to me."

"He could've had me," Ophelia said. "You were mad. He could have let you storm away; let you have your rage… I was there. I wanted to celebrate him, to thank him, to appreciate him… I would've done anything with him… for him… He didn't even want me near him."

Some parts of that night were vivid in her mind, as if they'd happened just moments ago. Other flashes were a blur. Harlow hadn't thought about Ophelia's feelings or how she'd view Ryske's reaction to her. Harlow had been so caught up in her own frustration and grief that she hadn't given the other woman much consideration at all.

It must have hit Ophelia hard that Ryske cast her aside to chase another woman. Harlow remembered him following her to the bar in spite of her ignoring him. She remembered him pursuing her down the street… and the kiss.

Harlow didn't know what they looked like from the outside when they were kissing. She could only imagine that witnessing Ryske appreciate a woman—when all he'd done with Ophelia was spurn her—hurt the socialite.

Ophelia had known him the longest; wanted him the longest. Yet, he kept on shunning her in favor of other women. First Anwen and then Harlow.

"I'm sorry, Ophelia."

An apology was the decent thing to offer someone who'd had their heart broken whether that rejection was intentional or not.

"It's okay," she said, wrapping her hands around the sherry glass. "Because it made me see the truth. It made me see that I had to change for him."

"For him?" Harlow asked, inwardly cringing at the idea of any woman contorting herself into someone else for the sake of a man. "I don't think Ryske wants you to be anything other than what you are."

Ophelia smiled. Her head tilted like a mother talking to a child. "Men don't know what they want," she said. "I don't mean that as an insult I… I'd been going about it all wrong. I was trying to be subtle, hoping that in time he'd see what we could be together… But, all along, he wanted me to take control."

"Take control?"

"Anwen told me how she had to be forceful with him to get what she wanted. I saw it with you. The worse you treated him, the more he wanted you… Even when you threw us out of your parents'. He was so mad. I've never seen him so amped and it was because you treated him like shit."

Nice. Harlow didn't like to think she treated anyone like shit, but she wouldn't be a push over, just like she'd told him. If Ophelia chose to view it that way, Harlow wasn't going to expend any energy trying to change her mind.

"I'll admit," Ophelia continued. "A part of me did think there was a stronger chance for us when you were behind bars…" Sudden irritation tensed Ophelia's jaw. "Of course, I didn't know then that Anwen had been lurking in the wings all along… Did you know? Did you know she was alive?"

Harlow shook her head. "No, I didn't."

If she'd had the slightest clue, she'd have been more likely to listen to her internal suspicions about Ryske's death. In the second she'd thought maybe it was a lie, she wouldn't have been so quick to dismiss the possibility.

"I can't believe it," Ophelia said, shaking her head and surging to her feet to storm toward the mantelpiece. "She lied to me all this time."

"Is that why you're mad? That she left and didn't tell you it was a lie? Believe me, I understand how that feels. I know you feel betrayed—"

"It makes me question our whole friendship," she said, slamming her glass onto the mantel and spinning around. "We were like sisters. The best of friends for years. Years, Harlow! I thought… I thought we meant something to each other and then… How could she do this to me? First, she steals the man I love, the man I am meant to be with, devastating my brother and our friendship in the process. Then, she runs off to set up a secret home with him! You do know that's what they were doing… The whole point was for him to join her. They were going to run away together, disappear together."

Harlow didn't buy that. "No. Why would they come back?"

"Because I took out my brother," Ophelia said. "I didn't even know what I was doing for them when I murdered my own kin."

"Ryske came back before your brother was dead."

"Ryske came back for you," Ophelia said. "I don't know how or why… Maybe he wanted you with them in his sick little love nest… or maybe it was money. I don't know. Maybe they didn't have enough to keep her satisfied. The dirty, money-grubbing little slut."

Ophelia spun, putting her back to Harlow who rolled her lips into her mouth. It seemed that Ophelia needed someone to hate and that was why she'd turned on Anwen. Without Jarvis as a focus for everything that was wrong in her life, she didn't have an outlet for her anger. Anwen's return had given her one.

"He's not with her," Harlow said, hearing herself make the confession before she thought it through. "He's with me."

Turning again, Ophelia peered at her. "I don't believe that," she said. "I saw your anger, the way you threw him out. You hate him now… Is that when you learned about her?"

"Yes, it was," Harlow said. "I learned about her, and I was mad. I wanted him out, and you bore the brunt of that too."

Nodding in understanding, Ophelia seemed to be on her side. "You probably thought I knew too. I understand why you'd be angry." A smile rose on her lips and she breathed out in relief. "Oh, you have no idea how good it feels to clear this up. I was worried that something had happened. That maybe you were going to…"

"Go to the cops," Harlow said, and all the pieces clicked. "That's why you came to my parents. You didn't believe the evidence was gone… Did you think I'd agreed to testify?"

"I don't know. I… I didn't think that, but I… I was concerned."

"I'm not going to lie to you and say I didn't consider it, because I did," Harlow said.

Becoming discerning, Ophelia folded her arms. "Telling them about my crime means confessing yours and Ryske's. You'd have to reveal everything about Pothos and where Ryske comes from…"

"Yes," Harlow said.

Just like she'd told Ryske, telling the truth about one thing meant unravelling everything else. Without the full story there was no way to put the pieces together for a jury.

"So we're at an impasse," Ophelia said, wandering back over to sit down on the couch.

"How so?"

"I came to your parents because I needed to ask you something, something I couldn't ask while you were in jail… Something I couldn't even ask Ryske because I didn't know what he knew…"

No one knew what she'd told Ryske before or during her time in jail. The guys might, but no one had raised it with her. "What did you want to ask?"

Careful, Ophelia slid closer, moistening her lips as she moved across the couch until her knee touched Harlow's. "The night it happened," she whispered like maybe someone could hear them. "I wasn't myself. I was emotional."

Ecstatic, if that was an emotion. Harlow still struggled to believe how high someone could be after murdering another person. "Okay."

"I wasn't thinking and I… I didn't think."

"Ophelia, I don't—"

"Where is the gun?"

Their eyes locked. The mask of the beautiful, demure socialite slipped to show the unforgiving creature beneath.

"That's what you want," she murmured. "You want

the gun… Why?"

Settling back on the couch, Ophelia straightened her skirt. "Shouldn't I want a memento of that night?"

"You have your victim," Harlow said. "Why do you need the weapon?"

"Animal needs his gun back."

If Ophelia was going to be glib, she wasn't likely to get what she wanted. "I doubt that."

"Why do *you* need it?"

Harlow's smile grew. Ophelia obviously didn't like it because she raised her hands and clapped. The door in the corner opened and Animal, also known in Harlow's mind as Alleyman, entered. Despite his size and menace, she didn't fear him, so her smile got wider.

"If he lays a hand on me, you'll never find the gun," Harlow said. "And Ryske will know exactly what kind of woman you are."

She didn't want to confess Ryske had seen what Animal did to Anwen. That would betray the woman's location and Harlow had already told Ophelia the couple weren't together. Claiming ownership of Ryske may be the only way Harlow could protect the woman who'd just come back from the dead.

"Ryske appreciates a woman who stands up for herself."

This woman would sink to any level to get what she wanted and could twist anything to fit her cause. Harlow wouldn't let herself be manipulated. She'd have to be smart and take advantage of every opportunity presented.

TWENTY-FIVE

HARLOW'S NECK MUSCLES relaxed and her head fell to the side. "You know what, Ophe, you're right. He does… He likes smart women. But you've forgotten what he doesn't like… vendettas. You asked him to ruin your brother after Anwen died because you blamed Jarvis for what happened. Ryske said no."

"Because he knew she wasn't really dead."

"Didn't take away from what your brother did. Jarvis still drove Anwen to feel she had no way out except to fake her own death… Ryske could have agreed with your suggestion and ruined Jarvis. That would've let Anwen return to him, if that's truly what he wanted… Except Ryske doesn't like vendettas."

Harlow had piqued Ophelia's curiosity and that was all she needed. "What are you implying?"

"You and me, we have the power to hurt each other…"

"Yes, we do."

"Both of us have to find a way to let it go," Harlow said.

She might not like being tagged as a murderer. Even if the charges had been dropped, she would always carry the legacy of what Ophelia did. But her anger had to take a backseat. Having been witness to the outcomes of Ophelia's volatile tendencies, Harlow couldn't take the risk that Ryske or Anwen could fall victim to them again.

Ophelia's chin rose. "If you bring me the gun, I'll consider it."

Shaking her head, Harlow wasn't going to surrender her only leverage. "I don't have it. I destroyed it."

After a moment of silence, Ophelia smiled. "Good," she said, and without looking waved Animal away, sending him back into the adjoining room. "Then all that's left to talk about is the future."

"The future?"

"Our investment is secure," Ophelia said. "The first shipment is due any day. I have been preparing the club, and we have some interested buyers... It's time for you to hold up your end of the deal."

"Pothos," Harlow said, almost incredulous that it was still on anyone's agenda. "You're going ahead with that?"

"It's our future," Ophelia said like it was obvious. "We put our money in and we will get a return. I'll admit, things stalled after we lost Jarvis. With you in jail and Ryske unreachable, we didn't know how secure our plan would be... But I've worked hard to keep both Parratt and Yarker on the reservation. I won't let my hard work be wasted. We have to be ready."

Ready. Pothos. Harlow only gave passing thought to the money she'd invested. Maybe because it wasn't her money, and she'd been freed from her deal with Rupert when she went to jail. He'd never been explicit in saying he didn't want to be with her anymore after her arrest. Sometimes it seemed he still had affection for her. But he was a businessman who'd understand she was no longer a stable investment.

Rupert couldn't have children with her and build a life with her knowing she could go off and do something crazy—like get herself arrested for murder—any minute.

Her mind wandered. Ophelia took a long breath, pulling Harlow back into the moment.

"The evidence that was lost... in the evidence locker

raid," Ophelia said. "Do you think it would be important to your case anymore if say… a witness stepped up?"

That wasn't a question, it was a threat. "I didn't shoot him, Ophelia," Harlow said. "Anything you say would be a lie."

"What if I said Ryske shot him?" Ophelia asked, stroking the back of the couch. "He and my brother were not friends. My brother made attempts on his life, maybe he responded in kind… Ryske knew I was unhappy, and everyone knows we're engaged…"

Shaking her head, Harlow didn't believe her capable. "You wouldn't do that to the man you love."

"Doesn't seem to be doing me much good," Ophelia said. "At least in jail I'd know where he was… and it wouldn't be with another woman, would it? I'd make sure to be the last woman loyal to him…"

If Ryske was in jail, Ophelia wouldn't have to worry about him faking his death or disappearing or refusing to return her calls. She'd be able to write to Ryske or visit him. His life would be on hold, just like hers had been.

Ophelia kept talking, "I have connections I could use to his advantage… He and I could come to some kind of… arrangement."

An arrangement that would lead to his freedom from prison only to walk into captivity with his liberator. The woman was smart.

The threat was enough to make Harlow take notice. "There's footage of me going into the building. They know I was there," she said. "I'll tell them you're lying."

Ophelia's smile was sinister in its satisfaction. "What footage? That evidence is gone, remember? Even if it did reappear, it wouldn't take much to convince a jury you were scared of Ryske or protecting him."

If she'd witnessed the crime, Ryske might have threatened her life, preventing her from speaking up, which would be backed up by her lack of response to the cops and lawyers. Or, if the jury believed she and Ryske were having an affair, they'd think she was protecting a lover… They could both go to jail.

"Why wouldn't you have said this at the time?" Harlow asked. "Why would you…"

The tape. She was the only one in the world who knew about the recording. Except she'd never had a chance to listen to it, to figure out if it could help anyone. In jail, she'd thought about that tape. Turning it over to authorities wasn't an option; she and Hagan discussed other crimes before Ophelia interrupted them.

Providing it was audible, the recording was guaranteed to do one thing: exonerate Ryske of Hagan's murder. She and Ophelia would end up in prison for sure. Harlow had no idea if the tape made it obvious who did the shooting and who was the accessory. Either way, they were both guilty of a crime. But Ryske would be cleared.

"I wouldn't snitch on my fiancé," Ophelia said. "At least not until I found out about his affair with you… or maybe until he hit me."

"Why are you doing this? Why would you want to hurt him?"

Lunging forward, Ophelia grabbed her hands. "I don't want to hurt him. I don't. I promise. Pothos will bring us closer. It will require us to work together, to build our empire."

Ophelia was selling off her brother's legacy in preparation for creating a new one with Ryske. Threatening him was just a way to get Harlow onboard. She doubted Ophelia's intention to hurt Ryske, but couldn't take the chance. She wouldn't wish jail on anyone, even for a short time.

Though the tape would exonerate Ryske of Hagan's murder, it could implicate him in other crimes. She needed to get to that tape. This wasn't as simple as snitching on Ophelia and having her arrested. They would all go to prison if the Pothos plot was uncovered.

Harlow wanted to protect everyone. The only way to do that was to give Ophelia what she wanted.

"Fine," she said. "I'm in until I get my money back, and that's it."

Pulling her into a hug, Ophelia made a sound of

delight. "Oh, that will be enough. I know it will," she said. "I just need Ryske to get the taste for it. Once he sees how much money we can make with Pothos, I know it will seduce him."

Into making more money? Or did Ophelia think he'd see her dynamic, capable businesswoman side and decide he had to have her?

Harlow was still in Ophelia's embrace when the door opened. Both women twisted to look over the back of the couch.

Ryske stormed toward them. "What the hell is—"

"Baby," Harlow said, leaping from her seat.

Running to him, she threw herself against his body, grabbing his face to pull him down for a kiss. Ryske hadn't expected passion, he was still running on rage. Ever the professional, he got over his surprise fast and let his palms slide around her waist so he could pull her higher.

One of his hands slithered up her back, into her hair. He tipped her head back, cradling it, angling her to push his tongue deeper into her mouth.

This was more than any standard hello kiss, but it served a purpose. Ryske would know she was running a con and was taking advantage of the moment just because he could. Despite that, she wouldn't show any signs this wasn't standard for them.

Pulling herself away, she grinned and puffed out a breath. "I missed you," she murmured, stroking his face.

His feral grin was exactly what she'd expect from a man who knew this was a play. "I'm right here."

Holding her head in both hands, he yanked her up and kissed her again. If she didn't slow him down, he'd take them all the way right there on Ophelia's floor.

Pressing her hands to his chest, she laughed. "Baby, take me home if you're going to kiss me like that."

"On it," Ryske said, snatching her hand to pull her toward the door.

They only got two strides.

"Harlow," Ophelia called.

Stopping to look back, Harlow had to say something. "Let me talk to him and we'll come back."

Ophelia nodded, then switched her attention to Ryske closer to the door. "Hey, stranger."

The smile on her face expected something. It dropped to disappointment when Ryske didn't respond. Instead, he turned and walked out, tugging her along behind him. He stabbed the elevator button with a knuckle and glanced back.

Harlow followed his glare to see Ophelia was at the door watching them. She stayed there until the elevator came and only disappeared from view when the doors closed allowing them to descend.

"What—"

"Not here," Ryske said and nodded at the camera in the corner.

The cameras had picture but no sound. Just in case there had been an upgrade, she was prepared to wait until they got out to talk. Always on the lookout for an opportunity, Ryske yanked her into his arms and held her close.

"What are you doing?" she asked, her arms trapped between them.

"Smile for the camera, Trinket," he murmured before swooping down for a kiss.

Instinct warred within her. The part of her that wanted to stand up for herself wanted to beat on his shoulders and kick his shins. But, as always happened when he kissed her, her resolve dissolved. The rest of the world became oblivion.

Sliding her hands up his arms, over his shoulders and into his hair, she whimpered. He pushed harder, demanding more from their kiss. The back wall of the elevator met her spine and when he crouched to pick her up, her legs wrapped themselves around his hips.

"Fuck, I never stop wanting you, Trink," he growled against her throat. "Not for one damn second."

She'd have let him slide himself into her right there if it wasn't for the sound of someone clearing their throat. Ryske twisted around, giving her the chance to peek over his shoulder. They'd reached the lobby. An elderly couple stood on the other side of the open doors waiting to use the elevator.

Sensing it was against his impulse, Harlow pushed on Ryske's shoulders, forcing him to put her down. It was on her to take his hand to lead him outside. They got to the alley where she'd parked Noon's car. She tossed him the keys before getting in.

Ryske reached across the center console for her thigh. Before he could touch her, she pushed his hand away. "If Ophelia thinks you're with Anwen, she'll kill her," she said. "Telling her we were together was the only way to protect Anwen."

He frowned. "How does that protect you?"

"It doesn't," she said, shaking her head. "I have other leverage."

"Leverage?"

The weight of the confession compressed her chest. In spite of her trepidation, she forced the words from her dry mouth. "The murder weapon."

Shock slid through him until his mouth opened an inch. "All this time… you've had the murder weapon?"

She nodded. "I have more than that… We need to have a meeting. It's time we came up with a plan… I need my crew with me for whatever comes next."

Maybe he sensed her apprehension and wanted to soothe her or maybe he was just proud. Either way, she was grateful when he caressed her cheek.

"'Til we're dirt in the ground, baby."

Turning her head, she gave his palm a quick kiss then shoved it away. "We need to get home, Crash… Take me away from here."

Ophelia had given her a lot to think about, which meant she had a lot to work with. Glancing at Ryske's determined profile, she was grateful to have an ally. For so long, she'd hidden things from him to protect him. That barrier of protection would have to come down.

Revealing everything to him could hurt him, which she really didn't want. Except she couldn't see any way to handle this situation other than to give it to him straight. Once he knew everything, he could choose to help her find a way out of this… or not.

In the past, he'd told her that nothing she could say would change the way he felt about her. Once they got home and she laid it all out for him, that promise would be put to the test.

TWENTY-SIX

RYSKE WENT TO gather the guys while Harlow rushed upstairs to the apartment to retrieve the things she'd stashed in the closet hidey-hole.

By the time the guys ascended the spiral stairs, she was in the living room on her knees with the TV behind her and the coffee table in front. Ryske was herding them, fielding their objections. Friday was the busiest night of the week, none of them should be away from their posts.

"Whatever the fuck it is…" Dover trailed off when he saw her kneeling in the living room.

Maze saw her too. "You better not have dragged us up here to tell us you're getting hitched or something."

"Yeah, you did the baby thing the other day," Noon said. "It's not funny to play with us like that again. If you say it, you better mean it."

"Sit down," she said, keeping her hands on her lap and her props concealed beneath the table.

"Nothing terminal, is it?" Maze asked, doing as she'd said, rounding an armchair to sit down. Noon took one too while Ryske and Dover elected to sit on the couch. "I mean, I know marriage is terminal, but…"

"You've got our attention, babe," Dover said.

"Whatever you need, we're there."

"Yeah," Noon said.

"Anything," Maze agreed.

Ryske winked at her as both a show of support and of triumph because he'd known the guys would rally.

Instead of responding with words, she sucked her lips into her mouth and took a deep breath through her nose. This was the moment of truth. The moment she would tell them everything and pray they would stand by her.

Slipping a hand underneath the table, Harlow picked up the gun and put it on top for them all to see.

"What is that?" Noon asked after they'd considered it for a few seconds.

Harlow hadn't taken her eyes away from the weapon, so she couldn't judge any of their reactions.

"It's the gun I gave her," Ryske said.

Lifting her chin, she made eye contact with him and nodded. Pushing it in his direction, she took her hand away.

"You can have it back. I didn't use it for anything. It's still loaded, just like you gave it to me."

"Anyone else touch it?" Ryske asked and she shook her head. Picking it up, he checked the ammo and the safety. "Why conceal it if it wasn't used in a crime?"

"Adrenaline," she said. "I wasn't thinking. It was already in there and I was just acting on instinct."

"In where?" Dover asked.

"Wait, where was it?" Maze asked. "Where was the gun all this time?"

"With this," she said, taking her purse from under the table to put it on top. Rolling down the edges, she showed them the bundle of material inside.

"What is it?" Noon asked, rising to reach over.

Harlow pulled the purse back before he could make contact with anything. "Ah," she said and turned to look at Ryske again. The other gun was on its side, supported on his thigh under his hand. "It's the weapon that killed Jarvis Hagan." The reaction to that news among the crew was more audible, but it was Ryske's scowl that kept her ensnared. "He took two bullets to the chest. I'll tell you anything you want to know."

"Then we could be here a while, 'cause I want to know everything," Ryske mumbled.

"That's fine," she said, slipping her hand into the purse behind the scarf, which earned her a lot of objections. "I've already touched the scarf, guys. I put it in the purse… haven't touched the gun though."

She'd been careful about that on the night. Sliding her hand out of the purse again, she held up the long skinny recorder, presenting it to Ryske.

"What is it?" he asked.

"I went to Hagan's because he implied to me he was responsible for Felipe being beaten. It was my intention to get him to admit that… on tape. I thought we could use the leverage."

If it was possible, Ryske's gaze darkened. "Are you telling me this whole time you've had the murder on tape, and we're just learning about it now?"

"Actually," she said, holding the recorder toward Maze. "I have no idea what it picked up. I've never heard what's on it. There wasn't time."

Maze slid to the front of his seat but seemed hesitant to take it. "Whose fingerprints are on it?"

"Only mine and my breasts," she said, trying a comforting smile. "Until now, no one else even knew it existed."

Maze grabbed it and went to retrieve a laptop.

No one said anything while he got the computer setup and plugged in the device. Despite her attempts to meet Ryske's eye, he seemed to be doing everything in his power to avoid looking at her.

It broke her heart that he stayed fixated on Maze's actions. She'd figured he would be mad, but how mad was he? Was he disappointed? Disappointing him would devastate her.

Maze paused. "Ready?" he asked.

Everyone gave some sign until all eyes landed on her. She'd come this far, she had to let them listen.

She nodded. Maze hit a key on his keyboard before settling back in his chair to listen. Every word was crisp and clear. More than once when Harlow closed her eyes, she could imagine herself back in the room, in the moment.

On the tape, when she was talking to Hagan about Ryske… about what it was like to have him inside her, her eyes drifted up to his. The intensity he returned in that gaze was so overpowering she could almost feel exactly what her words described.

He could consume her without ever touching her. Making her feel like the only woman worthy of his attention, Ryske knew exactly how to tease and coax her. Against her better sense, and despite her anxiety about what was on the tape, she forgot fear and worry. For a minute, she was just seduced by the notion of him.

The sound of Hagan smacking her in the face snapped the room to attention. Ryske, who was usually the face of composure, straightened and bounced to the edge of his seat so fast that the other three guys braced to pounce too.

"He hit you?" Noon asked.

Maze hit a key to pause the audio.

She blinked her eyes down.

"That's why your blood was at the scene," Dover said.

"Why you started to bleed when we were kissing," Ryske said.

They could be shocked about that, but she was more worried about what was coming next.

Crawling around the table, she stopped on her knees between Ryske's feet, and rubbed his thighs. "I didn't want you to hear this because I was worried it might upset you."

"Upset me? I'm pissed," he said, stroking her hair. "I'd kill the guy again if I could, but I've seen him hit you… and I've seen you fight back. I know you can handle yourself, baby… Doesn't mean I like anyone putting their hands on you in anger. That's no reason for you to go to jail. Was that really why—"

"Not that," she said.

Tensing, his hand dropped from her hair. "Trink, if I'm about to hear that fucker forcing himself on you…"

"No, nothing like that," she said, grabbing his hand

to press it to her face again. "Some of the things you told me… His version isn't the same as yours and I…" Ryske may know everything that Hagan was about to say. It was possible he'd lied to her, but Harlow chose to have faith that he hadn't, not about this. "It's about Anwen… The things she told you… they're not completely accurate."

Instead of responding to her, he tipped his head to Maze, giving him the go ahead to play the audio again. It came back on with a crash as the sound of glass shattering burst down the speakers.

"That's my wine glass," she murmured. "I dropped it."

Flattening her hand on his thigh, Ryske held it there. With the other, he encouraged her head down to his inner thigh, where she let it rest while the audio conversation moved to Anwen.

As the truth of Anwen's bruises came out, Ryske curled his hand around Harlow's fingers, tightening and squeezing either in a show of anger or in a subconscious plea for comfort. He hadn't known about Ophelia's violent tendencies, or he hadn't known one woman hit the other.

Maze lunged forward and stabbed at a key on the keyboard. The audio silenced. "This guy is something else. Everything is someone else's fault. All this, losing Anwen changed who he was, it's bullshit. He's always been a sadistic fucking asshole."

"It isn't bullshit," she said, lifting her head from Ryske's thigh. "That's about the only part I can verify from experience. What he just said about not caring what happens to him after he lost her… About trying to let it go, but struggling to live knowing the person who stole your love is out there. That's true. I've never lived through anything more difficult. It changes everything you think you know about yourself and about the world."

Although the men were growing more solemn and a sense of awkwardness was settling over the room, she wouldn't shy from the truth.

Ryske's hand rested on the back of her head. "I'm right here, Trinket."

Without looking at him, she settled her head back on his leg. He must have nodded at Maze again because the audio started. Harlow heard herself gasp and reference the SweSec event at which Hagan spurred her into action.

She wondered if he hadn't done that how long it would've taken her to ignite the fire to act. If she hadn't moved into Floyd's and used it as her base, betraying to the guys she hadn't just rolled over, Ryske may never have returned.

After her defense of Hagan's point, it probably wasn't good for the guys to hear him talk about the bond she and him shared. Not that she could deny that affinity. In a way, it was a shame Hagan had died before finding out he hadn't lost his love. Just like her, his love had faked their demise. Though his ignorance wouldn't be a negative for Anwen, who wanted to be free of the obsessed man.

Harlow might tell Ryske that he was overbearing, but the truth was, she'd be devastated if he became indifferent to her. In contrast, Anwen and Hagan's relationship from Anwen's point of view, was toxic. She didn't want Hagan's intensity, didn't covet it as Harlow coveted Ryske's. It could be a scary proposition. Harlow could understand Anwen wanting to escape it.

She could even understand Anwen's desire to protect Ophelia. The women were friends. It was probably embarrassing for both of them to admit Ophelia's juvenile tendency to lash out.

The problem came with how Anwen manipulated Ryske. She'd told him that Hagan ordered his men to beat her. Hagan said different. If it was a deception, Ryske's dislike of Hagan was rooted in a lie.

Maybe the men would never have been best of friends, but Hagan's cruelty allowed Ryske to justify the cheating. If Anwen's portrayal of Hagan as an evil monster was false, Ryske was the one conned and just a letch who'd stolen another man's woman.

Given how Ryske felt about his mother's cheating, he wouldn't want to believe himself capable of breaking up another person's relationship for nothing other than baser animal lust. He'd messed with involved women for a job; at least he'd implied he had. A prolonged affair for personal reasons was a more complex thing.

A new kind of tension vibrated through Ryske when she and Hagan started to talk about him attacking her. Ryske squeezed her fingers so tight that her mouth opened in a silent yelp. It couldn't be easy for him to hear that she'd gone through that experience because Hagan wanted to attack Ryske's dignity.

New clarity piqued her crew when Hagan mentioned his sister recruiting him for Pothos. Ryske sat up, releasing a whistle, prompting Maze to pause the recording.

"Ophelia talked him into it?"

Sitting up, she glanced at them all. "She was behind the whole thing. The contact was Parratt's, but somehow she knew about it… She was quick to suggest us sleeping with him and Yarker. Maybe she's involved with him. I don't know. But Pothos, the consortium, all of it was a way to… to be close to you."

Raising her eyes to Ryske, she couldn't ignore his scrutiny. "You told Ophelia we were together to protect Anwen," he said and she nodded. "And to protect me." He caught her chin when she tried to look away. "Trink, you've gotta stop doing that."

"Would you ever stop protecting me?" she asked, sure in her conviction. "I went to jail to protect my crew and I'll do it again if I have to…" Laying a hand on his chest, she pressed her palm against him. "And, if anyone ever tries to injure you again, I promise you they'll have to get through me to do it." Scooping his hand around the side of her head, he tried to pull her mouth to his. Harlow pressed hard to stop him. "There's more, Ryske."

TWENTY-SEVEN

SLIDING OUT OF RYSKE'S hold, Harlow slithered down to rest her head on his thigh again. Ryske slumped back, his fingers resting in her locks as Maze put the recording back on.

They listened to Hagan's admission he'd lied about his involvement in Felipe's assault and his discreet compliment when he showed admiration for Ryske's skills. The next part was about Gina and how Hagan basically bought off officials. That would clue Ryske in to how she'd known what she revealed during visitation in the jail.

The mood began to change during Hagan's warning. For a second, Harlow fixated on the urgency of his words. She hadn't given it much thought. The murder that followed was so shocking, that the strength of his determination had fallen out of her mind. Whatever he wanted her to know, he deemed it important enough to be classified as a warning. But what was it? What was the gift?

Why would Hagan want to warn her? How could she find out what he'd wanted to say? She didn't think he'd be smart enough to plan for his death, or rather his murder, but what if he had?

On the recording, Hagan started to say his sister's name; gunshots silenced him. Closing her eyes, she relived the moment he'd turned to her, then fallen.

The tone of Ophelia's name on her lips on the tape was like none she'd ever heard from herself. It betrayed her shock, her confusion, and her apprehension all at once.

The others around her shifted. Their movement opened her eyes. The three members of her crew she hadn't told about the real murderer showed their shock. Maze paused the recording again.

She tipped her head back. "You didn't tell them?"

"You before them," Ryske said, drawing a finger down her temple.

"Fucking hell," Maze said. "It was Ophelia."

"Yes," Harlow said, sitting up, though she remained between Ryske's feet. "It was Ophelia."

"And she just… came from nowhere?" Dover asked.

"We were sitting at the bar. There's a sunken door next to it that leads to another section of the apartment."

"You didn't know she was there?" Noon asked. "She wasn't backing you up?"

"I arranged to meet Hagan alone. I wanted to be alone with him… Obviously, Ophelia had other ideas."

"She was listening," Ryske said. "Ophelia wanted to silence him."

"You should hear the rest of the recording," she said and looked at Maze who waited for the nod from Ryske before playing it again.

There was an audible reaction in the Floyd's apartment to Ophelia's exuberant response when Harlow declared Hagan dead. Harlow peeked up at Ryske when the murderess mentioned him, but he didn't give much away.

It wasn't until the mention of how Ophelia got into Hagan's that he snapped his fingers at Maze to pause the recording.

"That's why she wasn't on the security video," Ryske said. "You came in the front way; they got video of you going in. Ophelia knew how to get in the back door."

"Yes."

"You left that way?"

"We did."

Cupping her face, he stroked his thumbs across both her cheeks. "You kept your head, baby. You did good."

"I was in shock," she whispered, confessing her shame.

Ryske smiled. "I'm proud of you, Trink. Fuck, baby, you are fearless."

Though he was smiling, she couldn't be satisfied under his pride. Being this close to him, with the memory of Hagan's death vivid in her mind, it was easy to be taken back to the night she'd lost him.

The memory of watching Ryske drop would never leave her. "No," she murmured, the truth in her eyes was enough to erase his smile. "I'm not… I feel like… like we're on the edge of losing each other again and I… I'm worried we won't come back this time."

"We always come back," he said, pulling her forward to press a kiss to her forehead. "We always come back."

On her knees with her forearms resting on his upper arms and her hands curled around his shoulders, Harlow closed her eyes. His mouth against her forehead gave her a focus, an anchor. Maze played the recording again. The room echoed with her and Ophelia's conversation, post Hagan's death.

At the time, it felt like it took hours for them to move through the apartment, down the back stairs, and out into the open. According to the recording, it was around a minute. The brush of fabric accompanied the distant sounds from the street. Their escape was caught on the recorder nestled between her breasts.

The women's final conversation was picked up too; Harlow told Ophelia to go home and say she'd been there all night. After Ophelia's final declaration of happiness, there was some more background noise and then it went silent.

The recording was over and her crew were taking their time to absorb everything they'd heard.

When the silence stretched longer than expected, she began to think that maybe they were waiting for her to say something.

"I came back here," she said. "I stayed off the main

streets, walked for a while, ran… I came back here, got into bed with Ryske, and you guys know everything that happened after."

"Where did you stash this?" Maze asked, removing the recorder from his laptop. "And your clothes? You slept naked and told us your clothes were unavailable."

Bending forward until she was almost flat on the floor, she slid a hand under the table to produce the bag with her clothes. "I didn't know what else to do. I just wanted to forget it happened… On autopilot, I preserved what I could."

"You did the right thing," Ryske said, his fingers moving into the length of her hair when she sat up again. "You did everything right."

"Including retreating to here," Dover said. "Now we have to figure out how to handle this."

"I have one question first," Noon said. Usually the least astute of the group, he had his moments of greatness, as he was about to display. "Why tonight? Why pull us out of casino night, the busiest of the week, to tell us this? Why the urgency?"

"Because she went to see Ophelia tonight," Ryske said, wrapping her hair around his fist in what she guessed was a sign of frustration.

Her back was almost to him. She could see everyone else, but Ryske was out of her field of vision.

"Ophelia didn't come to me in jail," Harlow said. "She showed up at my parents' house as soon as I got out. I found out why tonight… she wanted the murder weapon back."

"Why?"

She shrugged. "Because Animal wanted his gun back. That was the line she tried to sell me. I think it's more to do with her lack of trust in me. She committed a serious crime."

"The gun could be registered to her," Dover said. "Or to Animal… anyone know his real name?"

"We can't hand the gun over," Maze said. "It's useless for a conviction. There's no chain of custody. Though, if they found it here, it would implicate Harlow."

"Or Ryske," she said, swallowing her anxiety.

"Ophelia wants Pothos to go ahead. She told me if we didn't comply with the original plan that she'd implicate Ryske."

"How?" Maze said. "How the fuck can—"

"He wasn't even there," Noon argued.

Holding up both hands, Harlow calmed them. "I'm not going to let that happen. That threat was why I told you this tonight. We have to work out our next move, and if it involves me going to the cops with the murder weapon to confess, I will."

Ryske tugged her hair hard, forcing her neck to jerk back. "You're staying right fucking here. No one will cage you again… No one except me."

"Why not just hand over the recording?" Noon asked. "That proves what happened."

"Because there are things on that recording we don't want the cops to know," Dover said. "And if the cops get hold of Ophelia, she could make herself a deal. Sing about Pothos and get everyone in the shit."

With her neck at an awkward angle, Harlow couldn't nod. Ryske pressed his thumb into her pulse point and dragged it down, limiting her breathing. Having her in his grip distracted him. It was obvious that he appreciated her being under his mercy.

A shimmer of need heightened her awareness of her prickling skin. It agitated her hormones, warming her from within. Concentrating on this important discussion was difficult when heat gathered between her thighs. His thumb kept on descending, imprinting itself on the swell of her breast before it went down into her cleavage.

"There's nothing explicit said at the beginning," Maze said.

"It does confirm Ryske's engagement to Ophelia, and that Hagan didn't like it."

"Isn't that good?" Noon asked. "If Ophelia wanted to marry him and her brother was going to be an obstacle… that's motive for murder."

"Yeah," Dover said. "But they also named Parratt and talked about Hagan attacking Harlow. That gives Harlow motive too."

Ryske's thumb came into contact with the leather around her neck. Hooking it beneath his knuckle, he pulled it from her cleavage to hold up the mangled bullet hanging from the thin strap.

"What is that?" he asked.

Pushing away from him, she caught the necklace and tucked it away. "Nothing."

"Trinket," he said, his warning thick and impatient.

Facing him, on her knees, she touched his tee-shirt over the area of his chest scar. Clarity flowed through him.

"Anwen gave it to me," Harlow said. "I won't ever take it off. Don't challenge me for it, Crash."

Sinking forward, his elbow landed on his knee as his hand went up through his hair. "You wear a constant reminder of what I did to you."

"I wear a constant reminder of how precious life is… and of the pain I went through when I lost you."

"What is it?" Noon asked, though he was probably talking to Maze rather than her.

Putting her back to Ryske again, she sat between his feet and toyed with the bullet in her fingertips, propping her upper arm on his thigh.

"It's the bullet Animal shot into Ryske," Dover said. "I guess we left it at Anwen's."

"Wait," Maze said. "If Animal's gun shot Hagan, doesn't that make it the same one that shot Ryske?"

Everyone took another look at her purse on the table. It hadn't even occurred to her that the weapon could be one and the same. Somehow that made having it there all the worse. It actually made her nauseous.

"You're probably right," Dover said. "Not that it matters. Ryske didn't talk to the cops. There was a report of a shooting, but no statements or evidence. We couldn't link it now even if we wanted to."

"Again, there's no chain of custody," Maze said, opening an arm to Dover then letting it flop down. "Damn it."

"I say we give the cops the recording, let them deal with the psycho bitch," Noon said. "Who cares if Parratt's name is on the tape?"

"Naming Parratt links back to Pothos," Maze said. "If the cops ever hear that recording, they'll go to him. He's not going to hesitate to save his own ass."

"If that's true," Dover said. "Why did we ever think it was safe to get involved with him and Pothos?"

"Because Ophelia talked me into it," Ryske muttered, probably feeling responsible for the mess for so many reasons.

Twisting around to face him, she pushed up high on her knees, pressing her hands into his thighs and leaning closer. "This is not your fault," she whispered. "Crash…" He wouldn't look at her, so she slipped a hand onto his cheek to brush her thumb across his lips. "Do I need to blow you to get you out of this funk? My Ryske doesn't sulk… doesn't pout. Fight. Tell me how it's going to be. Hear what you want to hear. Tell me, Crash… You always know how it's going to be before I do. Baby…"

Her comfort, her support, it gave him strength. With her eyes locked onto his, she could see his determination growing. In that, in them, was the power Bale claimed she had over him.

"We're gonna own the world, Trink," he murmured, scooping his hand under her ear.

She tipped her head into his palm. "I love you," she mouthed.

It wasn't the same as saying the words loud. Yet, somehow, the moment called for it. She'd already told him she loved him, even in spite of them not being together. Her feelings hadn't changed since the last time she'd confessed them. If anything, her feelings for him had grown. Everything was out in the open and after hearing her tale, he hadn't demanded she pack her bags and get out of his life.

He winked at her, then shifted his focus to the guys. "Protecting the women is number one," he said, sounding almost militaristic. "Anwen might be a lying bitch, but she shouldn't die just because she fucked me."

Sinking back down, Harlow settled against him, her head on his inner thigh, her arms twining around his lower leg. She could relax and close her eyes; the guys would hash it out.

She'd contribute, of course, and assert her opinion if needed, but no longer being alone with her dilemma felt good.

She'd never known people so quick to jump to another's aid. Yes, they were all tangled in this web, but she was at the heart of it. Until confessing, Harlow had carried the burden alone. After talking about it, she felt lighter. If only she'd had the chance to tell Ryske before she was arrested, maybe she could've felt this way months ago.

In jail, she'd always been paranoid about someone listening or being recorded, in visiting or on the phone. Even if she'd wanted to tell him everything, she wouldn't have the gumption.

Even though the recording of the murder had been in Floyd's this whole time, there hadn't been a way for her to tell Ryske that. Not that she'd wanted to. Going for the gun meant risking one of the guys accidently touching it and possibly implicating themselves.

"Are you gonna talk to her?" Noon asked.

"You bet your fucking ass I'm gonna talk to her." Slipping a hand up the leg of his jeans, Harlow dug her nails into his ankle. "What?" Ryske asked, dropping a hand onto her hair. "You think I'm gonna let this go?"

"I think you should talk to her," she said. "I also think the truth is somewhere in the middle of all these stories. Just because Ophelia hurt her doesn't mean Hagan didn't order his guys to hurt her too. It's possible she was getting it from every angle."

"Why not tell me that?"

"Because Ophelia was her friend, and your friend too. Maybe she didn't want to admit she got beaten up by a girl. Maybe she worried you would take Ophelia's side. I don't know. Talk to her, yes. I'm just saying, don't jump to conclusions."

"That's fine," Dover said. "'Cept the past is low on the list of priorities. Anwen is still in danger if Ophelia did this to her for stealing you away."

"Harlow told Ophelia we're together," Ryske said, opening his fingers to capture her hair between them. "To take the heat off Anwen."

"Ophelia's still pissed about the whole fake death thing, right?"

"She thinks the plan was for you and Anwen to run away together," Harlow said, her eyes still closed. "She thinks you faking your death was the plan all along so you could be together off the radar."

"Fuck," Maze said. "That woman is insane."

Harlow sighed. "It isn't that insane."

"Then why did he come back?" Dover asked.

"Ophelia was less certain about that. She knows Anwen came back because with Hagan gone, she was freed. Her guess was that Ryske either came back to make money with Pothos or to drag me back to be his second wife."

"Second wife, huh?" Ryske said. "Can't imagine you in anything except the top spot."

She smiled because he was right. No way she'd be any man's second anything, except possibly his second in command.

"How do you want to protect them, Ryske?" Noon asked. "Safe house? Ophelia could decide any second that she wants rid of them. She snapped on her own brother."

"He's got a point," Maze said. "All of this is because Ophelia wants you, man. If you show her you have any interest in Anwen or Harlow, the littlest thing could make her snap."

"I'm not afraid," Harlow said.

Maze slammed his laptop shut. "You think you're indestructible, you're not. You've been lucky, that's it. If Animal comes for you—"

"I don't think I'm invincible," she said, pushing away from Ryske. "But I'll be damned if I'll cower in front of anyone. Especially the motherfucker who tried to take my heart from me!"

Until the thump of her heart betrayed how rage fueled her, the strength of it wasn't clear. Ryske's hands slid onto her shoulders from behind to squeeze.

His mouth landed in her crown. "I'm here, baby."

Tossing his hands from her body, she surged to her feet. "I need a minute."

TWENTY-EIGHT

LEAVING THE GUYS in the living room, Harlow went into the closet and closed the door. It quickly left the frame again to allow Ryske inside. "Trink—"

"Don't, Ryske," she said, pacing up and down the middle of the closet, despising the adrenaline amping her up. "I can't... I can't deal with us right now."

"Hey," he said, rushing over to catch her mid-pace to sweep her into his arms. "Just shh... Shh..."

Squeezing her body against his, he didn't say anything else. He just held her to him combing his fingers through her hair. Ryske had never comforted her before, not like this. Not calm and affectionate without expectation or urgency.

Her heart slowed. Adrenaline ebbed. She sank into him, letting him hold her up. After at least three or four minutes, she accepted she couldn't stay in his embrace forever.

Licking her lips, Harlow hitched her chin an inch. "You know I was kidding about the blowjob, right?"

He exhaled a laugh. "Damn, I just wasted three minutes on this hug. If I jerkoff will you catch and swallow?"

Smacking his chest, she stepped back to part them. "Want me to gargle it first?"

On a laugh, he swooped forward to snag her hand. "Let's get back to the guys."

Ryske only got a step before she spoke. "Crash," she said, drawing his attention. "I don't want you to have sex with her." His brows rose. He turned in a slow arc until he faced her again. "I know I said we don't have ownership over each other anymore—"

"You did say that," he said. Reaching out for him, she wanted an anchor and a distraction. Initiating physical contact wouldn't hurt his decision making either. Except, he didn't welcome her advance. He pushed her hand down to her side and let go of the other one. "Let's get one thing straight. I love you." That seemed like an odd opener given he'd just rejected her touch. "But I already told you I'd sacrifice whatever I have to, to keep you safe. If fucking Ophelia keeps you safe… Hell, if ditching the crew, marrying her and never seeing any of you ever again keeps you safe… I'm gonna do it."

So much for calming down, his words riled her again. Her hackles rose in time with the awareness that elevated her chin. If that was his position, he couldn't love her much. The idea of him touching Ophelia, kissing her and making love to her, it was sickening. She'd rather have found out he had fucked Lena after all.

"The woman manipulated you," she hissed, angry that he could even think about being intimate with her. "This Pothos crap, it was all a manipulation to get you back into her life."

Harlow had teamed up with Ophelia to topple Hagan when she wanted revenge for Ryske's death. Things were different in the light of new evidence. They couldn't trust anything about the woman who'd attacked her own best friend and murdered her brother.

"I didn't say I *want* to fuck her," he said. "But I will."

Harlow couldn't stop her suspicion from bubbling up. "You told her I was fearless. She's trying to show you she's the same thing… If this new dangerous side to her is attractive to you—"

"Yeah, that's it," he said, getting sarcastic and widening his stance. "Aren't you turned on? She beat the shit out of her friend, slaughtered her brother, and sent the woman I love to jail… Fuck, how did I keep it in my pants for so long?"

Restraining her rage wasn't easy. "She did those things for your attention. If you give it to her—"

"What? I'll encourage her? If I'm on the inside, if I'm with her, I can control her. That means you'll be safe… Shit, you always knew it could come to this. That I might have to be with another woman for an op. It doesn't mean that I—"

Jumping forward, she pressed the point of her ring to his chin, silencing him. "Don't you dare tell me you love me while you're even thinking about giving yourself to her…" The idea filled her with such disgust, she had to back away. "God, Ryske, how could you ever expect me to let your cock back into my body, into my mouth, after it's been in her."

"To keep you safe, that's a risk I'll take," he said. "Don't forget, you're the one putting a wedge between us. You keep reminding me we're not together. So my cock is none of your business."

Accepting that didn't lessen her anger. She folded her arms. "You know, it's easy for a woman to fake it with a guy. All we have to do is lie there."

His snicker was short and disbelieving. "If you're gonna tell me you were faking with me…"

"I wasn't talking about me, or us. I was talking about you. You'll have to get hard for her. If you didn't want her, you'd be worried about—"

"I have a good memory. Our shower sessions will come in handy," he said, folding his arms, his salacious gaze slithering down her body. "You'll be right there with me, baby."

Just the idea of being in his mind when he was with another woman made her shudder. His brazenness fueled her anger.

"God, it makes me want to throw up," she sneered. "You can't doubt me for being suspicious all this has got to you. When you met Ophelia, you had no trouble keeping your hands off her. Now it feels like you can't wait to get over there."

He exhaled. "I'm not saying it's a done deal. I'm saying we have to consider every possibility… We can't go to the cops. You knew that, baby. Despite all those studies of yours, you're becoming more like us every day."

The instincts of career criminals went against turning any responsibility for justice over to the cops. There wasn't only a lack of trust and a fear of their own crimes being uncovered, there was also a lack of credibility. Cops wouldn't be likely to trust her crew who were shifty, deceptive, and guilty of plenty themselves.

"So we fight."

Her fire seemed to amuse him. "Oh yeah? And what does that look like, Xena? You gonna go in there with the ninja skills you learned from Costello and whoop her ass? 'Cause I won't beat a woman, guys won't either. You could take Annie, but if you guys aren't willing to kill her, all you'll accomplish is making Fifi mad."

"Do you want me to kill her?"

The question was quick, but so was his reaction. All of a sudden, he wasn't playing and was in her personal space. "If anyone is ever going to pull the trigger on another person it will be me or one of the guys. Are you fucking nuts, Trink? I wouldn't ask you to do shit like that. None of us would. Just because the charges were dropped doesn't mean you're home. People have memories and that shit lingers."

Her memory of spending three months in jail was clear as crystal.

"I don't want to go to jail again," she said, pissed that he had to be told.

"You think I'd let you go back?" he asked, resting a hand on her shoulder. "I'll pull my weight with the kids, but let's not kid ourselves, you'll be better at looking after them. I'm irresponsible. Daddy will do prison. Mommy can do daycare."

"We don't have kids," she said, narrowing her eyes to a growl.

"Not yet."

He had the audacity to wink at her.

She shrugged his hand away. "You're so goddamn

cocky," she muttered. "How in the hell did I fall for a guy like you?"

Harlow wasn't sorry she loved Ryske. From the beginning, there had been an electricity between them that was impossible to ignore. Life would be easier if she didn't love him, but that wasn't the first time she'd had that thought. Yet, for all his flaws, she wouldn't change a thing about the frustrating idiot.

"You meant every word you said to Hagan about me," Ryske purred with a seductive lilt. Bowing down, he got close to her ear. "About how it feels when I'm inside you." Harlow didn't say anything, but did shove him back, getting an unwelcome view of his smirk. "You weren't bullshitting or saying it to get a rise out of him. You meant it."

Clenching her jaw, she heard her teeth grinding before forcing herself to speak. "Unfortunately, you're the goddamn love of my life too."

In that minute, she couldn't have hated herself more for that weakness. Her dislike was eclipsed by annoyance when Ryske laughed.

Leaving him to his amusement, she body-swerved around him and made her way back out to the guys in the living room. They stopped talking when she went to stand in front of the TV.

"The chances of Anwen finding Floyd's are pretty high," she declared. "She's eager to find out where Ryske lives and wants me to talk you guys into letting her stay here."

"Is that what you're doing?" Maze asked, sinking against the back of his chair. "We don't let women up here."

She waved a finger in his direction. "No, you don't let outsiders here. I respect that."

"Because you're not one of 'em," Dover said. "You don't understand it was a big deal for us to let you in… Floyd didn't let no one up here. The den downstairs was for hanging out with friends, fooling around with girls, whatever. No one was allowed up here."

"It's how we grew up," Maze said. "Just the five of us. That's where the rule came from; it's Floyd's rule."

Dover had been close to his father. All five of them

had been close. Floyd had been a surrogate father figure to them all.

"I'm not telling you to let her come here," Harlow said. "I'm saying that when she was talking about it earlier, I realized it wouldn't be difficult for her to find this place."

"We could let her stay in the den," Noon said. The suggestion wasn't well-received. Both Dover and Maze threw glares in his direction, making him blanch. "I'm just saying, Ophelia doesn't know where this place is, so—"

"Yes, she does," Harlow said, figuring it out.

"How the hell would she—"

"Because Animal knows where this place is," she said. "Think about it, Hagan kept Floyd's a secret from his sister because he didn't want her to get any closer to Ryske. With Hagan gone, there's no reason for Animal not to tell Ophelia. I don't know how she got his loyalty. Brash's too, if she has it. However she did it, she'll have found a way to get him to talk."

"If she knows where this place is, why hasn't she come looking for Ryske?" Maze asked.

Choosing to sit on the arm of Maze's chair, she tried to figure out Ophelia's reasoning. "Maybe she wants Ryske to chase her or she's afraid of what she'll find…" The person who could help them figure this out wasn't present. "Ryske!"

The closet door was open, so he'd probably been listening in even though he hadn't joined them.

Wandering in like he had all the time in the world, he slid his hands into his pockets. "Trinket?"

"Has Ophelia ever made a move on you?"

His attention went from her and around the guys as they turned to him. "Define move," he said. "We've kissed."

"I know you've kissed. I've seen you kiss her," she said, propping a hand on the back of Maze's chair. "I mean, in private, when you've been alone with her. Has she ever made a genuine move on you? Not one for show because there were people around… Has she ever been vulnerable, put herself out there for you?"

For a second, he thought about it. His lower lip slid out in sync with him moving his head side to side in a lazy shake. "No."

She could believe that. Ryske had disagreed when she told him about Ophelia's feelings for him.

"You might not have noticed," she muttered.

He smirked. "I notice when a woman's into me."

Harlow didn't hesitate to contradict his certainty. "No, you don't," she said, wishing to shake him… or slap him. "You think you do, but you don't. You notice when they're attracted to you, because they all are. Anything deeper, you miss. You missed how deep Ophelia's feelings for you are… You missed how deeply Anwen felt for you too… And you missed how deep my feelings went… You wouldn't have killed yourself if you hadn't… I don't know if you do it on purpose. You could be that oblivious, or it could be a defense mechanism that stops you facing how much you hurt the women you cast aside. But you do hurt us, Ryske. You marginalize our feelings by minimizing them in your mind. You're dismissive. You tell yourself we don't feel anything real for you. That allows you to act in any way you have to."

"Should we be here for this?" Noon asked Maze in a stage whisper.

Harlow smiled. "I'm not mad, honey," she said, leaning across Maze to pat Noon's hand. The statement wasn't emotional, just factual. "It's Ryske; that's the way he is. My point is, Ophelia might have thought she was showing him her feelings and he missed the memo… It's just as possible she didn't tell him. Maybe she's afraid of being rejected by him."

Noon's laugh was short. "Ryske doesn't reject women who want sex," he said and quickly flattened his smile in a panic. "Before you, I mean. He doesn't fuck around now, he's like totally yours."

Watching Noon freak and backtrack was funny and sweet at the same time. "We're not talking about sex though," she said and looked at Ryske. "She loves you."

"You said that before," he grumbled.

"You didn't believe me, and now look where we are… What did I tell you about scorned women?"

"They're dangerous," he said, strolling around the couch to stand in front of where he'd been seated before.

"I was right," she said. "Just ask Anwen and Hagan."

"If she wanted him so bad, why didn't she do something about it?" Noon asked. "After Anwen died, she could've made a move on him."

"Your lives went in different directions… Ophelia had to cook up the Pothos scheme to get Ryske back into her life."

"Why didn't she make a move then?" Maze asked.

That these men were so clueless was frustrating. Harlow tried to hold onto her patience. "You don't make a move on Ryske, not if you're smart," she explained to the men in armchairs. "If you want to fuck him, sure. Whip off those panties and grab his dick, he won't ask questions… But he won't call you the next day. He won't think about you ever again. Ophelia wants him to think about her. More than that, she wants him to be as obsessed with her as she is with him."

"As obsessed as he is with you," Maze said. "Like that?"

Though she couldn't exactly comment, she used a half-blink, half-shrug to humor him. There was a part of her obsessed with Ryske too. If there wasn't, she wouldn't still be there.

"I don't know how much time she's spent thinking about it," Harlow said. "At first, I'd guess she thought it would happen naturally. She was probably upset that he forgot about her after Anwen. He didn't care his life didn't include her anymore."

"So she cooked up Pothos to remind him she was there," Dover said.

"Or when she heard about it, it gave her an idea for this plot… It was perfect. A little bit dangerous. A little sexy. It would bond them in something thrilling and lucrative. She probably saw it as the perfect in."

"Why did she get her brother involved?" Noon asked.

"Money, I guess," Maze answered. "They needed premises."

"And the fact that the siblings always competed," Harlow said. "Anwen said the rivalry between them was insane. Forcing her brother to watch her hooking up with

Ryske would be a fuck you to her brother who despised the guy. In a backhanded way, it was a fuck you to Anwen too. Even though she thought her friend was dead, she was still stealing him from the woman who, in Ophelia's eyes, stole him away from her in the first place."

"Women are nuts," Maze muttered.

"Women in love are," she said, crossing her legs toward him. "Ophelia was smart. She probably decided early that she'd play the long game. She knew Ryske before Anwen, Hagan, me... She had a clear run at him when they met."

"I'm standing right here," Ryske said, opening his hands at his sides.

Harlow ignored him. "Ophelia thought she had nothing but time to draw him in... then Anwen came along. Her friend interrupting her plan must have really fucked her off."

"Do you think Anwen knew it was Ophelia's plan to seduce him?" Dover said. "Was Anwen competing too?"

Harlow could only shrug. "I don't know. I don't know her well enough to judge for myself. All the stories I've heard about her are so conflicting. I wouldn't put money on that either way... I don't think she decided to go out of her way to seduce Ryske. He was there and she wanted to have sex. If she did know about Ophelia's plan, she didn't care about it. Why she acted the way she did after that..."

TWENTY-NINE

A SENSE OF ANTICIPATION joined the men who leaned in, waiting with bated breath for her to finish the sentence.

"What?" Noon asked, being the one to break.

Aggravated in her sigh, she surrendered to saying it out loud even knowing what it would do for Ryske's ego.

"He's good. Ryske is good," she said, her eyes at the top of their sockets.

"Good at what?" Noon asked.

Maze backhanded his arm. "She's talking about sex, dumbass. Anwen wanted to get fucked, Ryske fucked her good."

Harlow opened her hand to Maze. "I'd bet the sex in the alley was impulse. Once she knew it was good, she wanted more… Still doesn't tell us if she was aware Ophelia had designs on Ryske or not. I don't think that matters. Ophelia was going to be mad whether or not she'd confided her attraction for Ryske in her friend. She wanted Ryske, Anwen had him."

"She was probably pissed at herself for missing her chance to make a move," Noon said, like he was getting it.

Except as he started to nod, she shook her head, which made him switch to mirror her. With the change came a look of confusion.

"You don't make a move on Ryske," she said again.

"Unless you want sex," Noon said to prove he'd been paying attention.

"She thought he was going to make a move on her," Maze said. Harlow put a hand on his shoulder. "Anwen interrupted that."

"It can't feel good to be the only woman at the party he hasn't fucked," Harlow said, twisting a quarter turn and extending her legs to drape them across Maze, curling her toes over the closest arm of Noon's chair.

"I haven't fucked every woman," Ryske said, dropping onto the couch.

"In this scenario? In our little clique? At the Pothos investment meeting, you admitted to fucking Yarker's wife, Parratt's mistress… and me, when they thought I was a hooker. Ophelia, in the back of her mind, was wondering why she'd been the only one denied the pleasure."

"Maybe Ryske knew, in the back of *his* mind, that she was a fucking psycho, homicidal slut."

"Maybe," Harlow said to Noon.

"I need a reason to fuck a woman," Ryske said. "I don't go around sticking my cock in pussy for no reason. Every woman you just listed, I fucked for a purpose. There was motivation behind it. I'm not just a man-whore who can't control himself…" Pushing up, he sat straighter, raising a finger as he did. "And, I gotta say, for the record… This year I've had less sex than in any other year since I started having it. And this is the first year I've ever been in anything close to resembling a relationship." He pointed at her. "That's on you, babydoll."

She wasn't stingy with her grin. "You are welcome, Gorgeous."

When she winked at him, he growled in response.

"Interesting as this is…" Dover said, folding his bulky arms. "What are we gonna do about it?"

"Yeah, we need a plan," Noon said. "What's the plan?"

"Ryske has an ingenious plan. He's going to fuck

Ophelia," she said, returning to the irritation of the closet. "Isn't that a magnificent plan from Mr. I-don't-go-around-sticking-my-cock-in-pussy-for-no-reason?"

"That's not what I fucking said," Ryske said, calling over the top of everyone's objections. When he whistled, everyone shut up. With command of the room, he started marking off points on his fingers. "We can't go to the cops, that's out. We can't kill Ophelia, because I'm not risking any of us going to prison just because she's psycho. So we get the women safe. Once they're somewhere we can protect them, we figure out how to take Ophelia down."

"And you think that involves fucking her?" Maze said. It was gratifying to hear his incredulity. "Are you using this as an excuse to get in her panties? 'Cause, fuck, man, apparently they've been on offer a long time. You could've saved us all a lot of shit, if you'd just—"

"She wants him in on Pothos," Harlow said, though it probably sounded like she was snitching. "She thinks if they work together that he'll be turned on by the thrill of the job, and her entrepreneurial brilliance—"

"And become obsessed with her," Dover said.

"Exactly."

"Pothos is dangerous," Maze said.

None of them knew exactly what the drug could do to people. It was still too new to understand the full effects. They hadn't seen it in action either. Still, Harlow didn't think Maze was talking about its pharmacological effects. Maze meant doing as Ophelia asked and seeing the deal through was dangerous.

"Because if he doesn't get obsessed and she gets frustrated, she could go to the cops and blow the whole thing," Dover added.

"Yeah, but she's in it too," Noon said. "It's supposed to happen on her turf. Once they're in it, they're all as liable as each other."

"Whoever turns on the others could cut a deal."

Maze was shaking his head. "Not in that circle. We're not talking a backroom drug deal in a crack house. This is a designer drug. The customers are going to be a high class of people. You might even get some city officials in there. Even if they aren't there themselves, the people using Pothos are going to have prominent figures in their pockets."

Like Hagan had.

"We're going to play nice," Ryske muttered.

While the rest of them were speculating, he was figuring things out.

"What do you mean?" Noon asked.

Ryske rolled his tongue in his mouth and then snapped from his reverie to talk to them. "We play nice. We do what Ophelia wants and we get Pothos off the ground. Let it run a while, couple of weeks, couple of months, whatever we need."

"And the exit strategy is…"

"Windsor's," Ryske said. "The club she plans to use, it's the same one Hagan used for his high stakes card games. Remember, our recce of the joint got me stabbed. I promise Fifi is keeping those events going. The people who go to those are the same people we'll want to crossover into Pothos."

"She's following her brother's plan to draw them in," Maze said.

Ryske nodded. "We get everything going, keep it smooth. One night we play a few hands… late night, maybe after hours… house rules."

"Anything on the table," Maze murmured.

They were figuring it out, but Harlow was a little lost. "I don't get it," she said. Noon didn't appear to either, but Maze, Dover, and Ryske were reflective. "What are we going to put on the table?"

"We might need some smoke," Maze said. "Make it a regular thing. A bonding exercise for the consortium to play a hand at the end of the night."

"Yeah," Ryske said. "I'll suggest we kick-start by blending the two. Rather than having a straight Pothos night and asking people to come for something unknown. Makes more sense to introduce Pothos during a cards night, invitation only. We bring in people we think would be interested, or at least people who we can blackmail to keep quiet."

"Cards isn't as intimidating as drugs and sex," Dover said. "Get invited for a card game, tell them there's a twist to the new special night. Have girls there ready to go."

Harlow interjected. "Willing girls who keep every cent they earn."

Though she didn't understand the exit strategy, she was beginning to understand the thought process. The Pothos night had already been discussed.

"Cards is already going on," Maze said. "Everyone's there…"

"If it's a weekly thing, no one will suspect anything," Dover said. "You'd have to stick by whatever you put on the table, money, whatever. Stakes would have to be honored… or we can't expect her to honor what she puts down."

"Windsor's nights aren't about money, that's what attracts people," Ryske said. "We can figure out the details as we go along… We'll know what's coming, we can prep for it."

"Okay," Maze said. "I'm in."

"Are we ever not in?" Noon asked and turned over his arm to show his stars.

They had a plan. While she didn't understand the specifics, she trusted every man present.

"Good," Ryske said. "Now we have to decide where to keep the women safe. Trinket could take Anwen to her parents."

She shook her head. "I thought about that, but I don't want to endanger them. Especially not with Lena in her condition."

"Nightingale is technically an investor," Dover said. "She has to be in the city and involved in this."

"Least you'll get Marlowe his money back," Maze said.

That was sort of a secondary bonus, but not one she'd snub. She appreciated them volunteering the funds when they could just as easily have decided to keep the cash for themselves.

"I could take her to Clyde's," Harlow said. "Except he only has one bedroom."

"He couldn't fight his way out of a paper bag," Dover

said. "He's all the way across town… We'd never be able to get to them if they needed us. One of us would have to stay there with them."

"In a one bedroom?" Maze asked. "Do we want to be scattered that far apart? It's been tough enough going back and forth to Bale's and he's in the neighborhood."

Costello didn't have space and neither did the Sotos. Not that Harlow wanted to endanger any of them either. Her crew were stronger as a group. They needed to find somewhere that they could protect each other.

"I could get an apartment," Harlow said. "Somewhere close… whatever size we need."

"This is your home," Ryske said before the idea could take root.

Leasing a separate apartment made sense. It would keep Anwen away from the men's sanctuary. But that wasn't the priority in Ryske's thought process. With their relationship in this state of flux, she guessed he didn't want to take the risk of letting her move out.

"I promise to come back and bake you cookies," she said, teasing while reassuring him too.

"Why would I want that?" Ryske asked in a flat tone, surprising her with his apathy. "You'll be too busy sucking my cock to bake." Sneering at him, she portrayed displeasure at his attempted joke. Her being unimpressed didn't dent his swagger. "Damn, you want me bad. Don't you, baby?"

"When was the last time you two had sex?" Maze asked.

If Ryske could be a comedian, so could she. "This morning," Harlow said, shocking them all. It served them right for being smart asses. "Yeah, if you ask Ryske, I fuck Costello every time I see him… or maybe it's every guy, not just Costello. Want to clarify that for us, Crash? I've seen all these guys today, does that mean I've fucked them too?"

Ryske's blink was slow. "They're still breathing, and I've got a gun right beside me, so I guess not," he said, glancing at the gun on the arm of the couch.

"I think he meant with each other," Noon said. "When was the last time you had sex with each other?"

"I don't know, Noon," Ryske said. "You like walking in on it so much, I'm surprised you don't keep notes in your diary. Want to tell me when her Aunt Flo is visiting too?"

"Anwen can stay here," Dover said, cutting through the bullshit. Once again proving that he was really the only grown up amongst them.

It took them a second to reorient to the serious conversation.

Noon got there first. "In the den downstairs?"

"That won't work if we want to protect her," Maze said.

"I'll sleep downstairs with her," Harlow said, in spite of what she'd thought about how awful it would be to sleep in the den.

"I sleep where you sleep," Ryske said. "I'm not leaving you open down there. Any fucker comes in, they'll get to you first. None of us would even know it."

"Putting them on the pull out couch up here won't work either," Maze said. "They'll be exposed without protection."

"I'll take the pull out in the living room," Ryske said. "The women can have my bed." A wave of nodding went around the room. "But the closet stays locked. Annie doesn't get in there and she is never left in this apartment alone."

"Agreed," Maze said.

"And we make it clear now," Dover said. "We're tied to Anwen whether we like it or not. She has no one because we kept her in hiding for so long. Otherwise, we wouldn't be doing this. If we don't help her, Ophelia could kill her. That's the only reason for this."

"Your point is we're never doing this again," Maze said. "I agree."

"Ophelia already knows we're here. I think Nightingale is right about that. If she didn't, I'd say we should be more cautious," Dover said. "Having all of us here gives us constant security, and there's a whole army downstairs if we need backup."

"Don't give Anwen your trust, none of you," Ryske said, hitting them each with a pointed look that stopped on her. "You hear me, Trink?"

Turned out that she hadn't got all of the sass out of her system. "If you're telling me not to fuck her, then I have some real bad news for you."

Noon gasped and shot forward in his seat, almost knocking down her feet. "You already did?"

"Guess it's news I have to break to you all gently," she said, scrunching her core to sit up straight. Taking Maze's hand, she gave them all a condescending look. "Guys, I don't know how to tell you this, but… I'm heterosexual."

Maze was the first to laugh. "You like cock? Well, that's a newsflash… right, Ryske?"

"Boobs are boobs," she said, giving hers a generous squeeze. "Never really did anything for me."

Ryske's laugh startled her. "Now who's the liar?" he said. "Bring 'em over here and I'll prove that's bullshit."

On a tsk, she rolled her eyes. "I like it when you play with mine, but I don't look at boobs and slide off my chair. Anwen's virtue is safe from me." She saluted and leaped off Maze's chair. "Can't say the same about the other cocks on the crew though. I'll slip downstairs and give you guys peace to talk about boundaries."

Crossing the kitchen, she ran down the spiral stairs and into the den. Having Anwen around would be more of a shock for the guys than for her. Floyd's had only been part of her life for a year, they'd all lived there much longer.

She needed a second to herself before going out to the bar. A nagging juvenile doubt liked being the only woman they trusted to be there. Harlow had been unique at Floyd's. That was over. She wasn't special or unique anymore. She was just another person and that was it.

Protecting Anwen was important. It was their responsibility. Floyd's was safe, no matter what. Harlow had so much faith in her team, but what was coming was going to challenge them all.

THIRTY

AFTER CLOSING, Ryske went back to Bale's to talk to the doc about Anwen's needs going forward.

Harlow and the rest of the crew stayed up through the night. She made more cookies and they'd cleaned the whole apartment while polishing off a bunch of booze Dover brought up from downstairs. Anything sensitive or personal was stored in the closet and the door was locked… this time with no one inside.

All of them slept late in the morning meaning a crush in the bathroom when their day did get started. Still, no one slowed each other down. Even she was used to moving around the guys to go about her routine. Their fun night had been re-hashed, with maybe a little jeering, during showers and coffee before they went their separate ways.

Later that afternoon, Harlow was sweeping the sidewalk outside Floyd's, something the guys made fun of her for, when she noticed Felipe running down the street pushing a stroller. She wasted no time hurrying to meet him.

"What's wrong?" she asked, finding him out of breath.

Baby Tiffy was awake and happy blinking up at the sky from beneath the stroller hood.

"My mom is gonna see my dad!"

Martina Soto had promised not to go anywhere near the man who'd broken his vow about never going back to prison. Over the last few months, she'd been true to her word and hadn't wavered… as far as she knew. How could Martina be going to see Pablo if he was still behind bars?

"But your dad's in prison… oh."

Martina must have planned to see him. Felipe's father had been writing to them, but Martina denied replying to the letters. Maybe she hadn't. Maybe something else was going on. Though if Felipe's distress was any indication, he hadn't known his parents were communicating either.

"Yeah! Auntie Camila is going mad! Says she won't have her baby in no house with a felon… She's going after her. I have to go. But with the baby…"

"It's okay, honey. You can leave her here."

Relief racked him. "Are you sure?"

"Of course," she said, making a face at Tiffy who offered a goofy smile. "Do you have—"

Felipe thrust a diaper bag at her and, in a surprise, leaped up to hug her. Before she could absorb what was happening, he seemed to realize what he'd done and jumped away.

He bowed his face to the ground. "Thanks, Nightingale. She'll be hungry soon," he mumbled and bolted away down the street.

Hanging the diaper bag over the handle of the stroller, Harlow made faces at the yawning Tiffy. The little one was polite enough to smile. Instead of taking the baby through the bar, because she didn't know the rules on that, she pushed the stroller along the sidewalk. Going around the outside of the bar, through the parking area, and down the side alley.

Leaving the broom just inside the door, she managed to carry the stroller upstairs. Although it was awkward, it wasn't as tough as she'd imagined.

When she got into the apartment, she parked the stroller beside the weight bench and searched through the diaper bag, checking everything was there.

Harlow had never had kids. She'd done some courses

on childcare with her work at family services. Back then, her role included coaching hesitant or vulnerable new mothers.

Deciding it was warm, she took Tiffy's blanket off and then went to the kitchen to heat up the milk. She called through to Tiffy reassuring the little one that she was there. By the time she got back to the stroller, testing the temperature of the milk on her wrist, Tiffy was beginning to fuss.

"Oh, sweetie, it's okay," Harlow said, scooping up the baby and slipping the bottle between her eager lips.

Tiffy was happy to gulp away. After a manic start, she settled into a rhythm.

Wandering around the apartment, she cradled Tiffy close and admired her enjoying her food. With heavy eyes, the baby's feeding slowed, but didn't stop.

In the living room, at the head of the coffee table with her back to Ryske's bed, Harlow heard footsteps on the spiral stairs. She tensed, hoping whoever was coming up wasn't going to make too much noise.

Tiffy heard them, or she felt Harlow tense, and her eyes opened. "Shh, honey," she said and looked up just as Anwen appeared from the funnel of the stairs.

The wonder in their guest's eyes faded to horror when she noticed Harlow in the living room. Ryske came up behind Anwen, her bag in one hand, and put a hand to her shoulder.

"Oh my God," Anwen whispered. "I had no idea you… you have a family. You have a baby together."

Ryske's head angled, matching the confusion of his expression. "Uh, I don't think that's ours… Unless there's something you want to tell me, Trink?"

Ryske pushed the hesitant Anwen forward, past the kitchen counter and the dining table into the living room. He tossed the bag onto the floor and kept on pushing Anwen until they were near enough to see the baby.

"She's… she's yours?" Anwen asked Harlow.

"No, a friend's."

"She's a cutie pie," Ryske said. The moment he spoke, Tiffy's eyes opened. She stopped feeding and released the bottle to blink past Anwen at Ryske. "Hey, heartbreaker."

Tiffy's smile spread and she opened her gummy mouth to let out a gargly laugh.

"Oh, God," Harlow said and reached over Anwen to sock his shoulder. "Stop flirting with her."

His mouth and hands opened in genuine innocence. "I didn't flirt with her! What did I do?"

Harlow tried to put the bottle between her lips again, but the baby was mesmerized.

"She's so precious," Anwen said. Harlow eased her aside to slide Tiffy into a surprised Ryske's arms. "I think I want one."

Harlow grinned. "I know, right?"

"Geez, ladies, form a line," he said, but was focused on Tiffy. The baby wouldn't stop smiling at him. Once he relaxed, Ryske smiled too. "You know, this isn't so bad."

He bounced Tiffy a little. When Harlow was confident that he was okay, she put the bottle in his hand and guided it into Tiffy's mouth. The baby took it first time.

"You're a natural," Harlow said and patted his arm before leaving him to go over to the weight bench to organize the diaper bag. "But she's a girl, so… Guess we know who'll be doing a lot of babysitting, Uncle Ryske."

"You look so good with her," Anwen beamed. "What's her name?"

"Tiffy," Harlow said.

"The kid okay?" Ryske asked.

Was he just figuring out who the baby belonged to? The kid he was talking about wasn't the one in his arms, he was asking about Felipe. He'd instructed them not to trust Anwen. Harlow didn't feel like doing a whole bit on the backstory anyway. So she didn't go into details.

"Just drama," she said. "I'll tell you about it later."

Ryske nodded and went back to making faces at the baby.

"Do you… need me to step out?" Anwen asked.

Harlow couldn't tell if she was being snide or not. "No," she said and left the diaper bag to open her arms to the apartment. "There's nowhere to go anyway, this is pretty much it." She pointed to a door. "That's the bathroom. The door doesn't close, but Maze said he'd work on a sign or something."

"I can use whatever you use," Anwen said, slipping an arm around Ryske to hold herself against his side.

Ryske was focused on the feeding babe in his arms. "You can use the restroom downstairs, Annie. Harlow's one of the guys. She doesn't give a damn who sees her pee."

That wasn't exactly true; she'd never been given a choice for anything else. As that morning proved, she was just used to it and didn't give it a second thought anymore.

"One of the guys," Anwen murmured. After a moment of hesitation, she laughed. "I can do that. Whatever Harlow can do, I can do."

"Don't say that," Ryske said. "She drives me up the wall. I can't have two of you doing that."

Anwen pouted up at him. "Would I ever do that?"

Witnessing the couple share a moment was awkward enough. Having the baby in the picture too made Harlow more queasy.

She'd looked away, but hadn't realized it until Ryske spoke, drawing her attention back.

"Something's different in here," he said. "What is it?"

If it was something they'd hoped to hide from Anwen, he'd just blown it. All of the curtains were pulled around the beds. Nothing beyond was visible, that was unusual. Ordinarily, they were open, or at the most, partially pulled across their rails. That was an obvious difference he should notice, so she hazarded a guess it was something else.

"We cleaned," she said. His mouth opened in understanding. "You're all pigs, by the way."

"You knew that before you moved in," Ryske said.

She smiled. "The guys might be hungover today. Cut them some slack if they're grumpy."

"You partied?"

Calling it a party might be overstating it. "We got drunk… very drunk… Well, the guys did. Noon threw up, though he refuses to admit it."

Tiffy's mouth lost suction on the bottle.

Ryske looked down at her again. "What now?"

Harlow headed over to join them. "Now we burp her," she said, draping muslin over her shoulder before scooping Tiffy away from Ryske. "Will you make coffee for Anwen?"

She was asking Ryske, but he was watching her bounce and pat the baby. "I think I want one," he murmured, wearing a stupid smile.

Anwen's presence gave Harlow a great out. "There you go, match made in heaven," she said, eyeing them both. "Ryske, meet your baby mama."

Heading into the kitchen, Harlow kept patting Tiffy's back and went about making the coffee at the same time.

"Come on," Ryske said, following her. "You really don't want a kid?"

"Not now," Harlow answered him.

Anwen's voice came from near Ryske's. "Really?"

Glancing over her shoulder, she saw both of them leaning on the kitchen counter. It was like they were joined at the hip.

"I think," she said, meeting Ryske's eyes. "You're currently in charge of protecting three females. Do you really want more on your plate?"

"We'd have sons too. We'll teach them to protect their sisters."

Harlow scoffed. "My daughters would run rings around your sons."

Tiffy let out a startling belch. Rubbing her back, Harlow checked the little one was okay. She was already drifting toward sleep.

Ryske came over and put one hand on her back and the other on Tiffy's, rubbing both females at the same time. "You're good at that."

She tried to nudge him aside. "I'm going to put her down in her stroller."

"Should've got you that crib after all," he said, taking the baby. "Give her to me."

"She could sleep for a couple of hours," Harlow said. "You take her now, you might not be able to put her back down without disturbing her."

"I don't mind holding a beautiful girl for a couple of hours," he said, caressing Tiffy's cheek with the back of his finger. "We'll just go take a nap."

"You're not swaying me, Crash," she sang, returning to the coffee making. "It's never going to happen."

"You said that about sleeping with me," he said, carrying Tiffy through to the living room. "Got that one wrong, didn't you?"

Harlow was smiling when she cast a look in his direction and caught a glimpse of their guest. Anwen stood by the counter that separated kitchen and dining table. The woman wore such a severe frown Harlow's smile dropped.

"Are you…" Harlow cleared her throat. "Are you sore? Do you need anything?"

"No," Anwen said, coming over to stand between Harlow and the fridge, blocking out the rest of the apartment. "I thought you and Ryske weren't together."

From the hushed tone, Harlow assumed they were supposed to be keeping this conversation a secret. "We're not," she said, going around Anwen to get the cream from the fridge, though their guest was the only one who took it.

"How long do we have this angel?" Ryske asked, lying down on the couch, holding the baby on his chest.

"Don't know," Harlow said. "At least until tonight… I know you're going out later, but Noon will be here. He's a big kid, so they'll get along great." Figuring Ryske couldn't be comfortable, she crossed the full width of the apartment and grabbed a pillow from his bed to take it to him. "Lift."

When he saw what she was doing, he crunched up to let her put the pillow under his head. Ryske got more comfortable and she returned to the kitchen to get the cookies from the cabinet.

"You still have sex?" Anwen asked.

For a second, Harlow didn't know what she was talking about, then remembered their conversation.

"Uh, no," Harlow said. "We flirt. I'm sorry if it makes you uncomfortable. I don't know what promises he's made you…"

That was sort of a lie. Ryske was averse to making promises to anyone. So the number of promises he'd made to Anwen with regard to their relationship probably equaled zero.

"Oh no, he… he hasn't made me promises," Anwen said, turning her back on the counter.

There was something in the concentration on Anwen's face that deserved a double take as she poured the coffee.

Once done, she handed one cup to Anwen and raised the cookies, gesturing for her to follow. "Pick an armchair."

She carried a cup of coffee to Ryske and moved the coffee table closer so he'd be able to reach the drink from his reclined position. Crouching in the narrow space between the couch and coffee table, she popped the lid off the cookie tin and took one out.

"You made cookies," he said, but his smile became a scowl. "Didn't I say you should do something else with your baking time?"

"You weren't here," she said, feeding it between his lips.

There was something about sitting there, feeding him, that reminded her of the soup she'd fed him at Bale's. Switching the cookie to her right hand, she kept her eyes on his while snaking her left hand up beneath the edge of his tee-shirt to graze his stabbing scar.

"You like taking care of me," he said, supporting Tiffy's tiny body with one hand while the other rose to brush her hair from her temple.

"I like it when you're laid up," she said. "Then you're not out there getting yourself in trouble."

His head shifted. "What happened to that dress?"

Somehow, she followed his thought. He was thinking of the dress she'd been wearing the night they fled Bale's.

"It's somewhere."

One corner of his mouth tilted. "Were you wearing panties that night?"

"Probably not."

"Damn, I never got to fuck you in that dress."

Stuffing the rest of the cookie into his mouth, she stood up, brushing her hands together. "And you never will, Crash… I'm going back to my sweeping. Are you okay with Tiffy for a half hour?" He nodded. "Shout if you can't handle her."

He swallowed and wiped his mouth. "She's female… females love me."

The baby did seem happy sleeping on his chest. "Don't fall asleep," she warned him and then spun around to smile at Anwen. "Keep an eye on them… I'll just be outside or downstairs if you need anything."

Leaving Anwen and Ryske alone was a good way to help Anwen get accustomed to her new surroundings. Chances were, she'd meet some resistance from the guys even though she'd been invited. Having a new person around wasn't in their comfort zone, but it wouldn't be forever… At least, Harlow hoped Anwen wasn't going to be there forever.

THIRTY-ONE

AFTER EVERYONE HAD played with Tiffy and fallen in love with her, Camila came to pick her up. By then, it was dark out and the baby was asleep. In a testament to how much the crew liked having the sweetie-pie around, they protested and tried to convince Camila to leave her for the night. It was probably a blessing she didn't; they had enough going on without adding a baby to the mix.

The only one unaffected by the little one was Anwen. Their guest was more affected by Ryske. She had such a bond with him that while watching him prepare to leave Floyd's, she'd been visibly uncomfortable.

Her dependence made sense. Ryske was the only one she'd been close to… intimate with. But he had to go out, there was no putting it off. Harlow would've preferred to be the one telling Ophelia that she was getting her way. Not because she wanted to be around to see the woman crow, but because she'd prefer to be Ophelia's point of contact. Ophelia's expectation of getting intimate with Ryske increased with every second they spent together.

Harlow didn't get what she wanted at home either. Instead of working the bar, as she'd have preferred, they'd had a quick crew huddle in the kitchen and decided she should stay upstairs with Anwen.

Dover went downstairs. Maze and Noon went out to do their sweep of the neighborhood, checking for information, helping out where they could. The women were left alone.

Hoping to distract the guest who'd become her responsibility, Harlow put on a movie and retrieved a bottle of wine. She probably should have cleared the alcohol with the doctor, especially since it was all for the guest. Harlow couldn't stomach it and elected for bourbon instead. Anwen was no longer taking antibiotics and vowed that she hadn't taken any pain pills that day, Harlow made an executive decision.

Later on, knowing the guys would be returning within the hour, Harlow helped Anwen get ready for sleep and showed her to Ryske's bed.

Once the guest was settled, Harlow made up the pull out couch for Ryske. She'd just finished when Maze and Noon got back. They huddled for a while in the kitchen talking about Anwen's first day and how Ryske might be doing with Ophelia.

When Dover came upstairs, he sent them all to bed. The last thing Harlow remembered was settling down on the edge of Ryske's bed, thinking that she'd never been so tense in it before.

At some point later, she became aware of someone rubbing her arm. Opening her heavy eyes, Harlow found Bale crouched next to the bed.

"Hey," he whispered. "Can I talk to you a minute?"

It was the middle of the night. Anwen was asleep, Noon too. It disturbed her that she couldn't check on Maze and Dover. The doctor's presence didn't usually herald good news. Though if someone on the crew was injured, she'd like to think that she'd know before him.

Bale slipped away through the curtain at the end of Ryske's bed. Harlow forced herself to melt out the bed and plod along in his wake. The chill in the air made her shiver. Ryske's shirt was the only thing she had on, but it was more than she usually wore in his bed.

Bale stood by the dining table waiting for her to join

him.

She pointed at an armchair. "Sit there," she whispered, seating herself on the side of the pull out where Ryske was sleeping. To combat the cold, she scooped up the sheet that was over him to wrap it around her shoulders. "What's up?"

"Will we wake him?" Bale asked, eyeing Ryske as he lowered himself into the armchair.

Harlow yawned and poked Ryske who didn't react. "I don't care. Probably not, he's a heavy sleeper."

"I wasn't sure if you'd want him to overhear…"

"Everything's out in the open now, doc," she said. "I no longer withhold… *he* still lies to me."

She poked Ryske again, though that one wasn't to prove a point.

Bale inhaled. "Your sister left a message at mine," he said. "I'm on my way out to work, so I thought I'd drop by and give it to you."

Floyd's and the hospital were in opposite directions when coming from Bale's apartment, though the trip didn't require a massive detour. He could've tried calling, but the Floyd's phone was downstairs at the bar. No one upstairs would hear it ringing. Even if they did, they wouldn't bother waking up to get it while they were sleeping.

"What did she say?"

"She wants you to go over there, tomorrow," he said. "Sunday."

"For dinner?"

"I don't know," he said. "She just said she wanted to talk and it was important."

"Like urgent?" she asked, tossing off the sheet. "Do you think it's my parents? If there's some emergency—"

"She sounded nervous, but not scared or in danger," he said, soothing her by laying a hand on hers. "If you wanted me to guess, I'd say it was about her pregnancy. You are the only one who knows, aren't you?"

That made sense, and she had neglected her sister that week. "Yeah," Harlow said, calming down. If there was a real emergency, Lena wouldn't be reserved about it. She'd freak and demand Harlow go over there immediately. "You're right. Sure, right."

Bale patted her hand and leaned in to kiss her cheek. "Want to have lunch on Monday?" Harlow nodded, still thinking about what Lena might want when Bale stood up. "Come to my place, we'll go from there… Get some sleep."

He bowed to kiss the top of her head again and then slipped out. Lena could tell her any number of things. Maybe she wanted to tell their parents about the baby and needed help coming up with a game plan.

Exhaustion slowed her mind. She yawned until her cheeks ached.

Picking up the edge of the sheet, she rolled onto her side and pulled it over her. Tired, and confused, she rested her head on the spare pillow by Ryske and closed her eyes. Lena needed her, so she'd be there, but, please, God, no more surprises.

***

RYSKE HADN'T BEEN sorry to wake up with her. His mouth on her neck betrayed his approval. Still half-asleep, Harlow hadn't been aware enough to argue when his hand slithered up her torso and onto her breast. It wasn't until Dover came over to offer her a steaming mug of coffee that she even really realized she was being seduced by her opportunistic ex.

She'd smacked him on the back of the head and taken the coffee from Dover. Harlow hadn't meant to sleep with Ryske. It took her a good few seconds to remember how she'd gotten there; her memory of Bale's visit was a vague blur.

Anwen was given access to the bathroom first. It was odd for the rest of them to sit around looking at each other, waiting for someone to finish in there. But the interlude afforded them a chance to make plans for the day and get debriefed by Ryske on his mission to Ophelia's the previous night.

As expected, Ophelia was ecstatic Ryske was committing to the Pothos operation. Ryske had tried to lay some ground rules. That had led to Ophelia telling him she didn't mind sharing him. Harlow *did* mind. Well, she didn't, couldn't, because they weren't really together. Except Ophelia didn't know that.

The next step would be attending a meeting with Parratt and Yarker to set a timeline and make some operational decisions. Pothos was really happening. They were in it. While Ryske was at Ophelia's, she'd arranged an investors meeting for the following Saturday night, in their usual meeting room at the hotel. From there, they'd figure out the next steps.

Harlow shared Bale's visit about Lena's message, so plans were made around her being absent that evening. Though she was worried about her sister, Harlow was confident if the situation was dire, Lena would've been explicit about that in her message.

Noon dropped her off at her parents for dinner. She'd been tempted to ask him to wait. Having him outside would give her a reason not to stay too long. As grateful as Harlow was for her parents' acceptance, even in spite of her murder charge, the memory of house arrest made her uneasy about going inside.

Sending Noon back to the city without voicing her trepidation, she promised to call later if she needed a ride back. It would depend how late her conversation with Lena ran. She'd already promised Ryske that if it got too late, she would stay overnight at her parents. He didn't want her traveling back in the dark alone. He didn't like them being separated and had even suggested that he join her. That was one explanation they wouldn't be able to sell.

Lena must have told her parents to expect her. There was a place set for her at dinner. To stop them from asking too much about life in the city, Harlow peppered them with questions about their vacation.

Her sister picked up on her cue and did the same, probably diverting from her own news. The youngest Sweeting seemed uneasy and on edge. Harlow noticed her anxiety. Given her parents lived with Lena, she had to guess they'd noticed it too.

Rupert joined them for dinner, as he so frequently did, and seemed happy to interject with comments about the company that kept Brysen busy for a while.

Her parents couldn't do coffee and brandy after dessert. They were having drinks with some client at the country club. Harlow figured Rupert planned to go with them. But after farewells were exchanged, her parents left and Rupert remained in the foyer.

His presence would make Lena feel awkward about having a private discussion. How could they politely ask him to get lost? Before she got the chance, her sister leaped to action.

"Would you like a drink?" Lena asked, scurrying into the kitchen to open the glass door of the illuminated drinks cabinet.

Harlow went after her, drawing her eyes off Rupert as she passed. "I'm happy with whatever," she said.

Lena yanked out a bottle. "You always liked this, didn't you?"

Wow, startling choice. Just how anxious was her sister?

"The… The Dalmore 45?" Harlow smiled and went over to her sister. "That's a forty-five year old single malt. It was a gift to Daddy from a client… It's a thirteen thousand dollar bottle of Scotch." Lena looked from her to the bottle like she'd never seen it before. "But if you want to drink it…"

The joke didn't earn her a laugh. Lena let the bottle drop to the counter. "I can't do this," she said to the liquor then looked up. "I can't do this."

Her sister wasn't looking at her, she was looking past her. Harlow turned around to see Rupert in the doorway, focused on Lena.

"It's okay," he said to her.

Stepping back, a chill of dread ascended her spine. "What's going on?" Harlow asked, recognizing her tone of trepidation. Lena and Rupert were still looking at each other. The longer they held their stare the more Harlow wanted to retreat. "Rupert?"

Breathing out in a resigned sort of sigh, he switched

his attention from Lena to land it on her. "It's me," he said. "I'm the father of Lena's child."

THIRTY-TWO

HARLOW HAD EXPERIENCE of the world going on pause.

Everything had stalled when Ryske was shot, when Hagan dropped, when the cops came to take her away. What she was enduring in her parents' kitchen was a new kind of pause. This time it didn't feel like reality had just taken a breath, it felt like the whole damn world had capsized.

Black was white. Up was down. Left was right.

For a moment, she stood there blinking into oblivion, trying to remember if she should breathe in or out.

"Harlow," Rupert said. "Did you hear what I—"

"I heard you," she said, holding up a hand, signaling him to keep his distance when he tried to touch her.

She didn't know when he'd moved from the door and gotten closer, but he must have because he was there with Lena at his side. Another score of seconds went by. Through the silence she could hear her sister panting. Still, she couldn't quite…

"I'm sorry, Harlow," Lena wailed. "I'm so sorry! I don't know how it happened I—"

"He spunked in your pussy, Lena," she snapped, "that's how it happened."

"She meant—"

"I know what she meant, Rupert," she said and forced herself to step away. "You had sex with my baby sister…" A reactive ball formed in her belly. Thick and full of lightning. The heat of rage merged with the fire of disappointment. "You fucking asshole."

Lunging forward, she had every intention of ripping him apart, except Lena leaped into her path.

"No! No, it wasn't him," Lena said, throwing out her arms. "It wasn't him, Harlow! It was me… I…"

"You seduced him," Harlow said and began to nod. "You know, I might believe that if I didn't know for a goddamn fact that that's what men want you to think. They want you to think it's you. Do you think if he didn't want it, he would've done it? He wanted you, Lena, and you walked right into it."

"It wasn't like that," Rupert said, putting his hands on Lena's shoulders. "It was while you were in prison. We both needed comfort. We didn't intend for it to happen—"

"And you've never heard of condoms? Shit! I can't fucking believe this."

Clutching her temples, Harlow tried to figure out how the hell this could've happened. Her ex-fiancé had impregnated her little sister.

"You guys broke up so long ago," Lena said, tears streaming down her face. "I know it was wrong. I know it was, but I… It felt so good and I—"

Shaking a hand, Harlow closed her eyes. "I don't need to hear what it was like…" she said and landed a glare on him. "I fucked him for six years. I know exactly what it was like."

Lena howled and spun around, burying herself against Rupert who held her while she wept.

"Harlow, you don't have to speak to her that way. We're apologizing," he hissed. "I know this is difficult for you."

But probably not in the way they thought. Lena couldn't know that until almost the day of her arrest, Harlow intended to go back to Rupert. Not because she was desperate to be with him, or even in love with him, but because Rupert asked her to be with him. Rupert had wanted her back.

As far as she knew, he'd never looked at Lena with lust. Harlow had never felt any need to be concerned about them being too close during her relationship with him.

While she was in jail, Rupert had come to visit her. She'd given him the speech about being off the hook with regards to her and their relationship. Was that before or after he'd bedded Lena?

It was embarrassing to think she might have been letting him down gently when he'd already moved on. Maybe her speech provided him the permission he needed to seduce the younger Sweeting.

She'd certainly made a fool of herself at least once. By the time she gave that speech at the top of the stairs about how they'd been when they got together, and how they'd ended up turning into their parents, Lena would've been pregnant.

Exhaling, she fought to get over her shock and accept that this was reality. "How many times?"

Lena peeked up at Rupert who was taking a sterner stance. From experience, rigid was his default. Even in a fight, even if he knew he was wrong, he could be unreasonable and dig his heels in. Usually, he'd come to her after the fact and apologize, acknowledging that his behavior had been wrong. God only knew how that would play out this time.

"It wasn't an affair," Rupert said. "It happened once and we both agreed it would never happen again."

"At roughly the same time you were deciding never to tell Daddy, right?" she asked, assessing the guilt and discomfort on both of their faces. "I don't think he'd be too happy to know you did a tour of the Sweeting women. Is Mom next?"

"There's no need to be vicious," Lena whispered, turning her face to Rupert again who put a protective arm around her shoulders.

"I stand up to my responsibilities, Harlow," Rupert said. "You're right, I have disappointed Brysen, and I've let myself down… I've let you and Lena down too. It was never my intention to hurt any of you."

She was disappointed in him. It broke her heart to feel that way because she'd always prided herself on not judging people. But, for some reason, she expected more from Rupert. He'd been her friend since the beginning of their relationship. She'd relied on him for so long. It wasn't right to hold him to a higher standard. Yet, somehow, he'd always seemed so much more righteous than others. It wasn't a pleasant sensation to discover he was as fallible as any other man.

"What are you going to do about it, Rupe?" she asked, knowing that no emotional outburst was going to change the predicament. Nothing would change the past. "Are you going to be a father to this child?"

"Of course I am. I would never abandon my child or its mother," he said. "I plan to talk to Brysen… We'll be getting married."

Sealing her throat, Harlow's stomach flipped. She forced herself to nod. "Married," she said. "When?"

"As soon as possible," Rupert said, "providing Brysen agrees."

The alternative meant casting out the man he thought of as a son. The man he'd groomed to take over his company. It also meant leaving his daughter alone to care for his grandchild. Her father might not like Rupert's behavior, but the men had a bond. This union would grant her parents' wish. Rupert would become a real part of the family rather than an honorary one.

Her sister was still cowering against Rupert. Although Lena was a grown woman, Harlow still felt as protective of her as she had when they were young.

"Well, he's not a millionaire," Harlow said, reaching out to touch Lena's hair. "But he'll always take care of you." Lena peeked out of her hidey hole behind her balled hands. Harlow smiled. "You won't find a better, or a kinder man, Le."

This was going to take some time to come to terms with. That was her problem, not theirs. They were in an unexpected situation and trying to make of it what they could. Her parents might not care about her opinion; she wasn't exactly daughter of the year. But Rupert was smart. His case would be easier to plead if he could tell the Sweeting father he had her blessing.

"You… you mean that?" Lena asked, letting herself turn. "You… you'll support us?"

"This is your life, Lena. You have to live it in whatever way makes you happy. If this is your choice, if it's what you want… Who am I to stand in your way?"

"Harlow…" Rupert said.

"I'm going to go," she said, creeping around the couple. "I'm just going to…"

Grabbing The Dalmore 45 from the counter because it was the closest alcohol, she made a beeline for the door. The revelation was enough for one night. She didn't want to talk it to death and definitely didn't want details.

The secret was out. Now she had to find a way to accept it, and the future in front of them all.

This wasn't as simple as getting over the fact Lena and Rupert slept together. They were going to have a child. A child who may one day come to her and ask if it was true that she'd almost married their daddy.

Rupert was going to be a daddy. Her sister was going to be a mom. Life for the Sweeting family was becoming picture perfect. Every family had their little secrets. Rupert switching sisters would become one that was whispered about through the years.

Still, if her sister was happy, she was happy. Harlow had said that and meant it. Yet, she'd never felt less like she belonged in the Sweeting house or their neighborhood. As much as she wanted to go home, to find her comfort, she wasn't ready yet. She was going to bury herself in the Scotch and walk. Eventually she'd thumb a ride or find a phone to call a cab. For now, Harlow just needed to walk.

THIRTY-THREE

HOURS HAD PASSED since Harlow left her childhood home.

The cold of the night caught up with her on her walk. So she'd hitchhiked back to the city, giving what was left of the expensive liquor to her driver before stumbling out of the car and walking the last of the way home.

Floyd's was locked, but she had a key for the alleyway door. Tiptoeing up the stairs, everyone was already asleep and the place in darkness. It wasn't easy to take her shoes off when the room was spinning. She didn't want to make any noise and did well until an urge to laugh almost overtook her. She slapped both hands over her mouth to stifle it.

Walking in a zigzag, she almost staggered into the kitchen and couldn't figure out how she'd ended up on the other side of the room from where she'd started. A dining chair assaulted her hip, forcing her to catch her weight on the back of an armchair. Ryske's bed was right there and exactly where she wanted to be.

She fell onto the pull out couch without even checking whether or not he was awake. It didn't really matter, Harlow had a plan. Yanking the zipper of her dress, she pushed the straps down her arms and tossed Ryske's sheet over her head to wriggle beneath it.

Though it was frustrating to find cotton over her prize, she didn't let it slow her down and rubbed her face against his groin while tugging at the fabric in her way. She'd just managed to get the head of his cock in her mouth when his knee bent and his fingers touched her hair.

The sheet left her shoulders, but she didn't check why, she just kept sucking.

"Trink?" Ryske grumbled.

"Take these off," she whispered, licking her lips. Raising his hips, he pulled his underwear off in a flash. Yes, mm, yeah, that's what she wanted. Climbing on top of him, she wriggled her way up his body, squeezing her fist around his dick. "Get hard for me, Ryske." The request was moot because he was already thickening and pulsing against her palm. "Oh, I need you in me so bad."

Finding his mouth with hers, she didn't care that her kiss was sloppy. All she could feel was the tightening of his fingers around her upper arms. The crushing sensation sent a bolt of need to her softening core.

Tugging at her dress, she tried to get free of it, and hated that she had to sit up. Even upright, she couldn't get it off. The skirt was confusing. The dress was coiled around her hips. What was going on? With her legs wide, straddling him, she couldn't get free of it.

Frustrated, she pulled at his hands, guiding them to the base of the zipper at her hip. "Rip this, Ryske. Get it off."

"Trink," he said, scooping a hand onto her face. Harlow pushed it down to the zipper again. "Trinket, are you drunk?"

"Rip it, Ryske."

Her volume was probably enough to wake anyone who was a light sleeper. Not that she cared. Ryske humored her and ripped the skirt from waist to hem, allowing her to free herself from the fabric.

Squashing his hands to her breasts, she flopped down and tried to kiss him again. Except he turned his head and took her arms to hold her back and examine her face.

"Trinket, answer me… How much have you had to

drink?"

Giggling, she tried to find his mouth again, but groaned when he rolled them over, putting her on her back. "Fuck me, Ryske," she said, coiling her arms around his neck to pull him down. "Be rough… Do me like you've always dreamed of, anyway you want… Use me to fulfil your fantasies."

"You are my fantasy," he said, his fingers touching her temple to comb her hair from her face. "Go to sleep, baby."

Were her eyes closed? Ah, maybe that was why she couldn't see him! Her lips curled when his touched hers. It wasn't a kiss of passion. It was a soft kiss. A goodnight kiss.

Determined and in need, her head flopped from side to side in an attempted shake. "No, no, no," she objected. "I want you to come inside me, Crash. My Crash. I need you to want me so bad you'll die if you don't have me."

"That's every day of my life, Trink," he said. His fingertips drifted from her temple down her cheek to her chin and over her breast. "You've no idea how bad I want you."

Exhaling a laugh of longing, her fingers sought his cock beneath the sheet. She was thrilled to find it engorged. "Fuck me, Crash. Please. Fuck me."

"Tomorrow," he said, pressing his mouth to her forehead. "We'll do it tomorrow."

She grinned. Her eyes still wouldn't open, she couldn't even move. His bed was so warm and comfortable that she could feel every muscle in her body loosening. "All day?"

"If you want."

There was some kind of pain in his voice she didn't understand. After a long, satisfied sigh, she couldn't bring herself to question it.

"I love you, Crash," she murmured, nuzzling him like she did when they'd slept together every night.

"I know, Trink," he said, pressing her head to his chest. "I love you too."

"I love you so much," she exhaled. "My Crash."

"That's me."

There was no drama when she was in Ryske's arms. He made everything better and that was what she needed. Seeking him out was natural. Instinct. No one could keep her as safe as he could.

***

THE VOICES WOKE her before she was ready. Harlow kept her eyes closed, wishing the weight in her head would subside. It wasn't sore, just fuzzy; she needed coffee.

Dover and Maze were talking about some sports something. The sound of their voices wasn't helping her head.

Rolling away from the body under her, she blinked open her unfocused eyes to try fixating on the pendant ceiling light.

"Hey, Princess," Maze said.

Tipping her head up, she spied Maze in his usual armchair that had been pushed back to give the pull out more space. His legs were out in front of him, resting on the end of the bed. When she stretched and pointed her toes, her feet came to rest on his calf.

"Coffee?" Dover called from the kitchen.

"I should probably shower first," she said, sitting up, holding the sheet to her chest. "Can someone get me a towel?"

"Naked again?" Maze asked, twisting to catch the towel Dover tossed from the laundry basket in the kitchen.

He threw it to her. She wrapped it around herself, leaving the sheet for the slumbering Ryske as she slipped out of bed.

Dover came through from the kitchen. "If you guys are back on, Noon will take the pull out. Anwen can sleep in his bed."

"We're not back on," she said.

"Yet you keep finding yourself naked in bed with him," Maze said, challenging her with a tease.

Backing up, her foot snagged on Ryske's underwear that must have been cast off during the night. She couldn't remember exactly what she'd said but did remember demanding sex and falling asleep.

Picking up his underwear, she dropped them onto the pillow she'd just vacated. He'd need them when he woke up.

The curtain at the end of Ryske's bed opened. Anwen came out in her satin babydoll nightdress.

"I'm going to shower," Harlow said, reversing to the bathroom, using it as an escape.

Noon was at the sink. "Morning."

"Good morning, honey," she said and slid back the shower door to slip inside.

"Everything go okay at your sister's?"

"Oh yeah, just peachy," she said and put on the shower.

Tossing her towel onto the top of the screen by the door so it was away from the water, Harlow stepped under the spray and turned down the temperature. The pressure grew as the heat vanished and the water became icy cold.

Folding one hand on top of the other on the wall, she rested her forehead on her knuckles and closed her eyes.

Maybe it was exhaustion; she was losing her grip. She could spiral, so easily. If she let go and allowed herself to slip, would she ever find her footing again?

The shower screen slid back, she rolled her head to see... Ryske's hair was a mess and his eyes were heavy, proving he'd just woken up. Coming inside, he didn't wait for an invitation, just closed the door behind him and discarded his underwear.

She planned to tell him they couldn't have sex, despite her behavior last night. Before the words came out, he stepped forward and slid an arm around her waist to pull her away from the wall into his arms.

Harlow was so rigid she couldn't feel him all over like normal. Though that might have been something to do with the freezing water.

"Shit, baby," he murmured, reaching over her to turn up the heat, so the water became lukewarm. Only when the heat of his embrace seeped through her did she feel anything again. "You're gonna hurt yourself."

With both arms around her again, he squeezed her tight and rubbed her skin, probably trying to stimulate blood flow.

"You shouldn't be in here," she whispered, staying nestled close.

"Forget about my cock, baby," he said, scooping her sopping hair away from her shoulder blades to press his hand against her. "What happened?"

There was enough sensation in her arms for her to relax and let them coil around him. "If I say it out loud, it will make it real."

"It was something big. I've never seen you so drunk."

Her head fell back to look up at him. "You should've known me when my boyfriend died. I hit the booze hard."

"Good thing he came back to pick you up then," Ryske said, using flat hands to push her hair and the water away from her face. "Now, talk to me, baby, or I'm going over to your folks place to get the skinny."

She glanced to the side. "Where's Anwen?"

"Kitchen, I think."

"She's not in here?"

He leaned sideways to swipe moisture and a thin layer of steam from the clear panel at the top of the shower screen to look into the bathroom.

"Maze is brushing his teeth," he said. "Want me to get rid of him?"

"I don't mind the guys overhearing us, you know that," she said, tightening her embrace around his torso as a way to encourage him to put his arms around her again.

Letting herself get warm, a sense of equilibrium oozed through her until she almost wanted to fall asleep again. That wouldn't be fair on Ryske who would have to hold her up.

"So talk, Trinket… or I'll start with my methods of persuasion."

She could already feel his erection imprinting itself on her belly, so she didn't have to ask what he meant.

Though she wanted to tell him, for some reason, shame held her back. "I'm so selfish," she admitted in a whisper.

"Selfish is good," he said, dropping his hands to rest

them on the top of her ass like he was proving a point about doing what felt good.

"I want to tell you what happened because I want your support. But it's insane… I'm worried you'll think less of me."

His chest moved in a scoffing laugh. "I already think pretty little of you, you know," he said in a tease. "You dumped me for crissakes. There has to be something wrong with you."

"I was wrong."

"For dumping me? I know."

Raising her chin, she forced herself to confront the truth. "Vane isn't the father of Lena's child," she said and bolstered herself. "Rupert is."

For a second, it was like he didn't know who she was talking about. The moment he figured it out, his expression hardened.

"Are you shitting me?" he hissed. "When the hell did they…?"

"While I was in jail."

"Oh, baby, I'm sorry." He trailed the back of his fingers up her cheek. "What did your parents say?"

"They don't know yet. I guess they wanted my approval first… Shit, Crash, I just… I don't know, it feels wrong."

"For the guy to be with you six years. Ask you to marry him. Manipulate you into agreeing to go back to him when you're at your lowest. Then fuck your sister when you need him most? What the hell is wrong with that?"

He urged her head to his chest.

She closed her eyes again. "I didn't need him while I was in jail, I had you then."

"You have me now," he said and kissed the top of her head. "You want me and the guys to kick the shit out of him?"

"I thought you didn't beat people up."

"I don't beat women up. Assholes who hurt my girl, I'm okay with that."

"He didn't hurt me, he hurt Lena…" She breathed

out and glanced up. "That's not fair, I don't think he meant to hurt her... I guess these things happen."

A muscle above his eye ticked. "Sex doesn't just happen," he said, coming over all serious. "There's never an excuse."

Given his mom's history, it was difficult for him to hear excuses from people who tried to justify their hurtful sexual behavior. Ryske was honest even about his most despicable acts. He'd confess they were wrong but wouldn't make excuses. His mistakes were his. He took ownership. Even if he didn't consider them mistakes.

Sometimes it was difficult to be sensible around Ryske. Sometimes? All the time. Her hormones always seemed eager for his attention; they liked the way he could torment them. But her hormones were easier to ignore than her heart. When he showed her himself, inside himself, the vulnerable part others didn't see, her resolve wavered.

It didn't matter if he masked that vulnerability in anger. She saw it and wanted it. Harlow wanted to be so safe for him that he'd always trust her with everything. Even his deepest, darkest secrets, and most depraved shame. That was probably why it hurt her so much every time she learned he'd lied to her.

The secret of Anwen was a big one. If he'd entrusted it to her, he'd have proven his faith in her was deep and true. But he hadn't shared it with her. He'd made the opposite choice.

With a gentle touch, she combed his wet hair from his face. "Sometimes you make it so easy for me to forget what an asshole you can be."

His signature smile adorned his lips, and he shook his head. "Idiot, I'll take. Fuckwit, is a possibility. But asshole? No, I won't accept that."

Skimming his hands down her back, he cupped her ass and pulled her to him. Raising her high onto her tiptoes until she couldn't balance herself anymore and had to hold onto him.

He got his mouth close to hers and let the growl in his voice turn feral. "You begged me to fuck you last night,

Trink. That dirty fucking mouth of yours got me fired up."

She smiled. "And you chose to say no." She spoke with teasing triumph, but tipped her head to kiss the corner of his mouth and rubbed her cheek on his. "Thank you."

Resigned and disappointed, he groaned and set her back on her feet, knowing he wasn't going to get what he was hoping for. If she gave him an opening while she was sober, he'd take advantage, without hesitation.

Harlow would've expected him to take advantage when she was drunk too. Except that didn't account for his cunning. Ryske was smart enough to play the long game. If he'd screwed her last night when she wasn't in complete control, she'd have every reason to be pissed at him in the light of day.

Instead, she was grateful.

If she could do it on the premise that it wouldn't mean anything then she might be persuaded to reward him with oral. But it would mean something. Being nude in the shower with him was blurring the already ambiguous line around their lack of a relationship.

Reaching past her for his soap, he held it up. "Let me lather you up?"

He wiggled his brows, making her laugh. "If you want to wash me, go right ahead," she said, opening her arms to present her body.

Ryske poured soap into his hands and began to work it into a lather. "And if I want to jerk off on you…"

"Don't push your luck," she said, turning around and scooping up her hair to pile it on her head.

His groan vibrated from a place deeper than his chest. "Trink, that's hardly nothing compared to what I want to do to you…"

Tilting her chin to her shoulder, she purred. "You want to eat my pussy."

"I want to fuck your pussy."

Returning to her teasing, she raised her elbows higher. His hands glided around her ribs up over her breasts. "What else is new?"

When he dipped lower to soap her belly and her inner

thighs, his teeth grazed the back of her ear. "Can I kiss you?"

"Hmm," she hummed. "You can soap my back."

"Prefer soaping these," he said, his hands slithering back up her body to her breasts.

When he had her nipples worked into tight peaks, he rolled and toyed with them, forcing her to sink back against him. Somehow, the technique of his fingers trickled down to torment her clit.

"Mmm," she moaned.

Next time when his mouth found its way to her ear, his tone was more sinister. "How bad do you want me now, baby?"

Biting her lip hard, she didn't let herself answer him. If she said a word, he'd know that he had her.

His hands went south until his broad forefinger traced a line on her outer labia, just next to her clit. "Right here," he growled, licking the rim of her ear. "That's where my name's gonna be… for every guy who ever thinks to touch what's mine."

Her lip slid free. "I belong to no one."

Her hand drifted back, brushing the scar on his outer thigh.

"No one but me, you got that right."

His knuckles grazed the curve of her ass where it ascended into her back. They moved back and forth, up and down. It took a few seconds to figure out he was doing exactly what he'd asked to do: jerking off on her.

"You can't do that," she panted and tried to pull away.

His hand flattened on her lower belly, forcing her back to him. Walking her forward, he put her face-first against the wall, crowding in so close she couldn't turn. With the hand that he didn't have on his cock, he found hers and slid it down her belly, curling her fingers against her clit.

"Crash," she whispered, her heart hammering against the inside of her ribs. "I can't do that."

His fist moved faster as his breathing grew more ragged. "You can, baby. Oh fuck, you can."

It felt so good to have him pleasuring himself against

her. So naughty. They were supposed to be friends. He wouldn't do this with any of the rest of the guys and she should be reminding him of that. Instead, her fingers opened, giving his space to move between hers. She twisted her finger around his, using it to push down over her clit.

Harlow opened her mouth in a mew of satisfaction, pushing her head back to his shoulder and urging his hand against her. Working it faster, she raised her foot from the floor to give deeper access.

"Oh, shit," she gasped.

Oh, this wasn't smart. That thought fled to be replaced by sheer gratification when he grunted in release, his spunk shooting against her.

Just the sensation of his liquid desire pouring over her skin was enough to fire her into release. She came with a deep, loud gasp; one she shouldn't really use when anyone else could be in the room with them. The guys had all heard her come with Ryske before... but that was before she'd put a stop to their relationship.

Turning around, she blinked her wet lashes. While she might have thought to express regret to temper his expectations, she couldn't. The sight of him, drowsy and satiated, was enough to erase all guilt. Somehow, he always reminded her not to worry so much.

Yeah, they weren't together, and playing with each other was against the rules. But the sun would rise tomorrow, and there would be actual real shit to worry about.

Resting a hand on his chest, she gave him a pat. "Get washed," she whispered and slithered around him.

As she was reaching for her towel, he swatted her ass hard, making her yelp. He moved under the water and winked at her outrage before closing his eyes and tipping his head back into the shower spray.

Ryske would always be Ryske, and she'd never take that for granted.

THIRTY-FOUR

Waiting wasn't Harlow's strong suit.

After the high of sharing the shower with Ryske, the rest of the week had a lot to live up to. The looming Pothos meeting became more prominent in all of their minds with every day that passed. Lena's predicament at least gave Harlow something else to ponder, though she hadn't got as far as calling home. Her family hadn't been in touch either, so she chose to let things lie. They'd kick off eventually. In no rush to deal with that drama, she was happy to keep her distance.

Ophelia and Pothos were more pressing. Each could involve life and death. Harlow hadn't wanted to get into the nitty-gritty of Ryske's meeting alone with Ophelia; the one where he'd told her they were in on Pothos.

Her reluctance only increased when it became obvious he was relieved at broad-strokes being sufficient to appease everyone. There was something he wasn't saying. Either something had happened at the meeting or he had reservations he hadn't shared. Harlow didn't want to probe too deep because she didn't want to force him into lying to her.

Saturday was going to be contradictory. On the negative side, Harlow didn't want Ryske anywhere near

Ophelia. She was also concerned about leaping into business with Parratt and Yarker. So many things could go wrong. As much as she trusted her crew to look out for each other, she was also terrified of losing any of them.

But there was a positive feeling too. One of anticipation that things were moving. The sooner they could get Ophelia out of their lives, the better.

Sleeping with Anwen was becoming easier. They were going to bed at the same time. Harlow didn't have trouble falling asleep anymore, which kept her out of Ryske's bed. That made it easier for them to keep their hands, and their mouths, to themselves.

Something pulled her out of sleep that night. Lying in bed, in the dark, the sheet pulled over her shirt-covered chest, she wasn't really thinking or fully awake.

Ryske's voice was the first thing her awareness snagged on.

"Fuck, Annie," he grumbled. "You gotta stop."

Turning her head, Harlow noted there was no one in the bed with her.

"Let me do this," Anwen said, a smile in her voice.

If Anwen wasn't in bed with her, and she was talking to Ryske, that meant she was in Ryske's bed.

Impulse pressed her hands to her churning stomach. If she moved too much, she could bring the couple's awareness to the fact that she was awake. So she squeezed her eyes closed and breathed. It wasn't so easy to close her ears.

"Annie, we can't," Ryske said, his voice low. "You've gotta stop."

What was she doing? Damn thought couldn't be erased. She didn't want to think about another woman being close to Ryske, enjoying him.

"Everyone's asleep," Anwen said, her volume increasing when she giggled. "We'll be quiet… I forgot how good you are at that…"

"Annie, we talked about this."

The whispered conversation was probably their attempt to be discreet. But in the open space of the apartment, there were no secrets.

"Is this about Harlow?" Anwen asked with sympathy. "I know you care about her, but she doesn't want you, babe… You're free… free to have me."

"You don't understand her," Ryske said, an edge in his tone that suggested he was fighting to restrain himself.

Anwen huffed. "If she wasn't here, you'd have me."

"If she wasn't here, I'd still be the same jerk I was last year."

"I never thought of you as a jerk."

"Then you didn't know me," he said. "Anwen, we were never gonna be more than we were."

"I don't get it," she said. It wasn't that she sounded offended. There was a curious tenderness in her voice. "I'm willing to give you everything she's not."

"You don't have anyone else, An. You're scared because you're back in the world again. You can have anything you want. You have to think about the future and what comes next."

"What's coming next for you?"

It felt rude to be listening in to what could be an intimate couple having a post-coital moment. Even without the sex, lying in the dark, in the arms of an attractive man was a powerful and intimate experience.

"This," Ryske said. "This is my life… it's atypical, but it's mine."

Anwen laughed. "Since when do you use words like atypical."

"Since my girlfriend gets prissy with me when she's pissy."

"She's not your girlfriend," Anwen said, irritating Harlow. It wasn't anyone else's job to comment on her relationships. "She told me if I could steal you, I could have you. What does that tell you?"

"It tells me she knows you could never steal me," Ryske said. "I know you don't understand it. I wouldn't have before Har. You can't know it unless you're in it. Unless you love like we do."

"She doesn't love you."

Ryske laughed. "Wake her up and ask her. I bet my

balls she'll tell you she does."

"It makes no sense. How can she love you and not want to be with you?"

"She does want to be with me and she will be with me… I'm just giving her space to find her own way back to me."

Harlow heard the smirk in his voice. It made her smile. He was repeating her words from their conversation on the sidewalk after the Costello debacle.

"I'm worried you're wasting your time." She sighed. "But if you're so sure…" Going sultry, Anwen sounded almost predatory. Harlow could envision her as a woman who'd do whatever it took to get her way. "Isn't making her jealous the best way to get her attention?"

"I don't play games like that with Harlow. She'd own my ass if I tried that bullshit," Ryske said. "An, I swear to fucking God, if you touch my dick one more time…"

Harlow pushed onto her elbows, driven by an urge to protect.

"You're wearing underwear," Anwen said. "Something I never imagined you doing when you slept."

"We never spent the night together, Anwen. You were never my girl. Harlow is my girl through and through."

Unable to even imagine words that might refute his statement, Harlow was distracted by the window at the left of the bottom corner of the bed.

They always had the eight inch vertical pane open. It was the last glass panel at the end of the window that stretched beyond the curtain and went into the living room. Movement caught her eye. Like the shadow of a specter, something crept in and floated upwards.

The words from the living room faded when the scent met her nose. Another waft, stronger smell.

Shoving her weight onto her hands, she watched it grow thicker and stronger. "Ryske," she hollered, forgetting about discretion.

Leaping onto the bed, she ran to the bottom corner and threw herself forward to open the window wider. The moment she did, a billow of thick black smoke surged in.

Catching the back of her throat as it consumed her, she coughed the dry air from her lungs.

"Trinket?"

Spinning around on the end of the bed just as he threw back the curtain to seek her out, urgency claimed her.

"Something's on fire," she said, panic gushing through her heart and forcing adrenaline into her veins.

His concern became more serious in a heartbeat. In the same moment he raised his hand toward her, he let out a long sharp whistle.

She'd seen the guys sleep through heavy bass and screaming arguments. Harlow had come in at all hours drunk and sober, making a fool of herself or seducing her man. On those occasions, she'd never seen her crew so much as stir.

But after that whistle, every man was scrambling out of bed to get up on his feet. Grabbing his hand, she let herself be tugged off the bed. Although she fell into his side, he didn't flinch and held her tight. Their hands stayed linked even when he coiled his arm around her to support her beneath her ribs.

"We've got fire," Ryske said when they all dashed into the living room.

Like it was practiced, Dover went for the stairwell while Maze crossed to the spiral stairs on the other side of the room. Noon made a beeline for the closet. Harlow's head was spinning.

Ryske gave her a shake and got her attention. "Tie your hair back, get a blanket," he said. "You hear me?" He turned to Anwen who was standing at the other side of the pull out couch wearing her skimpy babydoll nightdress. "Both of you, go."

"This way," Harlow said, remembering there were hair ties in the nightstand next to Ryske's bed.

She intended to go over there but didn't get far. Ryske kept hold of her hand, so she sprang back against him. "I love you, babe."

Sensing his apprehension for her safety, she smiled to lighten the tense mood. "I'll reserve my right to respond to that until after I've seen how hot the firefighters are." Sweeping his arm around her, he yanked her against him to give her a shake. Her fingers caught his jaw. He didn't want teasing, he wanted the truth. "I love you too, baby."

This time he did let her go. She ignored whatever look Anwen laid on her to head straight for the nightstand.

Pulling two ties from the drawer, she handed one to Anwen for her hair and nodded at Noon's bed. "Grab his blanket," she said and took her bullet necklace from the lamp to loop it around her neck. She always wore her bracelet, even in bed, so she didn't have to worry about retrieving that.

Anwen did as directed while Harlow pulled on the spare boxer briefs Ryske had in his drawer. Grabbing the comforter from Ryske's bed, Harlow pushed Anwen back toward the living room.

They found the men huddled in the middle of the room. From their grave expressions, the news wasn't good.

Ryske once again reached toward her. "Come here," he said. "We've got to move fast."

Harlow went to him and straight under his arm. She let him put her blanket around her and over her nose and mouth. He pulled her in front of him, so close that they were almost one person.

In convoy with Dover at the back and Maze at the front, the group went down the spiral stairs in a huddle. Noon was taking responsibility for Anwen. That couple were right behind her and Ryske.

The spiral stairs were blocked from the downstairs den by a thick curtain, which was probably what prevented the smoke from billowing up.

As soon as Maze pushed back the curtain, she saw the flames in the opposite corner of the den, eating through the door to the hallway that led to the bar. Flashes crept along the wall at the back of the room.

Maze went to the window at the other side of the TV and opened it wide. It wasn't a big window, only two feet wide by maybe four tall. Still, it would be large enough for them to get out, if they could get up to it. The sill was six feet from the floor.

Maze stepped back and pulled her forward, away from Ryske. He held her to him and gestured Noon forward while Ryske got hold of Anwen.

This had to be something they'd planned for. Without discussion, they each knew their role. Noon tossed a sports bag out the window first. He climbed up onto the ledge with Maze's support and paused to look back before jumping down outside.

Anticipating they'd try to evacuate her next, Harlow got Anwen and pushed her forward before anyone could move her.

Everyone was coughing and crowding in closer to the window. Almost overwhelmed by the thick smoke, the two women were cocooned by three men. Maze looked towards Ryske. With the smoke and the new vent they'd just introduced, time was running short.

Grabbing Anwen, he lifted her up, forcing her out to the waiting Noon on the other side.

Harlow didn't want to go next; she didn't want to leave her team, but there wasn't time to argue. The faster she went, the faster they would follow.

Letting herself be directed to the window, Maze bent down and boosted her up to the ledge.

Dover was the largest of the guys, the most bulky, and given what this building meant to him, she guessed he would be the last out. His heart would be breaking. The place he'd grown up in, the place his father cherished, his birthright, was going up in flames.

On the ledge, Harlow moved fast. Noon was there waiting for her. She leaned forward to grab his shoulders. He caught her weight and helped her down onto the cold asphalt.

The blanket she must have dropped followed in a ball that was pitched through the window. Days seemed to pass before Maze appeared, marred and disheveled with soot caked on his face and body, thicker around his nose and mouth.

"We've gotta get back, away from the building," Maze said, opening his arms to crowd her, Noon, and Anwen away.

Noon had his sports bag and was already heading toward the car parked at the side of the building, presumably to move it out of the way.

"Where's Ryske?" Anwen asked.

Harlow's heart pounded. Her breaths were sharp between coughs, but she hadn't taken her attention from the window. Neither Ryske nor Dover had come out.

Sirens wailed. The sweep of flashing lights came from the end of the alley to cross on the walls around the space she and the others escaped by. The firefighters would do their thing. But… where was Ryske?

Pushing on Maze, she tried to get past him. Fear compressed her chest, narrowing her airways. It didn't help that her head throbbed.

"I'm going back in," Harlow said.

Maze caught her shoulders and thrust her back just as Noon swung the car in an arc and stopped inches behind Maze.

Noon handed him a balled-up pair of jeans. Maze took them but didn't put them on. He opened the back of the car. "Get in. Go with Noon."

Grabbing the door, she thrust it shut. "Are you insane?" she said, getting up close to Maze. "You run and cower if you want. My man is in that building!"

Maze seized her arm and shook her hard. "You don't think I'm worried? We always said it was nuts to let Dover go last 'cause he'd never leave. There's no fucking way he wouldn't try to do something! And now Ryske's in there, he'll never leave Dover—"

"Oh my God," she breathed, figuring out what was happening. "They're trying to fight it… with… with nothing."

"Yeah," Maze said.

"Me before them," she whispered. Rage bolted through her so fast that she thrust her hands to his chest. "What the hell happened to me before them?"

"I don't know! But given you chose anyone but him, can you blame him for changing his priorities?"

"Yes!" she screamed. "Yes, I fucking can!"

"He loves you, Nightingale—"

"No!" she demanded, struggling against his grip. "Don't you dare! Don't you dare say his goodbyes for him!" She coughed. "The asshole…" Her throat narrowed. "He better face…" Another cough, each one hurt more than the last. "The fucker can say his own…"

Gasping, her chest grew tight. So tight until… she couldn't get a breath. Couldn't inhale. Clutching at Maze, she tried to pull in air to no avail. Something lodged in her throat stopping anything from going in or out. Pain clenched around her ribs.

Falling into Maze's arms, his panicked voice called her name. All she could think about was Ryske. She'd always told herself she'd never forgive him if he left her again. She hadn't considered that she might be the one to abandon him.

TO BE CONTINUED…

Thank you for reading this tale!
If you can, please take the time to review.

~

Ask your local library for more Scarlett Finn
novels!

~

For all things Scarlett Finn
check out:

www.scarlettfinn.com

BOOK FOUR

GO ALL IN

SCARLETT FINN

OUT NOW!